# Long Train
# Passing

# Long Train Passing

*A Novel*

## Steven W. Wise

Thomas Nelson Publishers
Nashville • Atlanta • London • Vancouver

Published in Nashville, Tennessee, by Thomas Nelson, Inc., Publishers, and
distributed in Canada by Word Communications, Ltd., Richmond, British
Columbia, and in the United Kingdom by Word (UK), Ltd., Milton Keynes,
England.

Scripture quotations are from The Holy Bible, KING JAMES VERSION.

**Library of Congress Cataloging-in-Publication Data**

Wise, Steven W.
    Long train passing / Steven W. Wise.
        p.   cm.
    ISBN 0-7852-7705-6 (hardcover)
    1. World War, 1939–1945—Missouri—Fiction.   I. Title.
PS3573.I798L6    1996
813'.54—dc20                                                95–23449
                                                              CIP

Printed in the United States of America

1 2 3 4 5 6 7 — 02 01 00 99 98 97 96

*For Miss Lillian Allen,*
*who was a saint long before she departed earth.*

There is no short road
to heaven or to love.

*Edward B. Pusey*

# Prologue

*Rural Missouri, December, 1922*

*THE TWO* men rode silently under the cold light of the moon. Despite the snow-filled ruts of the frozen road, the younger man allowed his mare to pick up her pace; she could smell the barnyard now, and she had trotted over treacherous roads for years. Better to trust her than the old doctor's balky Model T Ford. Behind him, intermingled with the crunch of hooves, the man could hear the slap of the doctor's bag tied behind the other man's saddle, but it was of little comfort. The baby was only ten days old, and she had fallen from the top of the kitchen table onto a floor as hard as the nails that held it together.

The light that beckoned from the two front windows of the small farmhouse was yellow and urgent, a man-made thing, unlike the clean moonlight that covered them now, and the young man despised it for a moment, swallowing against the dread in his throat. Harlon Allen was thirty-two years old, and he had already buried a son. The sight of another son standing on the open porch of the house lifted his spirits. Matthew had lived eight strong years now, and the promise of manhood was already about him. Good Missouri blood flowed in his veins, as it had in the veins of eight generations before him, and it flowed in the tiny veins of the baby girl inside the house. *Dear God, let it be strong now, good and strong and clinging to life.* The boy stepped forward as the men reined in the horses, and Harlon could see the worry in his face.

"Papa, I couldn't take hearin' her cry no more . . . there wasn't nothin' I could do to help . . . I . . ."

"It's all right, son. Take these horses around back and throw 'em some hay. Doc's here now."

Lester Dillow shook his head slightly at the reference to him. Even now, after thirty years of chasing into the night, the honor bestowed by a hopeful, trusting voice was as much curse as high title. They seemed to remember only the things that turned out well—the broken bones set, the wounds closed, the fevers calmed. But if the calamity was great enough, the fact that he was "Doc" meant very little. Very little indeed. And from what Harlon Allen had told him, he left town certain that a calamity of great magnitude had taken place inside this little house. But now he could hear the piercing cries of the infant, and they were beautiful sounds in the cold wind.

"Harlon, I thought you told me she was quiet when you left."

"She was, Doc, I swear . . . she *couldn't* cry."

"This cryin' is a good thing, Harlon," the old man said as he followed through the doorway.

Even as his eyes sought the infant's crib, Doc Dillow's left arm extended toward Madalene Allen, drawing the woman to him in a tight hug. "How you holdin' up, darlin'?" She nodded but did not reply.

Doc moved to the fire and opened his hands to the warmth. There was no urgency about the situation now; he had heard enough to know that. He smiled as he intercepted the worried glances of mother and father.

"Folks, this little girl's heart and lungs are sound as a dime, that much I can promise you. And very likely, all the other important parts inside her little body. Madalene, how long she been howlin' like this?"

"Well, Doc . . . for the last half hour at least, I reckon . . . nearly the whole time it took you to get here."

"Got these old paws warmed up now. Let's have a look."

He gently drew the blankets back from the tiny body.

"Settled on a name yet, Madalene?"

"Annabelle, Doc . . . this here's Miss Annabelle Allen."

The old man lovingly turned the baby from side to side in his great hands, all the while cooing sweet nothings to her. Satisfied, he wrapped her tightly in the white blanket.

"Folks, I'm pretty sure no internal damage has been done here. She's tellin' us she's hurt and mad to boot . . . but the way she's tellin' us, well . . . that gives me comfort."

"What about her head, Doc?" Madalene asked.

"Not worried about that either. She fell with the blanket under her didn't she?"

"Yes, it was mostly under her when I got to her."

"I think it bunched up some around her head. Soft as a little one's head is, I'd feel a flattened spot if there was trouble. I'm gonna stay till she gets calmed down and you can feed her, just to be sure."

Harlon and Madalene embraced, the woman resting her head on her husband's chest for a moment.

"Now, havin' said all that . . . I'd be wrong if I didn't mention the possibility of some . . . some spinal type of injury."

"What do you mean, Doc?" Madalene asked, instantly attentive again.

"Well, it's not worth worryin' over much . . . very unlikely, but somethin' like that could affect her . . . growth possibly. It's somethin' we won't know for a long time . . . months or even years. I don't want us to even bother with it. Great day, we ought to be thankin' the good Lord that it turned out so good." He paused and reassured them with his eyes. "How's little Hazel Lee doin'?"

"Still shut up in the bedroom," Madalene answered. "I can't do much with her now. It scared her to death . . . and I was yellin' for Harlon, and the baby was so quiet and still . . . it was a terrible time for a little while there. She thinks it was all her fault, but it was more mine than hers. When I laid the baby down on the table for washin' I must have set her down on Hazel Lee's nightgown sleeve. I figured she'd just stand beside her till I got some things together, but . . . for whatever reason . . . she turned to help me and when she did, the baby came with her. She almost caught her . . . but . . ."

"Well, it turned out all right. You tell her I said so."

"I will, Doc. It'll help."

Hazel Lee Allen wanted to rub her cold knees, but she resisted the urge as she prayed by the edge of her bed. Save for the moonlight, the room was dark, but Hazel Lee had never been afraid of the night in all of her seven years. She had prayed for her baby sister until she could think of nothing else to say, but the act of kneeling was an act of contrition and somehow maybe the discomfort would show God how sorry she was for having caused the baby to fall. Her mother had come to her and assured her that it was not her fault and that Doc said the baby was all right, but . . . the gnawing would not go away . . . something was wrong that even Doc or her parents did not know. Somehow . . . some way . . . something was very wrong, and it was her fault. Long, cold minutes passed until finally, in despair, Hazel Lee climbed numbly into bed and pulled the layers of blankets tightly under her chin and wept until merciful sleep took her.

Twenty-two years would pass before Hazel Lee would be able to tell her sister of the awful winter night.

# Chapter 1

*A*NNABELLE ALLEN studied her mirror image carefully under the unforgiving glare cast by the uncovered seventy-five watt bulb in the ceiling fixture. "How true it is that a mirror never lies." The words were a whisper in the room, and she listened to them as if someone else had spoken. In less than an hour, she would be a teacher. Four interminable years of squeezing the value out of every penny, four years of working two menial jobs while making good grades, four years of being more than she thought she could be. And now it had come to this. The twenty-seven sixth-grade pupils of her first class would stare at the image before her.

So Annabelle Allen stared at herself with all the intensity she could muster. She made her eyes dart furtively at every part of her body, the same way that the fifty-four all-seeing eyes would, the eyes that would miss nothing. Even in the two-inch heels of her new shoes, she stood only four feet, five inches tall; she would look most of her sixth-graders directly in the eye—a small rainbow in an otherwise dismal cloud, Annabelle judged. Her well-brushed brown hair was puffed over her brow in an effort to add to her height, but she had to be very careful; it was easily overdone.

The green of her eyes met the points of green in the mirror. If only they would concentrate on her eyes—if only *anyone* would concentrate on her eyes—then all would be well with her image. For Annabelle Allen's eyes were emeralds of inner beauty, ever dancing with delight or curiosity, ever probing gently for little signs of love in others. No . . . oh no, God had not taken her eyes on that fateful night.

Her other features were plain; there was no other word for it. The face a bit too broad for the nose, cheekbones somehow too high, a mouth that smiled easily enough but was not pretty—features worn without notice by a million other young women. But they would never be worn without notice by Annabelle, of that she was sure. The fact that she had no visible neck assured this. Her head appeared to rest squarely on her shoulders, some would even say *in* her shoulders. With arms and legs originally intended for a woman a foot taller, her compressed torso commanded the attention of every onlooker. Her neck was basically immobile; simple sideways glances required a proportionate movement of her shoulders.

And all of this from The Fall—an event so far removed in time that Annabelle often imagined that it had never happened. There were days when nothing mattered, save for the power of her mind as it locked onto Melville's white whale with Ahab lashed to its great flank, or Ulysses's struggle to return to his home in *The Odyssey,* or Saint Paul as he penned letters of hope and love from a Roman dungeon. Days with no onlookers or mirrors. Days of grace. Days, hours, even minutes, stolen from the reality of The Fall.

She reached up and smoothed the flat, white collar of her light green dress. Like all her clothing, it was a dress of her own handiwork; a result of the skill handed down by a mother who knew from her child's early years that store-bought clothing was not an option. The stitching was a thing of beauty within itself, but Annabelle realized that only someone with her skill could appreciate its perfection. Certainly it would not impress any of her students, but this did not matter; she had not stitched the dress perfectly to impress anyone. It was simply the way that the task should have been performed. It was Annabelle's way, and had been for as long as she could remember.

*Enough of this now,* she thought to herself. Stand here long enough and the little four-letter horror called "pity" would creep in and take a part of her. She huffed a short laugh at the silly thought. In the autumn of 1943, when blood spilled from thousands in the terrible war, surely her pity could be properly directed. She turned from the mirror and straightened her shoulders as she scanned the orderly space that enveloped her. It was the larger of two rented rooms on the second floor of a rambling turn-of-the-century house owned by an elderly widow named Sadie Armstrong. The room was used mainly for sleeping and necessary chores such as sewing and mending clothing. Like many older houses, the bathroom was on the second floor, and Annabelle and Mrs. Armstrong shared its use.

The tiny woman walked quietly, almost reverently, from the room and into another. The smaller of Annabelle's rooms had quickly become the center of her earthly life—a ten-foot square with a built-in bookcase on one wall and a large double-hung window on another. To the casual observer, it was nothing more than a common upstairs bedroom without a bed. For Annabelle, it was the storehouse of her literary treasures, with the big window allowing God's light to shine on the pages. An old rolltop desk that Mrs. Armstrong no longer had any use for had been moved into one corner. The only other piece of furniture was the rocking chair that Annabelle's father had made for her tenth birthday. It fit her body perfectly then and it fit perfectly today as she sat down and gently toed the hardwood floor. Annabelle wondered how any pilgrim in this life could manage without a good rocker.

Without looking from the window, she reached to the corner of the desk and found her Bible, resting it in her lap. The worn leather cover was soothing under her fingertips; back and forth they went, like a mother stroking the head of her child.

Annabelle Allen hoped to teach her students many things, some of which were much greater than the three Rs.

Jewell Cole stood half a head taller than any of the other students in the classroom. A dark brown shaggy mop of hair covered half of his forehead, drawing attention to deep set hazel eyes that held little light. The soft, round lines of boyhood were already giving way to the squareness of manhood. He was a handsome boy, though he had never considered himself either attractive or unattractive, nor could he remember anyone ever saying something that would give him an indication.

From his position beside the rear desk in the row nearest the door, he casually scanned his fellows as they stood waiting for the runt of a teacher to let them sit down. He huffed his favorite curse word under his breath; it had been ten seconds since he decided to sit down without permission, and now he was merely waiting for the moment when her eyes swept again to the left. When he was certain she was looking directly at his corner, he folded his body behind the small desk and plopped loudly into the wooden seat. Before a single head could turn in his direction, the teacher's pleasant, steady voice stole his moment of glory.

"Please take your seats, students."

She paused, waiting for the commotion to cease before continuing. "My name is Annabelle Allen, and since I am unmarried, you should address me as Miss Allen . . . or Teacher, if you like. We will try the seating arrangement you have chosen . . . for as long as it works. That is entirely up to you students."

She glanced down at the typed list of names in her hand and

then at the grid of small boxes she had drawn on another sheet of paper.

"I learn names very quickly, and I promise that by the end of the week I will know each of you. It will help me if you take note of where you are sitting today and be sure to sit in the same place every day. Now, starting here on the corner, please stand and say your name as I write it on my chart."

Annabelle quickly took her seat behind the desk and began to write as the children stood in turn and recited their names. Name by name, row by row, the small voices piped up the syllables until the room fell silent again. Only one child remained to be identified. Annabelle looked up at the boy at the end of the last row. The silence grew louder by the second as a few furtive glances darted toward him. Jewell Cole had no intention whatever of either standing or reciting his stupid-sounding name, and the hardness in his eyes told Annabelle as much. Somehow, the hardness did not look out of place on a boy so young, and Annabelle was momentarily taken aback.

"I . . . I, uh, believe we have one name left," she said, attempting a smile at Jewell.

Silence, then a few nervous giggles. Jewell enjoyed the mounting tension; his confidence was growing by the moment. He would break the runt early. He anticipated the trip down the hall to the principal's office. Old dragon face Bellman himself. He had already broken that old fool. Annabelle looked down at the papers on her desk and began to match the names on the list with those on the chart. When she found the missing name she pushed away from the desk and walked to the front of the room. She allowed her eyes to sweep the rows of faces, right to left, left to right, slowly seeking eyes, smiling pleasantly all the while.

"It is a pleasure to get to know twenty-six of you by name. The student on the end of the last row near the door will be called

Twenty-seven until I find time to match up the names on my list with our new chart."

More giggles, louder now, and without the nervousness. Jewell could feel his face begin to flush; things were not turning out as planned. He squirmed in his seat, attempting to settle on his next course of action; but he could not think clearly, and his irritation grew like a fever. The little woman had begun to speak to the class again, ignoring him, but her words were faraway things, lost in the haze of his anger. More than anything, Jewell wanted to jump up and dash from the cursed schoolhouse, never to return; in fact, the only reason he did not, and had never before, was that his father might find out.

The thought of the man eased his anger. Thoughts of his father were strange, whirling things, and Jewell could never predict how they would affect him. Fear was always a part of the puzzle, as it was now; but it had been there for a very long time, and he had learned to deal with most of it. He dealt with it now, simply by remaining in the stupid school.

It would not do to make Jubal Cole angry.

With a sharp crack, the snooker balls exploded across the felt-covered table, careening wildly and then slowing with clicks and clacks as they came to rest. These were sweet sounds to Jubal Cole; they were the sounds of money. Three of the big snooker tables were lined in perfect order, and then, like subordinate soldiers, six pool tables, each with a fluorescent light suspended five feet over the playing surface. Jubal watched from his place behind the long bar, a damp wiping cloth draped over his shoulder, the ubiquitous cigarette dangling precariously from the corner of his mouth. Four of the nine tables were occupied—not bad for mid-afternoon—but when the shift workers escaped from the jacket factory in another hour, the sounds would become even sweeter.

In truth, the direct income from the tables represented a small portion of Jubal's livelihood. It was the goods that he slid across the smooth bar top that really mattered. Beer by the mug and pitcher, endless packs of cigarettes, cigars, snuff, greasy cheeseburgers from the small grill, candy bars, soft drinks for the fainthearted—hour by hour, day by day in the smoky haze, the cash register clanged from noon until midnight in Jubal's Kingdom.

He huffed a smoky laugh to himself as he remembered the day ten years past when he hung the big hand-painted sign across the face of the building. What a beautiful rub in the face of the pious churchgoers who passed his place on their way to Christ Kingdom Baptist Church a block and a half down the street. The laugh faded with the memory of the visit the pastor had paid him the next day. Two thick smoke-yellowed fingers scissored the cigarette from his mouth, and then he shot a precise jet of smoke between the heads of two bar patrons, who seemingly ignored the stream.

"Sacrilegious," was the word that had set Jubal off, even though he did not know its precise meaning. It was the way that the preacher man had said it, the look of his mouth and the narrowing of his eyes when the fateful word oozed from his lips. The split second when Jubal's fist became one with the cheek and nose of the preacher was a marvelous remembrance.

To Jubal's mild surprise, no charges had ever been pressed, even though word filtered back that the preacher's nose had been badly broken. The fool was still there, down at his precious church house. Jubal had seen him a few times over the years, and twice they had passed on the same side of the street. Without having looked directly in his eyes either time, Jubal happily confirmed the unnatural angle to the line of his nose.

"Jubal . . . Jubal!" The sound of his name brought his thoughts back to the bar.

"Hey, I hear you, Henry. Ain't no need to yell at me."

"Seemed your mind had parted company with your body, and this here empty mug has a sad look to it."

Jubal swiped up the empty mug and turned away from the bar as he refilled it.

"Much obliged."

"I'll fill it as long as you can sit up on that stool, Henry."

"I was pretty sure of that, Jubal." He chuckled with the man beside him, but Jubal ignored them both, looking over their shoulders at the hump-shouldered man sweeping the floor around the unoccupied tables. The man named Henry turned and followed Jubal's eyes as they bore down on Emmett Tragman.

"Emmett!" Jubal's voice boomed over the country tune that twanged from the jukebox. The little man half-trotted to the bar with the broom still in his hand.

"Carry this burger down there to number five . . . guy in the red shirt." The words were heavy and measured. Jubal extended the paper plate, heavy with the sandwich and two dill pickle spears.

Silently, Emmett did as he was instructed and shuffled away with the plate of food.

"I don't know how you put up with him, Jubal."

"Me neither," his bar mate piped in.

"Idiot like that and all . . . even if he can do numbers in his head. He'd still drive me crazy, I tell you."

Emmett's ability to add the chalk-scrawled numbers of the snooker players at a glance had been the talk of the town among Jubal's crowd since the little man had been hired five months before. Long rows of two-digit numbers were totaled within seconds, and in the beginning, when this strange skill was discovered by the regulars, he was commanded to multiply three-digit numbers to the howling delight of half-drunken patrons of the Kingdom. Even though the novelty of it had already begun to fade, in truth, it was the only reason why Jubal Cole tolerated the man.

"Oh, he's kinda like a faithful dog or something, I reckon," Jubal drawled. "Does what I tell him . . . don't ever complain. And he is crazy smart with numbers. I get a kick out of that now and then."

"That boy of yours about big enough to do chores around here, ain't he?"

"Yeah, he's helping some, but I think I'll keep old crazy Emmett around anyhow."

"Whatever, Jubal," Henry said with a wave of his beer mug, "you're the one payin' him."

"That don't set me back much, Henry." Jubal laughed, and the two men joined him.

Jewell opened the unlocked door at the rear of the building and trudged up the creaking staircase that led to the two-bedroom apartment over Jubal's Kingdom. A song from the jukebox, garbled by raucous laughter, filtered upward through the staircase, but the boy paid little attention; it was a constant in his life now.

He looked about him at the dingy walls and ceiling that formed the living room area, the worn easy chair yawning emptily at him from the corner. It was his father's main resting place when he was not tending to business below. A small table to the left of the chair supported the radio, which scratched out news of the war, but the little table to the right was the most important piece of furniture in Jubal Cole's apartment. It was where the whiskey bottle rested.

Jewell scuffed through the room to the tiny kitchen. With a box of crackers in one hand and a jar of jelly and a spoon in the other, he walked to the smaller of the two bedrooms and sat on the edge of his bed. He solemnly ate six of the small squares smeared with the jelly before his mouth demanded water and he returned to the kitchen. Until now, he had been careful not to think about the runt teacher who had shamed him without speaking a word to him, but he could shut her out no longer. Not even the solid smack delivered to the back of Lester Thurman's head on the way home had helped much. Strange little woman, that Miss Allen. Before the end of the day, she had the others paying attention to her without raising her voice. Very strange. But it would change in time; Jewell knew that he would find a way to pay her back. He was very good at paying people back.

"Jewell!" the command thundered upward from the bottom of the stairs.

The boy trotted to the head of the stairs. "Yeah."

"Don't 'yeah' me, boy. Get your hind end down here and help him with the trash."

Jewell took the stairs two at a time and shouldered against the back door to the pool hall, barely avoiding a collision with Emmett, who was burdened with a garbage can in each hand.

"Watch it, Emmett, will ya. Liked to banged my leg with that can."

"Sorry, Jewell," Emmett said softly, "I got all but that one back there."

Jewell nodded his head silently and made his way toward the bar and the remaining garbage can.

"I thought I told you not to mess around upstairs when you came home from school. You're big enough this year to help me with this place."

"I was hungry."

"From what? I'm the one workin' my butt off down here all day. I imagine I know about how hard you work down at the schoolhouse." He paused and Jewell felt his stare on the top of his head. "And be dang sure you get the lids clamped down tight. I ain't interested in every blame cat in town helpin' himself tonight."

The boy looked down at his feet, allowing the words to glance obliquely off him. Satisfied with his admonition, his father turned away with a shake of his head.

Emmett was waiting in the alley as Jewell banged through the door. The boy shoved the open can to the brick wall and clamped on the lid before hopping up on it, his back resting against the wall. Emmett shuffled three steps to Jewell's resting place and leaned his back against the rough bricks. Jewell turned his head and stared at the man, making no attempt to shift his gaze from time to time. He knew crazy Emmett did not mind; it was a fact that everyone in the Kingdom had learned early on. It puzzled Jewell that a man could be stared at and not take offense, even if he was crazy. It was like a horse or some kind of show animal at the fair—just standing there, knowing that other eyes bore down on them from the side, but not caring, or if they did care, hiding it deep inside somehow, in a place where the eyes could not penetrate.

Jewell had stared at Emmett many times, but each time there seemed to be something new to discover, some new crease in his face, some new way that he gnawed at the corner of his mouth. The first time Jewell saw Emmett's face, he had been positive that it was an ugly face, but now, after many long starings, he was not sure. Emmett's hair was crudely shorn above the ears, with an unruly part on the left side. It was black, jet black, and did not fit well with a weathered, crinkly face always covered with a wiry stubble that hissed when he dragged a hand over it. His nose was ordinary enough, and the little mouth too, with the spittle collecting sometimes in the corners before he remembered to mop it with the tip of his tongue.

The one feature that kept him from being downright ugly was his eyes. Jewell settled the issue once and for all in his mind. It was the deep-set green eyes, with their bushy brows like wooly worms protecting them. They were soft when they looked at you, though Emmett never looked at anyone for more than a second or two. The eyes seemed fixed now at some point beyond the littered backyard of the house across the alley. He would wait to see if Jewell wanted to speak; not once had Jewell ever heard Emmett speak first to anyone. A little black and white spotted cur yipped an argument at an unseen foe beyond the house.

"Just what my old man sounds like when I open my ears."

"You oughtn't to call him that, Jewell."

"Talks to you the same way. Why should you care what I call him?"

"Just ain't right, that's all."

"We'll see what you're callin' him 'fore long, if he keeps you around long enough. Be worse than 'old man' I reckon."

The trace of a smile crossed Emmett's face as he cast a glance at the boy. "I don't call nobody no hard names."

"We'll see. Let's get back before he misses us—me especially, since I got to go up there and live with him tonight."

Emmett nodded and followed the boy back into the noise and smoke.

# Chapter 2

*A* WORD please, Miss Allen." The gravely friendly voice of Nathan Bellman caught up with Annabelle as she hurried past the school principal's open office door.

Annabelle stopped in mid–stride and did a quick pivot toward the man, now standing in the doorway. He gestured her toward a seat in front of his desk.

"So, now you're officially combat tested." He smiled. "How did yesterday go?"

"Very well, thank you, Mr. Bellman . . . for a first day, I suppose. A few minor trials and tribulations."

"If they were minor, you had a good first day in the profession, indeed. I remember, despite herculean efforts not to, terrible glimpses of my first day." He leaned back in his chair and clasped his hands over the mat of graying hair.

"The most vivid memories center around a boy who was entertaining his neighbors by drinking grape soda through a straw. No great thing, except for the fact that the straw was inserted in his right nostril instead of his mouth."

Annabelle laughed out loud as he shook his head thoughtfully.

"It was the right nostril; I'll always remember. When I loudly pointed out the error of his ways, he jerked his head up, and to my great dismay and the high delight of the students, the straw somehow remained lodged in his nostril and tipped the soda bottle over. Suffice to say, things went downhill from that point."

He laughed with her and tilted his body back to his desk, absentmindedly rearranging the position of a stack of papers.

"You've got a relatively good group of kids in there. I track them all from the very start. There is one, however, who deserves special mention."

Annabelle knew without a doubt the name she was about to hear. "His name is Jewell Cole." Nathan glanced up at her and saw the instant recognition. "Yes, I imagine he managed to introduce himself one way or another."

"We have some things to work out," Annabelle said evenly, flatly, she hoped.

"There's always one or two along the way that we really don't know exactly what to do with. I've about given up on this boy, I'll tell you frankly. He has been held back one grade, and beyond that he's nearly a man in stature already. He lives with his father over a pool hall and bar operation. Very rough place, to say the least . . ." His voice trailed off.

"Does his mother live there with them?" Annabelle asked.

"Been gone for years. If you knew Jubal Cole, you would know why."

Annabelle nodded but continued to hold the man's eyes. He was offering her an avenue of escape, should Jewell prove too much to deal with, and while she felt some appreciation, the stronger feeling was almost resentment. After all, she had taught the boy for only one day.

"Well, no need to belabor the point, but . . . if he . . ."

"Mr. Bellman, I appreciate your concern and thank you for the background on Jewell. He wasn't actually disruptive yesterday.

It was more of a communication problem. I think we can work it out." She smiled sheepishly as she realized how the last sentence must have sounded to Bellmam, a grizzled veteran, coming from a wet-behind-the-ears beginner.

"Well, good for you, young lady. Maybe you just can do something with him."

The encouragement was genuine; there was not a trace of condescension. Annabelle was very good at recognizing both traits.

"If you need me, I'll always be here to support you."

"Thank you, Mr. Bellman, I appreciate the help."

Annabelle stood and turned toward the door.

"Be sure to check them for straws before you start class."

Annabelle could hear him chuckling as she began the long walk down the corridor.

The second morning of class had gone rather well, Annabelle assured herself as she savored a bite of egg salad sandwich in the lunch room. Her brood was scattered loosely about the three tables in front of her, intermingled at the edges with the fifth-grade class of Lela Parker, who sat beside Annabelle. Student number Twenty-seven sat at the end of the far table hunched over a wrinkled brown paper sack, four feet of empty bench space on either side of him. There had not been the hint of a disruption during the morning session, but this gave Annabelle no cause for celebration; much of the day remained and beyond that an entire school year— nine long months of dealing with the issue that was Jewell Cole.

Annabelle could not refrain from glancing in his direction from time to time, indiscreetly she thought, but not so indiscreetly that Lela Parker did not notice. Her eyes twinkled behind dark-rimmed glasses slid halfway down her nose.

"So, how was morning number two with young Mister

Cole?" she asked after a soothing sip of scalding coffee from the red thermos top.

"Very good, really, Lela," Annabelle answered.

"Very good, meaning no spitballs or coyote howls, or very good, meaning you think he actually heard something you said?"

Annabelle sighed in resignation, irritated even before she heard the truth of her answer come from her mouth. "The former, unfortunately."

"Don't let yourself get too caught up in it, Annabelle. It just isn't fair either to yourself or to the other kids. I survived my year after I figured that fact out." Lela punctuated the last statement with two fingernail taps to the side of her thermos. "Some of them, for whatever reasons . . ." Her right hand drifted, open-fingered and lazy, away from her head in a helpless little gesture.

The delicate flavor of the egg salad faded to clay in Annabelle's mouth, and she chewed the last bite dutifully and swallowed before Lela continued.

"I know it sounds harsh, especially to someone so fresh to the battle, Annabelle, but, well, I really don't mean to squash your hopes, it's just that I don't—none of us—want to see your career get off to a bad start because of one hard-core kid . . ." The sentence sputtered back to life. ". . . who probably shouldn't even be in school."

Annabelle looked at the boy now, his square jawline slowly grinding away at the contents of his lunch sack, his gaze fixed straight ahead into nothingness. Although Annabelle could only imagine, she shuddered with the thought that the look would better fit in with a prison crowd down at the state prison in Jefferson City. She let her mind drift for a moment, powerless to stop the scene from materializing. The prison grays hanging loosely on the twenty-year-old, his eyes even harder now, darting furtively about at the hardened men packed uncomfortably around him.

From somewhere around the edges of the dismal scene, Lela's insistent voice crept in and shook Annabelle free. "Part of it is his age. Nathan claims that he is only a year older than his classmates, but I—and I'm not the only one—think he's two ahead." She paused and shook her head. "I don't really think it would matter anyway. He's like an angry grown man tied up in a boy's body . . . like he's never really been a child."

*Like he's never really been a child.* The words rang in Annabelle's ears like an echo. Dear God, how she knew what it was like to have never really been a child. Lela's voice chimed on, a faraway sound again.

The memories crept back like burglars in the shadows smiles at other children unreturned, empty swing seats, giggles behind her back and derisive laughter, and the one sight that forever convinced her that childhood would pass her by like a cold wind in December—the first time a classmate imitated her hump-shouldered walk, his head pulled down grotesquely as he entertained his fellow third graders. He had not known that Annabelle was watching, and he grinned stupidly at being caught; but it was finished, the deed done. And Annabelle let it go, allowing the elusive dream called childhood to slip quietly from her fingertips, like a wounded bird unable to survive despite tender care. She let it fall from her hand so that she would not have to watch it die.

Lela's voice again and with it her brown eyes from behind the glasses. "I'll declare, Annabelle, I seem to have put you in a trance with my rambling."

"Oh no, not at all, Lela. I'm sorry. My mind wandered. Listen, I do appreciate your concern, and I need all the insight I can get on, well, all of my students."

"Not much insight I can offer about him. I'm just trying to tell you how to survive. Whatever, time to reenter the fray, huh?"

"Yes, it is that time." Annabelle forced a smile.

"I promise I won't always be a boring lunch companion."

"Not at all, Lela. It was helpful. Thanks."

Lela had already turned away, her attention directed at one of her fifth graders. "Jeremy Canton, kindly stop mashing that sandwich on the table and put it in the trash can."

The plan began to form in Jewell's mind as Annabelle read enthusiastically from Cornelia Meigs's *Invincible Louisa*. She had announced yesterday that the first twenty minutes of class following lunch would be devoted to reading aloud. The whole scene was more than Jewell could bear: all the snivelling little stupid-heads hanging on every word, the runt teacher acting like she was some sort of actress; it was something that required his immediate attention. After all, he had allowed the morning to pass peacefully, but it was mostly from boredom. This opportunity was different though; soon the runt would know exactly who student number Twenty-seven was, and she would not soon forget.

Jewell fingered the rock in his right pocket; it had been carefully selected. Flat and smooth around the edges, the brown missile fit perfectly between his thumb and forefinger. He slowly slid the rock from his pocket and straightened his posture in the hard-backed seat, leaning slightly to the right and pulling his right foot back for balance. She looked up from the pages of the book too frequently to suit him, but it was of no real consequence; everyone, including her, would know who had committed the deed. Still, he wanted the runt to hear the rock whiz close to her ear just before it cracked like a rifle shot against the blackboard. Probably better not to hit her, but he had no misgivings about a target a couple of feet right of her head. After all, things like this should be something of a challenge.

Annabelle's head bobbed forward as her eyes found the proper line in the book. The knifelike jab of pain on the point of her shoulder came as one with the sharp report of the rock crashing against the blackboard, and her left hand dropped involuntarily from the book.

In the five seconds of dead silence that followed, Annabelle's mind whirred like a machine as it processed the incredible event: It had to be him, no doubt. Had he meant to strike her? Doubtful, probably bad aim. The pain was a little fire, but she could handle it. Stop reading and force the issue at once, or wait and pick her time? Later, but only a bit later. Bellman's office? The great question, that; really the only question. Was he salvageable or not? This could be the end for him. It was an act of physical violence. Her shoulder throbbed for answers.

With a tiny clearing of her throat, Annabelle reread the interrupted sentence from the beginning, and, to Jewell's astonishment as well as that of the students who realized what had just happened, she continued to read. Perfectly. Volume, tone, inflection—it was all there. Jewell could feel his face begin to flush; the thing was not turning out well at all. He knew the rock had hit her, and he knew how much it must have hurt; he had thrown it with all his might. And yet, there she stood, as if a fly had brushed her shoulder, reading like an actress again.

Annabelle read for ten minutes before coming to a suitable stopping place. "We will stop here for today."

A long pause, with nervous whispers breaking out in the last two rows.

"Student number Twenty-seven and I have some business to attend to. Please review your arithmetic assignment until we return."

Annabelle walked to the end of the first row, knelt to the floor, and picked up the rock. She continued down the outside aisle, stopping directly in front of Jewell's desk. He did not look up.

"Come with me."

For an instant, Jewell considered disobeying, just sitting there until she left for the principal and then dashing from the school.

What did it matter now anyway? He was as good as gone. He would have to figure a way to minimize the beating his father would give him, and he needed some time alone to work on that knotty problem.

But he obeyed. It was the voice—a soft sound, without malice, devoid of the sharp edges that should have been there. It was a voice of pain, not physical pain, but a strange kind of pain, distant somehow, haunting, and the boy could not disobey it. He followed Annabelle through the doorway, but instead of turning right toward Nathan Bellman's office, she turned left toward the outside door. She pushed it open and held it for Jewell. The warm breeze pushed gently at them, and Annabelle allowed it to caress her face before she spoke.

"Jewell." The sound of his name surprised him but it was good the way she said it. Other than Emmett, nobody ever said his name. She turned to face him now, his eyes fixed downward at the toes of his shoes. "No long speeches, Jewell. No trip to the principal's office. Just you and me. I know word of this incident will leak out, but I'll find a way to fix that."

A cool ripple of relief passed through Jewell; maybe his father would be denied the opportunity of thrashing him.

"Look at me, please."

The tousled head came up slowly, the dark eyes furtive, unable to lock on hers for more than a moment, but long enough to see the single tear slide from her eye and down her cheek.

"We are very much alike, you and I, Jewell. We are familiar with pain. Not this so much," she brushed her right hand over her throbbing shoulder. "No, I mean the real kind, the kind nobody else can understand. Believe me when I tell you that I have dealt with more of it than you. And believe me when I promise you that I want to help you with yours."

She paused and backhanded the tear stain, taking in more of the breeze. "You cannot make me dislike you, Jewell. It is a waste of your time. If the rock had split my head open, I would stand here and tell you the same thing."

The tiny burning sensation in Jewell's throat grew, and he knew he would soon have to deal with it. Words came inside his head, words of apology, words that begged for release, but he would not free them. He swallowed against the burning; he could overcome it.

"I would like for us to return to the class and finish out the afternoon."

Jewell managed a nod, and Annabelle sensed a bit of promise in it. She opened her hand and looked at the rock, holding it so that Jewell would be forced to see it.

"This is a keepsake for me now. I will put it in a special place, and when I take it out and look at it, I will remember how we are alike, and I won't remember the pain."

Annabelle gestured toward the door as she began to walk, and Jewell fell in step behind her.

# Chapter 3

*T*HE FACT that Annabelle Allen had found a room only three blocks from Christ Kingdom Baptist Church was a comfort, especially on Sundays. It eased the burden that came with living alone, nearly one hundred miles from her family. Harlon and Madalene Allen were as much a part of Randolph County, Missouri, as the sturdy cedar trees that lined the gravel driveway leading to the farmhouse. Like the trees, her parents were deeply rooted, a part of the landscape, a part of life so precious that Annabelle could almost close her eyes and return to them. Almost. But the church was there, visible, softly beckoning, and its members had quickly extended their arms to the newly arrived young teacher. It would become the place where Annabelle carried all of her burdens and laid them down. It had always been so.

The image that stared at her from the mirror was suitable: a powder blue dress of simple yet attractive cut, the flat white collar just so, the white belt to match, and a smile that came easily and without pretense. Bible and purse in hand, she walked from the house into the soft yellow of late summer.

The man was standing in exactly the same spot as last Sunday, a step from the street sign and looking down Hodge Street as Annabelle walked up the sidewalk toward the church building. His attire could only be honestly described as shabby, but the effort he made to keep it clean was not lost on the keen eye of Annabelle Allen, nor was the nearly imperceptible nod as she neared him. The sleeves and lapels of his suit coat were worn slick, and his white shirt collar was badly frayed from contact with his neck whiskers. When she sought his eyes, he shifted his gaze almost immediately, but it was not furtive. It was done in deference to Annabelle, and there was a warmth about the man that touched her, perhaps more than it should have.

"Good morning," she said.

"G . . . good mornin' to you too."

"I'm fairly new here, and I don't believe we have met. I'm Annabelle Allen." She extended her right hand, and he wrapped his calloused hand gently around hers.

"My name is Emmett Tragman, and I . . . I'm pleased to know you." He bowed his head slightly with the introduction.

"I'm a new schoolteacher . . . sixth grade," she said.

"I work around town, do most anything needs doin', but mostly I help down to the pool hall."

Tiny alarm bells sounded with the mention of the pool hall. "I see . . . well, it's good to meet you, Mr. Tragman."

His smile broke wide and sheepish. "I'd a lot rather you just call me Emmett, ma'am. Ain't nobody ever called me mister."

"Emmett it is then. And drop the 'ma'ams' for me too, all right?"

He nodded in reply.

"Have you been a member here long?" she asked.

"No ma . . . , no, couple of months or so, but it's a good church. They ain't afraid of the truth."

"Well, that's good to hear. My beginning impressions are very good also." Annabelle glanced at her watch. "Better get inside, I suppose. It was very nice getting to know you, Emmett." She nodded a smile at him before she turned to leave.

During the service, Annabelle glanced casually about the congregation, already putting faces with names. An outstanding feature, a mannerism, style of dress—there were dozens of things with which to glue a face and name together. She would certainly have no difficulty remembering Emmett Tragman. By the end of the service, she had not yet located him. She decided that he must be above her, in the balcony, even though there were empty spaces in some of the pews on the main level, and she made a mental note to look up there.

The pastor called on someone to pronounce the benediction and quietly walked up the aisle past Annabelle. With the "amen," she turned to look behind her toward the balcony. He was still seated in the far corner, the others about him already chatting and moving away. Somehow the fact that he appeared so alone, even in a crowd, did not trouble Annabelle, and she wondered why. He stood and pressed his hands over the lapels of his coat, slowly allowing them to slide to his side. Just before Annabelle decided he had not seen her, Emmett lifted his right hand a few inches from his side and moved his fingers in a tiny wave.

When the Sunday evening twilight oozed through his open window and softened the harshness of his room, Jewell was at once thankful and disheartened. Soft, late summer sounds came to him and were not drowned out by the weekday clamor rising from Jubal's Kingdom. The scratchy radio voice that brought news from the war drifted in from the next room. The absence of thick layers of tobacco smoke gave freedom to his sense of smell, and from somewhere west of the apartment he drew in the aroma of frying meat—chicken, he was nearly certain—and he felt the saliva form a delicate pool under his tongue. Yes, these were needful things for a boy who had learned to appreciate even the poorest offerings of earth. But even as he accepted them, he could not shut out the infernal tinkling.

The little screaming sounds came in intervals, sometimes seemingly only minutes apart, other times perhaps a half hour apart. They were like razors in his ears, yet the boy knew that he must listen to them closely and not only count the sounds but gauge their very timbre. If the neck of the whiskey bottle touched the rim of the glass too few times, with an ever deepening tone to the tinkling, it meant that the comfortable haze was not coming to Jubal quickly enough and that he was likely to rise from his chair only half-drunk. And Jubal Cole half-drunk was a living nightmare to anyone close to him. But if the tinkling remained soft for eight or ten times, and if the sounds were spaced fairly evenly, it meant that the man would not rise before morning. Jubal Cole dead drunk was a large harmless lump.

Jewell's tension eased as the thin light melted away; the darkness also helped with the problem, and there was no light from under his closed door now. The neck of the bottle softly tapped the rim of the glass for the eighth time. To anyone except Jewell, the sound would have been musical, like a fragile wind chime touched by a faint breeze. It was not musical to the boy, but it was a good sound; it was a safe sound. He could relax now, allow his guard to drop and be thirteen years old.

He stretched back on his bed and clasped his hands behind his head on the grimy pillow. He shook off his shoes; there would be no need to move quickly and without slipping tonight. Soon, Jubal Cole would be dead drunk. Jewell turned off the alarm system in his brain and listened to the friendly yapping of a dog in the alley, now intermingled with the singsong voice of a girl, and he knew that they were frolicking together. He allowed himself to tap into the pleasure of it all, to see himself playfully cuffing the mongrel about the ears. Jewell rested now, floating with the pleasant offerings from the alley; he knew that tonight there would be no more tinkling of glass in the next room.

But when the great church bell at Christ Kingdom Baptist began to toll, Jewell Cole counted the peals. The bell tolled eight times.

To the amazement of his fellow students, but not to Annabelle, Jewell had caused no further problems the following week. Although he had not spoken a word or shown any apparent interest in the subjects discussed, Annabelle caught him in a look of cautious inquiry from time to time, and smiled inwardly.

Nathan Bellman had spoken with her about the incident with the rock, and she had skillfully minimized the entire affair. Just another attention-seeking ploy, the tossing of a small rock toward the front of the classroom. Nothing more. She had given it scant notice, not even missing a sentence in the story being read. The boy was disappointed with the results. She had won the skirmish.

Annabelle glanced casually about the classroom at the heads bobbing up and down in thought. The geography quiz covered the locations of the countries engaged in the European theater of the war. Annabelle had made a rough sketch of the national boundaries and drawn a rectangle in the middle of the countries, with the assignment being proper identification. She pushed away from her desk and began to stroll the aisles, looking discreetly over shoulders and offering quiet encouragements.

As she neared Jewell's desk, he began to fidget and Annabelle fully expected to see a paper filled with doodles, if anything at all. She was badly mistaken.

"May I see it, please?"

Jewell offered no resistance as Annabelle picked up the paper and studied it. Several heads turned cautiously in the direction of Jewell's desk. Annabelle stared in amazement at the paper. The inexact boundary lines of her sketch had been redrawn, and she knew with the first glance that they were much more accurate than her own. The paper was too thick to allow for tracing and, besides, she was certain that none of the boy's books had been taken from the shelf under his seat. In fact, she had yet to see a book on any subject on his desk. The jagged northern coast of Germany, complete with the finger of Denmark, the elongated isle of Great Britain, the leg and boot of Italy with Sicily balanced on the toe, the sweeping coast of North Africa. She shook her head at the sight of it. The proper name was in every box, some misspelled, but all recognizable.

Annabelle's heart pounded with excitement as she leaned forward and spoke softly in Jewell's ear. "Jewell, this . . . this is wonderful work." She walked quickly to the front of the room.

"Students, please put your pencils down and listen. It appears that Jewell has drawn a much better picture of the countries than I have."

Twitters and whispers darted about the room as several sets of eyes dared look at the right rear corner of the room. Jewell, eyes fixed at the top of his desk, continued to fidget; this was not the sort of attention to which he was accustomed. The teacher's voice pierced the room, but he was not yet certain if it was a good thing.

"What I would like to do will make those of you who were having trouble happy. We will take the quiz again on Monday, and I will copy Jewell's drawing for our map. He has done an excellent job, and I think we all should benefit from it."

Jewell felt his face flush, and for an instant he could not distinguish between anger and pride before accepting the latter. He risked a peep about the room. Several heads were turned toward him, some with mouths dropped half-open in bewilderment, others with brows furrowed in puzzlement. He looked back to the safety of his desk.

"We will use the remaining time this afternoon to review this lesson and practice for Monday." She looked at Jewell. "Jewell, would you please stay for a few moments after the bell?"

He nodded but did not look up as the whispers broke out again. The thing had gone very far within the space of only a few minutes. The result of words spoken by the tiny woman teacher . . . nothing more than that, and yet this confused adrenaline rush within him. It was like watching pieces of a puzzle float about, and his mind reached for them and began to sort them. He needed the bit of remaining class time to steady himself, relieved that the whispers had died away.

He remained seated as the others filed from the room. Annabelle waited for the last child to leave before walking to the rear of the room and taking the seat beside Jewell.

"Jewell, I'm so proud of you. This is wonderful work." She laid the paper out on the desk, carefully smoothing the crinkled edges. "How did you manage to learn so much about this?"

"He keeps the radio on all the time at home . . . they're always talking about the war . . . and . . . I like to look at the maps in the papers and magazines."

The thrill of hearing his voice for the first time was something that Annabelle Allen would always hold as a dear treasure, locked safely away in a chamber of her heart. In the years to come, she would replay the marvelous words many times. She said a silent, thankful prayer for the beginning.

"Well, I must say that you pay attention very well when you choose to." She tested a tiny smile on him, and although he did not return the gesture, he managed to thank her with his eyes.

"What I would like for you to do this weekend is to take a clean piece of paper and draw your map out. Use a big dull pencil so that the lines show up well, all right? Then use your book to correct the spellings of some of the countries; that's the only thing keeping it from being perfect. I'll blank out the names of the countries and have copies made for the class quiz." She paused and held his eyes for a moment. "Of course, you have already made a one hundred on the quiz."

The flush began to creep back into his face as Annabelle continued. "What I want to do is to post your work in the hallway on the display board. It will be a very good example of geography work for the other students to see." She paused. "Could you do this for me?"

Jewell hesitated and swallowed against the rising tension. He realized the significance of the moment; it was clearly a crossroad. If he went along with her and allowed his map to be posted in the hallway, he would become a real student, and other things would be expected of him. The only reason geography held his interest was the war. Arithmetic, grammar, history—he would be touched by all that too. And what of his bag of tricks? What would become of that prize possession, and the fearful respect of the others that came with it? The pounding came to his ears; the little woman was waiting for an answer.

Annabelle knew precisely of his dilemma, and she allowed him to struggle with it, to sort through all the implications. She desired a meaningful decision, one that would last. But she could not allow the silence to grow too loud; he was, after all, a child.

"Jewell, I said something wrong a minute ago. I asked if you would do this for me. What I'm really asking is if you will do this for *you*. And I do know what I'm asking, believe me. I will help you every step of the way. I promise you that, and I don't make promises lightly."

Annabelle neatly folded the paper in half. The muffled sounds of shoes scuffing along in the hallway and the chatter of children came as welcome intrusions into the silence. She would say no more; Jewell would have to decide. Annabelle prayed another short prayer to the Keeper of all children.

Jewell shook his head from side to side as Annabelle's heart dropped with the misinterpretation of the gesture.

"Heck, I reckon it'll be okay with me."

# Chapter 4

THE LETTER from Hazel Lee came the following Tuesday, and Annabelle held it lovingly for a moment before beginning to read.

*Dearest Sister Annabelle,*

*So how does it go with you, now that you are a TEACHER?! I am dying to know how the first days have gone. My little sister up there in front of all those mean little nasties! Ha! If only I could see you, how proud I would be. Same for Mom and Daddy. Mom will write soon, if she has not already. I worry about Daddy, and I know that you do too. It's hard to believe that Matthew has been dead for nearly two years. Daddy grieved so long and so hard. If only we could have had his body back, I think Daddy would have taken it better.*

Annabelle looked up from the letter through eyes clouded with tears. It did seem so long ago now, the bloody affair that forever changed the enchanting name of Pearl Harbor into a searing poker in the collective brain of America. Matthew, the tall, strong brother with the quiet demeanor, the gentle giant of the family, gone for all time. Matthew, her protector, the brother who could discourage any unfriendly attention directed toward Annabelle with a mere glance. When the U.S.S. Arizona slid beneath the swirling waters of the bay, it became Matthew's tomb, and that of more than a thousand other brothers and husbands and sons. A flag had come home to Missouri in Matthew's place, but it was not enough.

*Anyway, write to him—lots, Annabelle. You seem to be the one who still softens his heart.*

*I pray for Charles every day, and I know you do too. His unit is moving north through Italy. Thank God at least Italy is out of it now. Now for that black-headed monster in Germany. Someday soon, he will get his.*

*Little Anna wants to see you and says hello to her "Aunt Teacher." She's almost old enough to be truly proud of you—heavens, maybe she already is. Only the smartest five-year-old in the universe, of course.*

*Oh, Annabelle, don't let it be like college for you—weekends studying and working and never coming home for a visit. You've DONE IT now, sister. A job and a paycheck and security—they will never find another teacher like you—all that, you have earned more than anyone I have ever known. So take some time for yourself now, and us. My peach cobbler is almost as good as Mom's now, if I do say so myself. Just get on the train and roll on back here SOON!*

*Anna is hanging on to my dress like a little monkey, so I'll end it for now and get this in the mail. Please take care of yourself. Write immediately and buy a train ticket very soon.*

*Much love,*
*Hazel Lee*

Annabelle refolded the letter and placed it on the corner of her desk. She would read it again before bedtime, with a cup of hot tea, and she knew that she would weep again over Matthew's memory. It was not a disturbing thought. Some people were worth the shedding of tears, and Matthew was worth enough to fill the ocean that covered him now.

Lela Parker sat across from Annabelle, munching a cheese sandwich, her jaws working mechanically and without enjoyment. Jewell Cole's geography map had been posted for a day and a half now, and the faculty was atwitter. Whether from sheer disbelief or being stricken mute with bewilderment, no one had yet broached the subject with Annabelle. Several teachers, and even Nathan Bellman, had danced around the question, but Annabelle had offered no assistance in providing clues to the great mystery. But the way Lela's jaws were working her sandwich now told Annabelle that the details of the great coup would soon be available to the public. Lela plopped the half-eaten sandwich on her paper napkin and folded her hands under her chin, waiting for Annabelle to look up from the bowl of soup.

"Okay, I can't stand it any longer. Two questions. One, is it really his work? Two, if it is, how exactly did you trick him into it? I'm waiting, but not patiently." Lela wore her best Cheshire cat smile.

"Well, I'm glad that someone finally had the courage to ask these simple questions," Annabelle answered with a wry smile of her own. She daubed at the corners of her mouth with her napkin after a sip of milk. "Question one. Without doubt, it is Jewell's work. I had drawn a rough sketch of the European Theater countries for a geography quiz, and when I walked the aisles to make a progress check, lo and behold, I look over his shoulder to see that he had improved on mine considerably. I was thunderstruck, to say the least. My first thought was the same as yours. But his books, as always, were under his seat, closed as clamshells. *His* work, no doubt."

"So question two doesn't apply?"

"Not in the slightest, Lela."

"This is too much for a poor old teacher like me to comprehend." Lela picked up the sandwich and flopped it down again. "But . . ."

"Lela," Annabelle raised her hand, "turns out that it was the war."

"The war?"

"His father evidently has the radio on all the time at home, and it piqued Jewell's interest. He says he likes to study the maps in the papers and magazines."

Lela shook her head. "I'd have bet the two hundred acres old Uncle Clarence hasn't given me yet that Jewell Cole couldn't locate the Atlantic Ocean on a globe."

"Well, Lela, you would have lost the farm."

"And the spelling and all . . ."

"I'll admit, I did allow him to correct most of the spellings, but he had them all correctly labeled, I assure you."

"I suppose you intend to play this for all it's worth?"

"Like a violin, Lela. Like a fine violin."

Lela picked up the sandwich and absently bit out a half-moon and resumed chewing. She finished the sandwich in silence, but not without shaking her head from time to time. The bell rang in the hallway.

"Back to the trenches," Annabelle said as she cleaned up her place at the table.

"Not before I ask one more, Annabelle . . . while I'm being totally nosey and all."

"Fire away."

"There is a version of the rock incident floating around that claims you were struck."

Annabelle pursed her lips into crooked smile. "Lela, I didn't even miss a line in the story I was reading aloud to the class."

"That's not an answer."

"It will have to do, Lela. Got to run now."

Within a week's time, Jubal Cole began to notice subtle changes in Jewell's habits. The boy had never been one to have his nose in a schoolbook. Jubal had seen him looking, idly he assumed, at newspapers lying around or at an occasional magazine, but not a dreaded schoolbook. Jubal swiveled his head away from the hiss of hamburger patties frying on the grill and looked at the two laden garbage cans at the end of the bar. *Maybe that's where he is now,* Jubal mused, *filling his head full of high learning while the garbage spills over onto the floor.*

"Lester, watch these burgers for a minute while I get my kid, will you?" The ruddy-faced man with the sweaty cowboy hat looked up over his mug of beer.

"Jubal, I ain't never passed for no cook."

"I ain't askin' you to start now, Lester. Just holler for Emmett if the smoke gets too thick over this thing."

Jubal was four long steps from the bar before Lester could renew his protest. He turned to his bar mate.

"Can you tell 'all right' thick from 'too thick', Harry?"

"Cain't."

"Emmett, get on over here!" Lester bellowed in the direction of the snooker tables.

Jewell heard the heavy steps pound up the stairs. He snapped the book shut and scrambled to the floor in search of his shoes. He had one on and was struggling with the other when Jubal banged the door open with a closed fist. Jewell flinched as a big hand darted in front of him to the bed and snatched up the book.

"Gee . . . og . . . er . . . fee. Well, now ain't this some surprisin' thing here?" He thumbed the pages slowly, looking mostly at the illustrations. "I don't reckon it tells in here where to find garbage cans runnin' over in my floor?"

The boy shook his head silently, not yet ready to venture a look at Jubal.

"I don't reckon it does either, boy. I don't reckon it says much at all about helpin' me scrape a livin' out of this place." He tossed the open book to the bed, face down, and it flopped open, creasing several pages. "Boy, the only thing that matters much to me is that I don't get no trouble from the school people. And I ain't had none for a long time now, and it don't seem to me that your book studyin' had nothin' to do with that. I don't plan on it gettin' in the way of your chores around here, you understand me?"

Jewell nodded without looking up. He could feel his father's eyes boring down on him, waiting for an answer. Should it be the truth or something that would just make him go away? The seed planted by the new teacher was living in the warm soil of his brain, and he very much desired to nurture it. But at what price? Was it worth risking his father's wrath? He could remain silent and be more careful about studying; Jewell could simply wait until he was drunk. But the nagging little desire to share the wonder of the seed grew stronger by the second. The man was his father after all, and Jewell knew that the man had never had any formal schooling. Surely some hidden part of him, some reminder of happier times, could be freed by the knowledge of Jewell's seed. He drew a quick breath; he would risk it.

"I got me a . . . new teacher this year. She thinks I can do some things right . . . and . . ."

"And she's gonna turn your backward ways around, huh? Just like magic. All those years of horsin' around and not payin' attention to nothin' . . . and this magic worker's just gonna make it all go away?"

"I didn't say that. I just said she . . ."

"Listen here, boy. In a couple more years, you'll be past eighth grade, and you can walk away from that school just like I did when I grew up. And you can make a place for yourself around here. If you show some gumption, before long you and me'll be runnin' this place together. And one day, it'll be yours."

Jewell looked up at him; the great, sagging face resembled a picture of George Washington, the heavy, solemn features weighted down by unknowable sorrows. His eyebrows joined above the bridge of his great nose, forming a dark woolly line that seemed to split his face into two distinct parts. The mouth, often given to cruel lines, was ordinary now. There was no use in Jewell's attempting to explain his feelings. In the only way he knew, the man was offering the promise of a life for Jewell, and the fact that it held little attraction for the boy mattered not a whit. Jewell nodded again and lowered his head.

"Now get your hind end down here and help Emmett with the trash and the floor sweepin'."

Jubal stomped from the room and down the stairs. Jewell reached for the geography book, turning it over and smoothing down the pages. He would have to be more careful now that Jubal considered schooling a threat. Jubal Cole did not take kindly to threats.

The neck of the whiskey bottle sounded its Sunday evening chime against Jubal's glass for the fourth time, but it was a hard sound. The warm blanket of alcohol should have already enwrapped him by now, and the fact that it had not was a wiggling thorn in his flesh. His mind sought restful images—quiet, sleepy, floating things that took away all the cares of life, but they would not come. The crackling drone of the radio, usually a comforting sound, only added to the growing torment.

The images that did come were irritating beyond measure. Jubal could see his son smiling in class at school, holding a textbook in front of his face. He could not understand the words, but he knew that they were the right words by the way his teacher was nodding her head. There were no distinct features to her face, and Jubal promised himself that very soon he would know her features, this bothersome woman who dared to make his son a high-minded thinker, better than his own father. Yes, he would get to know her soon.

But the features of his son's face were vividly clear, and the face behind the image was only steps away in the next room. The thought that the boy might be reading a schoolbook squirmed like an insect that had somehow gotten inside Jubal's skull. He had to know—now; he must gather himself and silently move to the door before the boy had a chance to hide the book. The voice coming from the radio would conceal the sound of his movement.

Jubal drew two long, steadying breaths and began to shift his weight forward in the old chair. He made sure the squeaks were tiny things as his sock-covered feet groped for the floor. Carefully, he bent his long frame forward, his weight over his feet now, and tested the standing position. The teetering sensation passed quickly as he drew himself to his full height. It would be easy now; the door to the boy's room was only four steps away.

Jewell studied the shape of the Italian coastline, marveling at the distinct shape of the boot. He thought of the man named Mussolini, now imprisoned in his own country by people who once followed his commands. This thing called war had many twists and turns. Jewell had a hundred questions with no answers, but he would soon seek answers from a teacher who seemed to know everything.

When he heard the turning of the doorknob, Jewell realized that there was no time to hide the book. The glass tinkling was only up to the count of four, and he was thankful that he still wore his shoes. Something very ugly was about to happen. The door crashed open as the soles of his shoes found the floor. He had learned long ago not to look at his father's face at a time like this. It was a paralyzing thing, if only for a fraction of a second, and he could not spare fractions of seconds. He fixed his eyes on the man's belt buckle; if he could manage to keep the buckle at least five feet from his body he would be safe. Sooner or later, the man would make his lunge and leave the doorway uncovered. It was in that moment that Jewell would find a crack of space and slither through it.

"You little . . ." The belt buckle moved with frightening speed, but before the gap was closed, Jewell ducked to his knees and spun with all his might toward the wall. To Jewell's horror, his father halted his lunge and spun in a tight parallel movement. When Jewell was one step from the open doorway, the blow came quartering from behind him. The pain was white hot, just below and to the rear of his left eye. The force of the blow hurled him through the opening, preventing further abuse. Jubal slipped with the effort of it all, and his groping fingers only brushed the boy's ankle. Still stunned, Jewell gathered his feet under his buttocks and sprang toward the staircase. Even the pounding of his shoes on the stairs could not overcome the pounding of his heart. The curses chased after him from the top of the stairs, but Jewell knew he was safe; his father would never risk the stairs, even if the night was only four chimes old. Jewell walked unhurriedly to the end of the alley, allowing his heart to return to a normal pace.

When he reached the corner of the last building and turned toward Main Street, his thoughts turned to the geography book. There was little hope that Jubal would not turn his attention to it. The book would receive the punishment instead of Jewell. No, there was little hope at all.

Emmett Tragman's measured pace was brisk as he listened to the scuffs of his shoe soles on the broken concrete sidewalk. When he drew within a half block of Jubal's Kingdom, he spied the slouched form against the concrete block wall at the edge of the alley. The head was down and the left hand covered the side of his face. Emmett's pace quickened; whoever it was seemed oblivious to his approach.

Emmett was only ten steps away when Jewell became aware of the sound of footsteps. His left hand shot downward from his face as his posture straightened.

"Hey, Jewell." The words were spoken quietly and without apprehension despite the knowledge that something was badly amiss.

"Hi." The voice was as much a part of the shadows as of a boy.

"You all right?"

Jewell nodded quickly, much too quickly, and the stupid little gesture caused a deepening of the throb that now owned half his head. He was reasonably certain that the trickle of blood was lost in the dirty light at the edge of the alley, but the need to reach up and touch it was something he could not ignore for long. In the few seconds of silence that followed, Jewell struggled with two urges, equally strong: Just dismiss Emmett with a word or two and pretend to walk down the alley toward the apartment, or reach out to him and accept his help. His legs were trembling now that the crisis had passed; he would have to make the decision immediately.

But the little man who was no stranger to sorrow saw the blood and heard the anguish in the one word the boy had spoken; Jewell would not have to make the choice.

"Your daddy?"

The tousled hair bobbed up and down, much slower this time.

"He didn't follow you down the stairs, did he?"

"No."

Emmett stepped forward and enveloped Jewell with his right arm. Jewell batted against the hot tears and lowered his head to hide them. He saw the flash of white handkerchief and felt the firm but gentle pressure over his wound.

"It's all right now. I aim to help you. Come on to my place, and I'll take a look at this for you."

Emmett felt Jewell's head move against his chest in affirmation, and the two began to walk.

"Here, you hold this tight up there yourself, and we can walk better."

# Chapter 5

*T*HE MAN and the boy passed no one as Jubal's Kingdom fell into the shadows behind them, and then another block of storefronts and an alley melted into the shadows. Another block, and they stood at the corner of an old two-story rooming house. Emmett motioned toward the rear of the house and led the way. The unlocked outside door creaked a wooden protest as it opened to a staircase much like the one Jewell had just fled from. At the top, Emmett opened another unlocked door and stepped into the one-room apartment, flipping a switch. Jewell squinted at the glare from the bare light bulb and winced in pain.

He glanced around the small room that was home to Emmett as the little man puttered busily in the top drawer of an old dresser. The panes of the single window were clean, as was the sill, but the flimsy cloths that passed for curtains were tattered and stained with age. The furnishings were sparse: the dresser, nearly devoid of varnish and with a diagonal crack in the half mirror, a metal frame bed only a foot above the wooden floor, and two armless chairs squeezed under a square table with fold-up legs. A two-foot-square metal wash basin hung under a single cabinet in the middle of one wall, beside the toilet.

Jewell's eyes swept slowly now; there was no need to peek at things. He had been invited into the room as a friend, someone who would surely understand the meager surroundings and not attach them to the man who lived in them. A doorless closet was tucked into one corner with a modest scattering of shirts and trousers, neatly arranged. It was a room whose very walls should have moaned with loneliness, but somehow Jewell decided that they did not. He was surprised when his gaze wandered to the old black leather Bible resting on a corner of the dresser. He had always assumed that Emmett could not read despite his wizardry with the snooker scores down at the Kingdom. He rolled the thought over in his mind. No, it was likely that Emmett could not read after all. The Bible was the only reading material of any sort in the room. Besides, many people kept a Bible around like some sort of holy ornament, an object intended to assure anyone who saw it, even its owner, of a life of some worth. That was probably it; the Bible was something that made Emmett feel better about himself.

"Sit down over here under the light."

Jewell sat down in the chair that Emmett pulled out from the table. He flinched at the touch of the cool, damp cloth as Emmett daubed gently at the wound. The laceration was less than an inch in length, but it was deep, with jagged edges.

"What's it look like?"

"I seen worse," Emmett answered calmly.

"Can you fix it with tape? I ain't goin' to no doctor." He had no fear of needles and thread; it was the questions that the doctor would ask—questions that would eventually lead to his father. He must not allow this to happen.

"Reckon I can, Jewell, if that's what you want. Ought to be sewed shut though."

"No. No doctor."

Emmett worked silently as he cleaned the gash and held a cloth firmly in place until the bleeding had subsided. He then placed a small square of cloth over it, securing three strips of tape to the undamaged flesh above and below the wound.

"Best I can do."

"Thanks, Emmett. Thanks a lot." Jewell started to rise from his chair, but Emmett clapped a hand on his shoulder and patted him back down.

"Ain't no hurry. Catch your breath a while."

Emmett fished a clean glass out of the cabinet and filled it with tap water, placing it in front of Jewell. The boy sipped at first before beginning to drink greedily; the cold water was wonderful. For the last half hour, except for the throb behind his eye, his physical needs had ceased to matter. The quenching of his thirst was a cleansing thing, and he became aware of his entire body again.

"Ain't got no ice," Emmett said. "It'll puff up if it ain't got something cold against it."

He took the empty glass and refilled it with cold water. "Here, hold this on it for a while. Coldest thing I got around here."

"Thanks."

Jewell allowed the last of the tension to fade away; it no longer served any purpose. He was safe now with Emmett. It was a strange thing to ponder, and he smiled inwardly at the thought. If Jubal Cole was still sober enough to guess that his misbehaving son might be with Emmett, terrible things could happen, but Jewell doubted that his father was sober enough to make such a guess, much less find his way to Emmett's room. But the possibility remained, looming like a distant cloud formation not yet black enough to warn of a storm. His father was strong enough to literally tear the door from its hinges and use it to grind them both in the floor. Yet there was a definite feeling of security about the place, something in Emmett's words and actions that was strong and quiet, like the way creek water pushed through your fingers after a spring rain.

The silence was not uncomfortable for either the man or the boy, and they sat for several minutes, each absorbed in his own thoughts. Jewell broke the silence.

"Reckon I ought to head on back before long. He's likely passed out by now."

"Not so sure about that. Not a half hour ago he moved fast enough to tag you pretty good."

"I can wait at the top of the stairs till I hear him snorin' good. I can tell when he's down for good."

"I wished you'd just stay here for the night to be on the safe side. Lay yourself down on the bed and rest easy for a night. Cut starts actin' up again, I can tend to it."

"No, I can't . . . do that. Where would you sleep?"

"I slept on lots worse things than this here floor in my time, Jewell. Won't bother me a bit."

"No, I ain't gonna make you . . ."

"You're not makin' me do anything, Jewell. It'd really be a favor to me. This way I won't have to worry about him and you for the rest of the night."

Jewell set the water glass down on the table and considered the offer. It would be a good thing to close his eyes in total peace, a very good thing indeed. He looked across at Emmett and nodded his head.

Jubal sat in semidarkness, but not in his drinking chair. He had chosen an uncomfortable straight-backed kitchen table chair from which to conduct his vigil. The whiskey bottle was fifteen feet away, untouched during the long wait. It had been nearly two hours now since the ungrateful son had escaped his rightful punishment. Surely he would come creeping back up the stairs soon. He would count on his father to be asleep by now, but he would be dreadfully wrong.

Jubal's tongue passed slowly over dry lips as he stole a glance at the bottle. He closed his eyes and anticipated the taste of the brown fire that would soon slake his thirst and reward him for his diligence. The boy could not stay out all night. The seconds oozed by and grudgingly formed minutes, but the minutes were tormentors, and the man began to hate them. Five more passed, and his lips grew drier still and he nibbled at them with his front teeth. The thought that the boy might not return had grown from a tiny seed into a distinct possibility. Five more of the dark minutes crept by. No, he was not coming back tonight; Jubal knew.

His right hand formed a great fist as it slowly rose to the height of his head and then crashed down on the table. His left hand found the edge and flipped the table across the room. Six long strides before the bang of a fist against the door to Jewell's room. The book rested mockingly, near the foot of the bed. The feel of the shredded pages in his fingers was satisfying, and when he tore the book in half and tossed it to the floor, a great deal of the rage passed with the finality of the act.

Before the last remnant of a page floated to the floor, Jubal's thoughts turned to his beckoning chair, and the glassy smoothness of the bottle waiting beside it. A man who had just put up with all that he had deserved the treasures of the tall bottle. Just the thought of it was a calming thing, a needful thing, and Jubal muttered assurances to himself as he hurried from his son's room.

Jewell awoke to the aroma of baking bread, but at first he thought it was part of a dream and he attempted to stay in it. His eyelids cracked open to the thin light as he became aware of the soft fingers of a breeze pushing through the open window. The bread smell was not a dream but a tantalizing delicacy rising from somewhere below. A light blanket covered him from chest to toes. He did not remember it being there when he drifted off last night. He reached up tentatively with the forefinger of his left hand and touched the area around his wound. The swelling had gone down considerably and the throb was more memory than reality. He sat up and looked around the room. He was alone, but a glance at the table assured him that he would not be for long. A cloth place mat lay at one end of the table, with a shiny, golden-skinned apple sitting on the upper right-hand corner.

Measured footfalls on the old wooden stairs now, light and precise. The door swung open and Emmett pushed through, his trailing hand wrapped around a small basket with a checkered cloth draped over it. Jewell's mouth began to water; the room was overflowing with the wonderful fragrance.

"Better get yourself on over here and try some of the best biscuits I ever ate."

Emmett set the basket on the table and stepped to the cabinet, peered inside for a moment, and withdrew a jar of grape jelly and a dinner knife.

"Help yourself."

Jewell flipped the cloth from the top of the basket and closed his fingers around one of the browned biscuits. Without waiting for the jelly, he crammed half of it into his mouth and closed his eyes with satisfaction. Emmett smiled at the sight of the boy's stuffed mouth.

"Last time I saw cheeks puffed out like that they was on a squirrel."

The words were muffled by the still large wad of biscuit. "Emmett . . . where'd you get these?"

"Landlady down below. She makes 'em every morning. Even better with this here jelly. She makes that too."

"Mmm . . . best I ever tried, I reckon."

Emmett watched as four more biscuits, smeared liberally with the jelly, disappeared from the basket. When Jewell reached into the basket, he realized that only one remained. He grinned sheepishly at Emmett.

"I . . . I'm sorry . . . I shouldn't a hogged that many down. You ain't had a one."

"Clean 'em up, I had mine downstairs," Emmett lied. "Ain't no sense in leavin' that last one."

Jewell's hand darted into the basket for the last time. Emmett got up and filled a water glass and placed it in front of the boy. Jewell picked his apple up and carved out a juicy bite. They sat in silence for several minutes, the wet cracks of apple bites the only sounds. Slowly, like a well-tended fire, thoughts of the night just past grew ever greater in Jewell's mind. He began to fidget with the apple core.

"About a half hour before school starts," Emmett said.

"I can't go in today."

"Why not? Young'uns all over that place scratched and banged up from somethin' or other."

Jewell shook his head. "They'll know. Ain't none of 'em big enough to give me a shiner. I just don't want them lookin' at me for a while—maybe a couple days or so. They don't really care if I come or not . . . least, most of 'em don't."

"I wouldn't be so sure of that. You been tellin' me your studyin's been lookin' up lately."

"That probably don't matter anymore now."

"Why's that?"

"It's what got me this." He pointed to the patch behind his eye. "He thinks I'm layin' off my chores to read and such for school. Thinks I'm wastin' my time. He caught me readin' a schoolbook last night. I was pretty sure he was drunk enough . . . almost down for the night, but . . . I didn't listen close enough."

Emmett sat stone-faced, and the emotion that welled up within him was well hidden from Jewell.

"I'm goin' down to the Kingdom and work straight for a couple of days, till he gets this off his mind. Then I'll go back."

Emmett nodded, but not in affirmation.

"There's one more thing I wish you'd do for me," Jewell said.

"What's that?"

"If you could go down to the school and find my teacher and tell her . . . that I got sick or something. I don't want her thinkin' I just skipped out on her."

"I ain't much good at lyin', Jewell."

"It's not much of a lie. I mean I am kinda sick from it all. I just don't want nobody goin' to him and makin' it worse, that's all."

"I understand that, but I can't promise exactly what I'll say down there. It just depends."

"On what?"

"On what kind of feelin's I get from who I talk to."

"Emmett, you're not makin' sense about this."

"I am so. You'll just have to trust me to take care of it proper. If you don't think I can handle it . . ."

"No . . . I ain't sayin' that at all . . ."

"Well then?"

"I give up, okay? But just remember if you mess up and it gets back around to him, they'll be more holes in me for you to patch up."

"Ain't no need remindin' me of that, Jewell. I ain't gonna get you in another pickle. Been studyin' people for a long time, and I'm pretty good at it."

"I hope so."

"What's your teacher's name?"

"Miss Annabelle, we call her. Annabelle Allen. And don't let 'em send you to the principal."

❧

"Could I ask you a question, young fella?"

The eleven-year-old boy looked quizzically at the homely little man standing near the front door of the school. The man surely looked harmless enough, and even though the boy did not take well to strangers, he decided that it would be all right to talk to him.

"Reckon so."

"I got to talk with a teacher named Miss Annabelle. You know where her room is?"

"Reckon so."

"Will you tell me where?"

"Ain't you supposed to go to the big office?"

"I'm in kind of a hurry. Besides, me and her know each other. No use in goin' through all that stuff."

The boy looked away for several seconds, acknowledging a classmate as he passed by. Emmett shifted from one foot to the other, his hands thrust to the bottom of his trouser pockets. Finally the boy looked back into his eyes.

He pointed as he spoke. "Go in that side door yonder. On your right-hand side, second room you come to."

"I thank you."

Emmett peeked around the open classroom door. Annabelle was writing on the blackboard in long flowing script. The twitters from the children nearest the door caught her attention even before the sight of Emmett's face did, and she turned her head in surprise. The recognition was instant; she placed the chalk in the tray and walked to the door.

"Why, good morning, Emmett. Are you looking for someone?"

"Well, yes ma'am . . . er, Miss Annabelle . . . I was lookin' for you really."

"What is it?" She stepped out into the hall, calming the students with a look and a small hand gesture.

"It's about Jewell." The cloud of apprehension passed immediately over her features, but Emmett was certain he saw concern; it was a good sign.

"Is something wrong?"

He hesitated, but only for a moment. There was no use in steering her away from it all, coating the truth with a flimsy veneer of lies, even though this would have been acceptable in dealing with some people. Miss Annabelle was not just any person; Emmett Tragman had known that from the beginning.

"Can this stay with me and you?"

"Yes, certainly."

"I reckon you've heard about his daddy?" Annabelle nodded as the lump grew in her throat. "I work for him some, down at the pool hall. He's a hard man. Has trouble with the bottle some. He and Jewell had a run-in last night and Jewell . . . he's all right mind you . . . he'd just rather not come in for a day or two. Took a lick on the side of his head. He . . . uh, didn't want you to think he was layin' out for no reason."

Annabelle swallowed against the thickness in her throat. Her eyes filled with moisture, and Emmett's face blurred for a moment before she blinked it back into focus.

"Are you sure he is not hurt badly?"

"It ain't bad. I tended to it myself. Mostly, he'll have a pretty good shiner . . . maybe a little scar."

"This is a very difficult thing for me to hear, Emmett."

"Yes, ma'am, I figure it is."

The last of the arriving students scurried behind them and into the open door. The friendly chorus of sounds in the corridor was a fading echo.

"Well . . . uh, will you please tell him that I'm very sorry for his trouble and that I trust he will continue to keep up with his studies? I will help him catch up in no time."

"Well, that there is another thing, Miss Annabelle. You just as well have it all laid out at once, 'cause I figure it's gonna take us both to help him with his studyin'."

"I don't quite follow."

"The reason his daddy cuffed him up was on account of his studyin'."

"You must be mista . . ."

"No, I ain't mistaken at all. He sees it as a kind of threat . . . the boy gettin' a lot of book learnin' and all. He figures on him growin' into the pool hall business and all someday . . . bein' a big help to him. He don't allow how any book learnin's gonna be much help down there."

Annabelle shook her head in bewilderment, and she twice started to speak before finally organizing her thoughts.

"Emmett, I gave you my word that I would keep this between us, and I will. But I make no promises about any future incidents. Jewell is a child, maybe in a man's body . . . but a child . . . and he has great potential . . ." She stopped before her emotions swept her too far and drew a measured breath.

"I'm sorry, Emmett. I don't mean to take it out on you. Forgive me, please. You said both of us would have to help him. What did you mean?"

"I'll find ways to get him some studyin' time without his daddy findin' out. You just keep him on the right track here. Me and you and the good Lord'll work it out."

Annabelle smiled at the earnest words pouring forth; Emmett was a good soul, and he obviously cared deeply for Jewell. They would give it a try, the three of them.

"I'm glad you included Him in this, Emmett."

The insistent clanging of the bell filled the corridor and Emmett turned to leave but stopped after two steps and turned back a final time. "It's my habit to have Him in things."

# Chapter 6

*JUBAL COLE* awoke in hazy stages on Monday morning. Full knowledge of the world around him was something he neither desired nor could even tolerate before mid-morning. It was twenty minutes before he allowed his mind to focus on the nasty little scene of the night before. He wondered if the boy was at school. He was surely not in his room; Jubal could see pieces of pages on the floor through the half-open door of Jewell's room. The man had no clear recollection of how hard he had struck his son. It was not a solid blow, that much he could remember, and he hoped that no lasting damage was done. It had been a simple thing when the boy was younger, before he had spurted into a man-sized body, just to smack his rear or box his ears when he needed some sense pounded into him. Now, it was a very difficult thing to deal with—just how hard to hit him when he needed some direction.

He sorted out the morning sounds from the street below and soon realized that sounds were coming from the pool hall. It was too early for Emmett to report; eleven o'clock was his usual starting time. He gathered himself in the chair and rocked gently forward, testing his balance carefully before standing. When he opened the door to the Kingdom, Jewell stood five steps in front of him, broom and dustpan in hand.

"How come you ain't at school?"

"I . . . I, uh figured I'd help out around here for a couple days."

"I don't want no trouble from them people, boy, you know that."

"They won't be no trouble. People get sick now and then. Nobody'll say a word."

So the cuffing had done some good, Jubal assured himself. This was a good sign, the boy showing some responsibility for a change without being asked. Jewell held his head slightly to the left, shielding his puffy cheek from his father's gaze.

"Lemme see the other side of your face."

Jewell slowly rotated his head to the right. "It ain't nothin', just a scratch. Put some tape on it."

Jubal nodded. He truly wanted to say something to the boy, but the only words he could think of would sound too much like an apology, so he remained silent until the thought died away.

"You get done with that, start sweepin' them tables. Always some fool droppin' ashes on 'em. I may make me a rule that no pool shooter can take a shot with a cigarette hangin' outta his mouth. Dumbheads, that'd fix 'em." Jubal grunted a laugh at the idea, momentarily pleased with himself, but when he sought approval in Jewell's expression, he found nothing of the sort. He grunted again, but without the laugh.

"Get on with it then. Emmett'll be along in a little while."

On Thursday morning, two minutes before the last bell, Jewell slipped quietly through the rear door to the classroom and took his seat. Annabelle smiled directly at him, but only for an instant, and then spread the smile to the other twenty-six faces. Before her eyes could sweep back to Jewell for a final glance, the thin face of Helen Lanning came to her, the child's puffy eyes red with grief. Annabelle was certain that no small thing had painted that kind of sorrow on her features. It was a face that Annabelle knew well; it was the face of war. So there were two mournful faces in her classroom this beautiful September morning. One, the stony face of a private war, fought in a dingy room over a pool hall, the other, with open grief, fought on the stage of the world. So different and so alike, the two faces.

The morning session passed slowly, at least for Annabelle. With the first glance at the two faces, she longed for the freedom of recess, a time when she could be more than a teacher of arithmetic and grammar. She sought Jewell first as he leaned against a little maple tree at the fringe of the activity on the asphalt playground. Thirty yards away, Helen stood alone, facing away from the friendly sounds that rose into the morning sky.

"Welcome back, Jewell, I've missed you."

"Me too," he nodded and turned his head to the left. His hands were jammed deeply into his trouser pockets, and Annabelle could see his fingers fidgeting behind the faded denim.

"Jewell, I don't want you to become discouraged by this. Emmett explained everything."

His look asked a wordless question.

"Yes, everything," Annabelle repeated. "Emmett said that he would attempt to find a way for you to continue your studies in spite of your father's . . . wishes."

"Yes, ma'am. I think me and him got it worked out."

"Good, but I want you to know that I would be more than willing to speak to your . . ."

"No. No, there ain't no reason for you to do that, Miss Annabelle. I figure me and Emmett can work it out, quiet like. It'd be better that way."

"Well, I hope it proves suitable, Jewell, but please trust me to help you if it does not."

Jewell lowered his head and swallowed, his fingers busy again in his pockets. "There is one thing."

"Yes, Jewell?"

"I ain't . . . er, I don't have a geography book anymore."

"Well, you will before the day is over. I'm a pretty fair finder of books. Now soak up some more of this sunshine. It makes brains grow, you know."

She smiled and winked as she turned and walked toward Helen Lanning. The girl had not moved since Annabelle had first spotted her, and she did not seem to notice when Annabelle gently touched shoulders with her.

"Do you want to talk about it, Helen?"

Helen moved her head a quarter turn toward Annabelle and then back straight ahead before answering. "I don't know."

"Sometimes it helps. I know we haven't had the chance to get to know each other very well yet, but I'm a good listener."

They stood in silence for two long minutes, and Annabelle decided to leave the child alone. As she turned to leave, the tiny voice stopped her. "Wait."

Annabelle circled an arm around Helen's shoulders. "A soldier came last night, right after supper. My . . . my Uncle Del . . . his bomber . . . it got shot down in Germany." The squeaky words tumbled out now. "My daddy . . . it scared me so . . . I never seen him cry before . . . he shook all over . . . Momma had to hold him tight . . . the sounds he made . . . it was the awfulest day of my life." Her chin quivered as she paused for breath. "Momma told me and my brothers to come on to school this morning . . . just to get us away from Daddy, I reckon. It was so scary, seein' him like that."

Annabelle held the child tighter. "Helen, I just wish there was some magical thing I could say that would make it all better, like some fairy princess with a beautiful wand. But it can't happen that way. The way it finally gets better is that people just cry together. I lost a brother way back when this thing started. I know what I'm talking about, child."

"Will my daddy get all right again?"

"Oh yes, I promise. From what you say, I know he loves your uncle very much, and when a man can love like that, it's a very wonderful thing. You're lucky to have a daddy like that."

Helen sobbed quietly and leaned her head against Annabelle's shoulder. "You can help your daddy very much in the days to come. Let him cry it out for a while. Your mother will tend to him at first, but then you and your brothers will be able to help as much as anybody."

"Uncle Del . . . Daddy always said he spoilt me. I'm the oldest and all, and he didn't have no kids yet. It seems strange that he won't be comin' home."

"Yes, it does seem strange."

"Part of me wants to be home with Daddy, but part of me knows it wouldn't help right now. Momma's right."

"Yes, I expect she is. But you remember . . . your time to help will be here very soon. He'll need you, and I know you'll be there for him, won't you?"

"I will."

"Tell you what I'd like to do, if it's all right with you. Some-time—maybe we'll wait a week or so—see if you can bring a picture of your uncle to class. We will pass it around so that everyone can see him, and then I would like for you to tell us something special about him . . . sometime when he did some of that spoiling you spoke of, maybe. And I'll tell something special about my brother Matthew, and we can look at his picture. Would that be okay?"

"Yes, ma'am . . . I think I'd like that."

"It's a deal then. You just let me know when you feel like it, okay?"

Helen tried to smile, but it would not form properly and she let it go.

"Don't worry about your daddy, Helen. The sooner he cries hard, the sooner he can start to get better."

The beauty of twilight offered little solace to Annabelle as she sat on the top front porch step, elbows resting on knees, chin cupped in both hands. Her eyes stared upward through the fading light as it painted faraway clouds in shades of amber. The talk with Helen had taken a part of her, and although it was a part willingly given, it was something irretrievable, like all things taken by war. Annabelle accepted the risk inherent in allowing herself to be lost in the sky when she first came out onto the porch. It beckoned, the great expanse, beckoned her to its very top, five miles high, where the air was as thin as a razor's edge and cold enough to consume uncovered flesh. It was the very whisper of death that beckoned her to the crystalline space from which young men fell.

The thoughts had crept into her mind an hour before, safely inside her room, where she could not see the sky. But she could not remain indoors; she had to go outside and look up, and risk mourning for Helen's uncle, the young boy named Del, loved so deeply, and for Matthew. Annabelle had to look up into the sky that joined the other sky, and the great ocean that touched it, the sky and the ocean that claimed young soldiers.

"Awful thoughtful, young lady." The soft voice of Sadie Armstrong, the landlady, startled Annabelle. "Can I sit with you a spell?"

"Please, sit down, Sadie. I could use some company."

"You look like it."

Sadie wiped the last of the moisture from her hands on the faded apron. "War things?"

Annabelle nodded and smiled ruefully. "One of my students lost an uncle. His bomber went down over Germany."

"Boeing B-17," Sadie said, "they call it the Flying Fortress. My baby sister's youngest is a tail gunner in one."

Neither woman spoke for several moments, allowing the sounds of evening to whisper to them. Annabelle spoke first.

"Somehow, the fact that this sky touches the sky over Germany haunts me. It's like a giant stage that stretches for thousands of miles . . . and these men, boys really, they play out scenes of life and death on this aerial stage miles in the air. There's no one to cheer, no one to weep, no one to witness their sacrifices. It just doesn't seem right."

"No . . . no, it doesn't seem right," Sadie said. "My sister's boy—he's nineteen—he wrote her and said that when the German fighter planes come, it's like their bomber is standing still in the air. He said the fighters reminded him of wasps diving around his head." She paused, lost in the air with Annabelle. "It would be a lonely way to die . . . in the other sky." In the silence, Sadie twisted the corner of her apron in the fingers of one hand. "Great day, listen to me, will you? A big help I am, huh? I'm sorry . . . I . . ."

"No, don't be sorry. I'm not really looking to feel better now, I just want to *feel* . . . to feel deeply enough so that somehow they know we hurt with them in our own way. Does that make sense?"

"Yes, Annabelle, to me it does."

"My brother Matthew in the bottom of Pearl Harbor. Helen's uncle dashed to the earth in Germany . . . oh, I hope they knew how much we cared before the end came."

The women wept silently, reverently, but spoke no more as nightfall came, quietly and lovingly, like an humble friend, and paid its tribute to the honored dead.

# Chapter 7

*T*HE FIRST determined snowflakes of winter swirled earthward as the northwest wind rattled the two big windows. Jewell looked up from the half-completed arithmetic quiz pinned under his left hand. He smiled to himself; there were no questions that he could not answer. It was now simply a matter of being careful with his calculations, and there was ample time remaining. He had the luxury of stealing a long look at December's beautiful offerings. The flakes were as big as nickels and quarters, airy things that collided gracefully against the glass panes and clung for a second or two before being swept away.

Annabelle watched the boy for a moment, lost in his innocent reverie, but there was no concern. Jewell Cole would grind out the little quiz just as he had all the others for the past several weeks. In truth, Annabelle's pleasant problem was with inventing ways of challenging him in the classroom. Within days after the crisis with Jewell's father, Emmett had concocted a seemingly foolproof plan for his young friend's studies, filling Annabelle in on the details after Sunday morning services.

"He's gonna keep all his books and things at my place. I've

fixed a little table and such for him," Emmett explained to Annabelle. "There's plenty of chores that allow for him to be outta' his daddy's sight for long spells. He does a bunch of inside stuff right after school, under his daddy's nose, so he gets satisfied right off with things. And then, instead of workin' out back or in the storeroom, he just slips down to my place, not but a few minutes' trot. Ain't no trouble for me to do his chores too. We mix it up a little . . . to be on the safe side, but it's gonna work, I guarantee."

Emmett. Annabelle's thoughts turned to the strange, gritty little man. He possessed a depth of character that was well hidden from most of the world, but not from Annabelle. She knew that Jubal Cole and all the regulars at the Kingdom considered him but a weird scrap of humanity, and yet he had never spoken ill of them to Annabelle—not a single word. But more than that, Annabelle had yet to hear a word of self-pity creep into their conversations. It was clearly a tool of no use to him, a lowly, empty thing that could serve no purpose in his life, as it could not in Annabelle's.

Annabelle's gaze swept slowly away from Jewell as she judged the progress of her other students. When she looked at him again, his head was bowed over his worksheet, the tip of his tongue poking from the left corner of his mouth, the pencil working methodically on the paper. Jewell Cole, grinding out his arithmetic—a most wonderful sight for a teacher to see.


Lela Parker shook her head in slow cadence with a sliver of carrot held between her thumb and forefinger.

"Annabelle, this cannot be as simple as it appears. Jewell Cole actually smiled at me in the hall yesterday—and I swear to you—nodded his head a little."

Annabelle smiled through a bite of apple, finger held up in a plea for a few seconds to clear her mouth.

"Yes, his manners have improved some. When you feel better about yourself, I think, almost always, your manners improve."

"Well, true enough, I suppose, but . . . there's more there than that, Annabelle."

"It's not a complicated thing, Lela. An opportunity presented itself, and I jumped on it, just like you or any other teacher in this school would have."

"The only thing we other teachers were worried about was being jumped on by Jewell." They both laughed. "Nathan says it's getting mighty lonely in the principal's office without Jewell's regular visits. He'd never come right out and tell a first-year teacher, but I think he's a bit in awe of this whole thing. You're becoming a legend *before* your own time."

"Oh, for heaven's sake, Lela . . ."

"No, I mean it. You know, if I weren't such a paragon of virtue myself, I'd be jealous."

"It's not all smooth sailing. I've had problems crop up out of the blue with other kids who shouldn't be having problems. How did such a genius teacher allow that to happen? Have I paid too much attention to Jewell? Have some of the other more perceptive kids picked up on it?" Annabelle tossed the apple core into the paper sack. "I promise you, I don't have a bag full of magic tricks."

"Maybe . . . maybe not," Lela smiled, a Cheshire cat in a woman's face, "I'll render a final opinion in about five years or so."

"I can save you the wait if you'd just listen."

Lela's eyes darted beyond Annabelle's right shoulder to the next table where one of her fifth-graders was preparing to apply a glob of grape jelly to the pigtailed head of an unsuspecting neighbor. "Clinton Cunningham, don't even *think* about it!"

Her gaze shifted automatically back to Annabelle as if no disruption had taken place. "Oh, don't spoil my fun. Every staff has to have a little mystery of some kind." She paused and dabbed at her mouth with a paper napkin. "Kidding aside, Annabelle, you should feel really good about this boy. I honestly think he might have a life now . . . in spite of his father."

"Yes, that's the real question now, isn't it?"

"Sadly, it is."

"I've learned that Mr. Cole intends for Jewell to drop out after eighth grade, so he can begin the process of making him a co-operator of the pool hall without any more . . . silly delays, shall we say."

"Not surprised at that. I am surprised that Jewell can find enough time for his studies."

Annabelle smiled ruefully. "That's yet another story, Lela. Suffice to say that it takes a bit of doing on Jewell's part . . . and the part of a wonderful friend of ours."

"How in the world could anyone be in a position . . ."

"He works at the pool hall. Emmett Tragman is his name. I actually met him at church before all this transpired. Sort of an ordinary little man, not much at first meeting or glance . . . but there is much more to him than anyone might guess. Anyway, he and Jewell have connived to manage the work load so that Jewell can study at his place, all unbeknownst to Mr. Cole."

"Great day. Strange how things can work out sometimes."

"Yes, isn't it though?" Annabelle drifted in thought for a moment, and Lela honored her short journey. "You know, Lela, I'm going to have a difficult time keeping my mouth shut if this little arrangement begins to fail."

The lines in the older woman's brow furrowed as she reached out a hand and placed it over Annabelle's. "Annabelle, you just do the best you can for the boy . . . while he's here in school . . . that's all anybody could ever expect." She waited until Annabelle looked directly into her eyes. "Leave Jubal Cole alone." The words hung in the air like four heavy musical notes. "You can't reason with a man that hard, especially one that lives half his life in the bottle."

"I've never met anyone who wouldn't listen to a respectful . . ."

"There's a preacher in this town with a crooked nose who thought the same thing."

"I've heard the story."

Jubal Cole felt his usual afternoon pride as the factory shift workers began to push through the front door of the Kingdom. They came in twos and threes mostly, a few singles here and there, banging one another on the back, knocking each other's hats off from behind, cursing either good-naturedly or in earnest—the real pride of the town as far as Jubal was concerned. These were the men who did the real work, not the high-minded sorts who were too good for the Kingdom, the ones who turned up their noses at the manly necessities Jubal provided. These were the men who could appreciate a few hearty beers and strong conversation before finding their way home to nagging women and whining brats and the like.

They were mostly older men like himself; the war effort had claimed many of the younger ones, but this was all right. Men such as these always made better customers in the end. They drank slower than the younger ones, but they were much steadier— unhurried and with a purpose to their endeavor. When the empty mugs and shot glasses were tallied in Jubal's head, the steady drinkers always made him more money. He had observed men drink for many years, and there was no doubt that slow and steady was better for business. Such men drank for all the right reasons, and this gave Jubal pleasure beyond the collection of their bills and coins. The slaking of their thirst was soon handled, usually with the first mug of beer or shot of whiskey. It was the part that came next, the steady part, the part that really satisfied, that made Jubal's customers real men.

There were many things in life that required the soothing touch of the bottle, the gentle quieting of the working man's brain. Alcohol was medicine for the soul of a working man. The fools in the church houses could slobber all over each other with their loud singing and praying all they wanted, but they would never know the peace of mind given by the sweet medicine of Jubal's Kingdom. It was his gift to the town, the real men of the town. Jubal could not imagine how they would get by without his Kingdom, these good men. But that worry had been fading for many weeks now.

The boy had stepped up and was working with Emmett like a thankful boy should. No more laying around with his nose in a silly book. Yes, the Kingdom would pass to him smoothly in the years to come. He might even find a decent woman who wouldn't drive him crazy, one who would bear him a son, and on and on it would go, Jubal's Kingdom, growing with the town as the years passed, and some of the honor would always be passed back to him, the man who put up the first sign.

It was a heady thought, and Jubal allowed himself to be lost in it for long, wondrous moments. No, he could not imagine a town without the Kingdom, his Kingdom. Needful things had a way of going on and on—maybe forever.

# Chapter 8

*T*HE PREMONITION passed over Annabelle like a chill breeze in autumn—an early promise of the cutting winds to ride down from Canada, things unavoidable, things dreaded. And it all had to do with a grade card, a small piece of white paper tucked proudly in the hip pocket of Jewell Cole's faded denim trousers.

"Annabelle, something wrong with my stew?" Sadie Armstrong's soft voice jerked her into the present.

"Oh . . . oh, heavens no, Sadie, it's wonderful as usual, I suppose I'm just a little drained from the end of semester and grades and parents and evaluations and such." Annabelle laughed tiredly.

"I can imagine, young lady. Why don't you go on upstairs and curl up with a book you want to read for a change. I'll putter around with these dishes later. Got all evening."

"No, I'll help."

Sadie shook her head firmly and smiled. "Consider it a very minor contribution to the education process."

"Well, it does sound appealing, I must admit."

"Off with you then." A kindly wave of her hand.

Annabelle sat stiffly on the edge of her bed, the nagging thought back in the center of her brain. Jewell had insisted that he take the grade card with him to show Emmett. He promised that he would be careful with it around the Kingdom. Surely he could manage that. And it was only for one night. Surely . . .

Annabelle shook her head at the image reflected in the window pane. It was not worth the chance. She could have shown it to Emmett herself, maybe even met him and Jewell somewhere so that the three of them could have shared a time of triumph. That is exactly what she should have done. Should have . . . should have . . . should have! Two of the ugliest words in the English language.

There would be no book for a companion this winter night; when worry was a companion, it allowed no room for any others.

The two figures huddled together in the alley, heads nearly touching in the pale beam cast by the streetlight.

"Can you believe it, Emmett? Look at those grades, will ya?" Jewell's voice chirped loudly over the low moan of the cold wind. "Top marks in four out of five classes."

"No surprise to me, Jewell. I knew you could do it."

"Miss Annabelle says I can head right on into seventh grade without givin' an inch up to anybody. Says I'll be all caught up with where I ought to be by the end of the year."

"I'm proud of you, I surely am, Jewell. You bring home another one like that in the spring—maybe even all top marks, huh?"

"Maybe I just will at that. Maybe I just will."

Emmett glanced over his shoulder. "Let's get on back in there 'fore he misses us now. You tuck that thing away good tonight and give it back to Miss Annabelle in the mornin'."

"I will."

"Why don't I keep it for you? I'll run it back over to the school myself tomorrow."

Jewell thought for a few seconds, the precious paper extended in his right hand. "No, I want to keep it tonight . . . look at it some more when I get a chance."

Emmett bit the inside of his lip and cocked his head slowly. "Well, just you be careful, young fella."

They walked quickly to the back door and slipped into the storeroom. Jewell's hand passed protectively over his right hip pocket; not even a sliver of the grade card protruded. He was sure.

"Emmett!" Jubal's voice rolled back to the storeroom like an iron wheel.

"You finish stackin' these here crates, Jewell. Careful with these down here. They're pretty heavy."

"I'll get 'em. Go on, tend to him up front."

Jewell worked steadily with the heavy crates and soon developed a rhythm. Squat, knees nearly touching the concrete floor, then a solid grasp as his hands slid through the openings, blow out some air as he stood with the weight, and on to the stack with a final heave. It was a man's job, and he smiled to himself with the knowledge that he could handle it. The stacks grew, and despite the chill in the poorly heated storeroom, beads of sweat formed on his brow and upper lip. It was finished; a proud exhalation escaped his lips as he turned to leave.

Two inches of the grade card jutted whitely above the top line of his pocket.

Darry Banks was pleasantly drunk. Hunkered over snooker table number two with his two playing companions, all things had gradually become hilarious; it had taken six mugs of beer, his usual late afternoon fare. The other two men, though in high spirits themselves, were no match for Darry in either voice or deed. They had given up any attempt at keeping score of the game; it just did not matter any longer. The grand idea now was to challenge one another, in turn, with difficult shots. It made for great fun.

From behind the bar, Jubal had watched out of the corner of his eye for several minutes since Darry had managed to strike the cue ball far too low and launch it onto the floor. The game had almost gone far enough for Jubal, who had no intention of dealing with a torn patch of velvet on his snooker table. If the cue ball clacked to the floor again, the little game would be finished for the evening.

Jewell bounded from the storeroom with long strides, arms swinging jauntily from his sides. When he was ten feet from Darry's table he heard the unmistakable sound of a poorly stroked cue tip scraping underneath the ball, and as he turned to the sound, the dull white cue ball arced gracefully toward him. He should have caught it cleanly on the first bounce, but the sight of Darry leaping after the ball like a laughing bear caused him to flinch. The ball bounced out of his cupped hands toward Darry, who by now was wheezing with laughter as he swiped at the moving target. The man and the boy collided at the hip, spinning Jewell a half turn away from Darry as the boy latched onto the cue ball. In the spirit of merriment, Darry reached out and plucked at the three-inch strip of paper poking from the boy's pocket. Jewell felt nothing.

"Whew, what we got here, a love letter from sweetie?" Darry crooned to the other two men as he sniffed the folded grade card.

Jewell was rolling the cue ball back across the snooker table when the word *letter* screamed into his brain. His right hand shot to the empty hip pocket as he spun toward the laughing man.

"Give me that!" Jewell lurched at the man who was now certain that he held a precious note that would provide for even more fun.

Darry held the paper high over his head and howled with delight. "What's the little darlin's name, Jewell? Bet she's a sweetie sure enough."

Jewell jumped up and snatched at the paper just as Darry

passed it to one of the other men, who held it over his head and joined the taunting. The man intended to pass it along to the third member of the little party, but the next hand that received it was Jubal Cole's. The great hand closed over the smaller man's like a flesh-colored vise as the laughter died away around the table.

"You three quiet down now, hear? Darry, you dang near tore a piece of my velvet loose."

"Didn't mean no harm, Jubal. Just havin' a little fun with the boy." Darry's smile was crooked now, and it did not feel right on his face. He dragged the top of his shirt sleeve over his mouth and wiped it away. The three men melted away toward the bar.

"Don't need all this commotion," Jubal said evenly, as much to himself as to the departing men.

Jewell's heart beat in his throat, and he fought against the rising wave of nausea. Within five seconds, it would be done, one way or another. Jewell fanned a flickering flame of hope that Jubal would toss the paper aside and return to the bar. He had heard Darry's taunts about a love note. By all rights, he should simply hand it back to Jewell or toss it aside. But he did not. Slowly, the long fingers unfolded the paper and the cold gray eyes focused in. It was an eerie silence that followed—a tiny circle of silence within the din that swirled about the walls of the Kingdom.

Jewell measured the distance from his father—two full steps. He could move now, before it all came together. He could be out the back door and into the alley in a flash. He moved his eyes but not his head. Emmett, ten feet away at the next snooker table, pretending to sweep the velvet, his free hand extended slightly, palm down, moving up and down ever so slightly. "Stay calm," said the hand, "don't run. Maybe we can work something out. All is not lost."

Jubal's hand closed over the grade card like a pneumatic press, so quick that it barely made a sound.

"Somethin' don't figure, boy." There was malice in his tone, but not as much as Jewell expected; it was mostly bewilderment that leaked through the words. "You better get your hind end back to work. We'll sort this out after closin'."

Jewell half trotted back to the storeroom, spun through the doorway, and slapped both hands against the cold wall in frustration. He was able to form no useful thoughts, only hurtful stabs of self-reproach. His hands formed fists now, pounding methodically on the concrete block wall. Long minutes of despair passed, the dank room a chamber of timelessness. When the hand touched the back of his shoulder, he spun in defense before he realized the hand was Emmett's.

"Easy now . . . easy now," Emmett said.

Jewell crumpled forward into wiry arms that easily caught him and held his weight. "I don't know . . . I can't figure out what to do." Words and sobs intermingled.

Emmett patted him firmly on the back and held him at arm's length. "Listen to me now, Jewell, I *do* know what you have to do. Calm down and listen."

Emmett fished a handkerchief from his pocket and stuffed it into Jewell's hand. "The main thing is not to let on like you *know* you've done somethin' wrong. He sees you actin' like this, he'll know somethin's up, understand?" Jewell nodded and swiped at his red nose. "Far as he knows, you might just be smart enough to get those marks by workin' extra hard at school."

"Never did before," Jewell sniffed, "he dang well remembers that too."

"You sure about that? How many grade cards he looked over in the last year or two?"

Jewell furrowed his brow and thought back. "Well, I don't reckon that many."

"Does he even sign 'em?"

"No, they know at school how he is. They don't say nothin' about them not gettin' signed."

"That's about what I figured. So you stop actin' like somethin's bad wrong and get yourself straightened out. The more ordinary you act, the better it'll go later."

"I'll try."

"I brought a can full of garbage back here. You take it out back and stay for a few minutes in the cold. It'll help you get your head straightened out."

The boy nodded, sniffed again, and handed the handkerchief back to Emmett. "Thanks, Emmett." He paused and rubbed his hands on the sides of his shirt. "No matter what happens, I ain't gonna give you up on this . . ."

"I was comin' to that. Now you listen here. If it starts to go real bad with him, you *will tell* him that I covered for you . . . that it was my idea . . . it *was* my idea, Jewell. Just tell him I snuck your books to you and let you read in the storeroom and upstairs some. We'll save my place . . . no need to give that up. You'll always have that to fall back on."

"I can't tell him . . ."

"Listen here, Jewell. You can and you will, if need be. I was lookin' for a job when I found this one, and what's more, I ain't as scrawny as I look. I ain't afraid of no man, includin' your daddy."

"I don't know . . . I . . ."

"I don't think it'll come to that anyway. Just stick to your story that you've worked real hard at school. He don't really know what to make of it all right now."

Emmett patted him on the back again, firmly, the way a man pats another man. "One more thing. Be better to deal with all this before he starts drinkin'. Don't hide from him."

"I know."

# Chapter 9

*L*OCK THIS place up after you sweep out. I'm goin' on up for the night."

Emmett nodded at Jubal's command, the big man's eyes hard as they swept over him. Emmett listened to the heavy thuds of footfalls, ever higher, and finally to the floor above—the floor that also held Jewell. Long before he finished sweeping, Emmett knew that he would not leave the Kingdom anytime soon. Finished with the chores, he turned the lights off, opened the door to the alley, and slammed it loudly from the inside. Then he turned and took two silent steps to the foot of the stairs and sat down.

Jewell's body tensed when the door to his room squeaked open. Not a single word had been spoken during the hour that passed after closing time. The scratchy voice from the radio and the tink of the bottle against the glass were the only sounds that prevented silence. It had not worked out well; Jewell could not be the one to broach the touchy subject without giving it added importance, and this had to be avoided. And Jubal had chosen to fortify himself.

"You tell me straight just how you got those marks, boy."

"Well, I know you wanted me to work harder around here . . .

so I just been workin' extra hard at school. I ain't let down around here."

"No, it don't seem like you have, but I've been thinkin' hard on this, and seems to me like I ain't been seein' near as much of you up front. Can't be that much to do in the back and outside."

"It's just . . . worked out like that, I reckon. Emmett's needed up front more'n me . . . ain't nothin' different about that."

At first, it sounded good to Jewell; there was no tension in his voice that he could detect, but he saw a shadow of anger pass over his father's face with the mention of Emmett. If he had had only another two or three seconds to gather himself, he would have avoided the grave mistake he was about to make. But he did not; the man retorted quickly and with just enough venom to knock him off guard.

"Emmett." He half spat the name. "You two been awful chummy the past few weeks."

"NO." The word shot out of Jewell's mouth much too loudly, the tone far too protective. He attempted to cover it, but the damage was done. "No, I mean . . . I been pullin' my load . . ."

"Shut your mouth, boy. You two must think I'm some kind of fool. Who's he think he is, that idiot, coverin' for you behind my back!"

"It ain't like that, I swear . . ."

The big hand snapped forward, open-handed, like a striking snake, and Jewell could not move his head quickly enough. The force of the blow knocked him flat against the bed, and he drew his knees up close to his chest as he struggled to clear his head of the ringing echo. The fingers of his left hand touched his cheek, but he could feel nothing. Jubal's face hovered over him like a fuzzy apparition and then words came from his crooked mouth with the sour smell of his breath.

"You got to the count of five to start talkin' the truth or I'm gonna pound it outta you."

The rage came to Jewell from a place within him that he could not identify. It grew from a spark to a flame with blinding speed—a mysterious force somehow separate from him and yet so much a part of him that he could smell it, red hot and acrid. And with the hellish rage came the certain knowledge that his life would forever change within the next few seconds. Never again would he grovel on his back like a helpless, wounded animal, waiting for the hurtful blows to rain down on him. Never again would it be so. He would die first.

In the instant before Jubal Cole could count for the fifth time, he saw the boy curl into a ball, his shoes gathered over his chest, and Jubal thought he recognized a defensive posture. He had never made a more incorrect assumption. The shoes became a blur as the blow covered Jubal's throat from his Adam's apple to the point of his chin, and he was hurled backward into the wall. The shock of the pain was secondary to the realization that his son was fighting back. The flesh of his flesh had just delivered a terrible blow, and his mind reeled with the horror of it. He sucked for air through his wounded throat, but only wheezing sounds came before the man-child clawed into him, all fists and fingernails and elbows and flailing knees—a being gone insane. Jubal braced himself against the wall like a giant bear under attack by a smaller animal, unaware of the strength in his own arms and hands, which could have turned the tide of battle in a moment. The man-child screamed curses as he ripped and pounded.

"You lousy, stinkin' drunk! I'll kill you! I'll kill you!"

Jubal felt a sudden void; the wild blows ceased completely and instantly as the screaming voice left the room. He slumped to the floor, his lungs pleading for air, his mind a horrible whirl. He blinked with great effort, as if coming out of a deep sleep, but he could not separate nightmare from reality, and in the netherworld between the two, he could not decide if the strange sight now before him was real. The vision was his son standing over him, a butcher knife in his clenched right fist. When the knife and hand rose high above Jewell's shoulder, Jubal knew that it was not a vision he saw.

The first knife thrust was never made. As Jewell's body lunged forward, the steely bands of Emmett's fingers locked around his wrist and spun him away from his father.

"Let go of the knife, Jewell."

The words were faraway sounds to the boy, and it was several seconds before he realized who had spoken them. Even after Emmett's features materialized before him, the red sea of rage churned inside Jewell's head. Slowly, like a fiery sunset succumbing to dusk, the rage began to melt. He felt the knife slip from his hand, and as he lowered his arm, he began to tremble, his body a limp rag as it slumped to the floor near the bed. Emmett stood between the two combatants—bloodied, fallen soldiers in a battle that produced no victors.

Emmett, poised against any attempted renewal of the struggle, looked first to Jubal. His long face was crisscrossed with deep scratches, one of which had nearly cost him an eye, and his upper lip was more pulp than flesh. The wide chest heaved inside the torn shirt; his breathing was no more than a discordant chain of wheezes. He did not appear to acknowledge Emmett's presence, the gray eyes unfocused now—dim, lifeless things that saw nothing, cared for nothing. There was no fight in Jubal Cole.

Jewell wept quietly, the horror of the scene clear to him now, his face buried in his hands. It was the sound of the weeping that gouged at Emmett's soul, for the boy wept as a man—deep, shuddering sobs wracking his body as he struggled against them, unwilling to allow them to cleanse him, unwilling to accept the healing tears. Emmett Tragman knew well what he was witnessing, and he accepted the burden of it with a heavy heart. It was a solemn occasion when the last vestiges of childhood were taken from a thirteen-year-old, but it was sometimes the way of the world. Emmett stood silently for three minutes, the same way that he had stood at the grave sites of loved ones, and then he turned and knelt in front of Jubal.

"Jubal, can you hear me?"

The empty eyes, still unfocused, blinked twice, and then a third time before his head slowly rolled a quarter turn against the wall toward Emmett. The tip of his tongue mopped at the crushed lip, and he attempted to spit out the blood that had pooled in his mouth; but he could not, and it dribbled over his chin.

"Jubal, can you understand what I'm sayin'? Do you want me to go for the doctor?"

The eyes cleared perceptibly, seeking Emmett's face, and the words came from him in grotesque whispers. "No . . . just get out . . . don't ever come back . . . and take him with you."

Jubal's head rolled the quarter turn back to its original position. It was clear to Emmett that the man would speak no more. Emmett knee-walked to Jewell's side and slid an arm around his shoulder. He spoke in steady, soothing tones, all the while patting the boy on the shoulder with a gentle, circular motion.

"Come on now, it's over. Nobody's hurt bad. Let's get you up on the bed. That's right . . . sit right there for a minute."

Emmett walked to the small closet, looked inside, and pulled out Jewell's only other pair of trousers. He moved to the dresser and opened both drawers, quickly stuffing socks, underwear, and shirts down the trouser legs. Jewell's coat lay at the foot of the bed, and Emmett snatched it up, wrapping it around Jewell's shoulders.

"Let's go now. Come on."

He gathered Jewell in one arm, the other enveloping the wad of clothing, and as one, they moved to the doorway without looking back. The cold wind that whipped down the alley was welcome to Emmett, a clean, powerful friend that chased away the memory of the close, bloody air in the room over the Kingdom.

"You're doin' real good, Jewell. Just keep walkin' steady. We'll be at my place in a few minutes. It's gonna be all right . . . all right."

Under the bare bulb light fixture over his table, Emmett made a close inspection of Jewell as the boy sat stiffly in the straight-backed chair. The only mark on his face was what Emmett reckoned to be the result of a strong open-handed slap; some redness lingered as did a slight puffiness. Emmett had closely observed Jewell's movements as they walked to the house and climbed the stairs. There was no sign that he had sustained a body blow of any consequence, just weakness from having spent nearly all of his energy, both physical and mental. The only parts of his body that had absorbed obvious damage were his hands.

They lay palms down on the table, like two soiled instruments that had served their grisly purpose, now set aside for cleaning and repair. Jewell stared at a point on the table beyond his hands. He had not responded to Emmett's little phrases of consolation, nor had he looked directly at his caretaker. For the first time, Emmett marveled at the size of the boy's hands; they were clearly larger than his own, the fingers long and thick. The blood that nearly covered them had dried in a ragged pattern extending be-yond his wrists, and even the ends of his shirt sleeves were tainted. The middle and forefinger nails of his right hand were badly torn, as was the thumbnail of his left hand. The left ring finger was swollen and bruised between the knuckle and the last joint.

Emmett filled a shallow pan with warm water and plopped in a bar of soap. He set the pan and a towel on the table beside Jewell's hands and returned to the small cabinet over the wash basin. He poked through the collection of loose objects on the bottom shelf for several seconds before finding the tiny box of razor blades and pulling one free. He slid a chair close to Jewell, the razor blade carefully hidden in his right hand.

"Let's see if we can't fix these paws up a little, Jewell. You got a few nails that are just hangin' by a thread or two. Be better if you'd let me trim 'em off so they wouldn't snag on things."

Emmett waited for an acknowledgment of some sort, but it was apparent that none would be forthcoming. Gently but firmly, he cradled Jewell's left thumb in one hand and carefully cut away the dangling nail. Jewell did not flinch at the pain, nor did he when the process was repeated on the two fingers of his right hand. Emmett laid the blade aside and lifted Jewell's hands into the pan of water.

"There now . . . let's clean these hands up a little."

The warm, soapy water soon began to dissolve the dried gore, and when Emmett finished, the water had turned light red.

"Dry 'em off now a little, all right? I got some salve that's the best stuff you ever saw."

He returned from the cabinet with a small circular tin of dull white salve.

"Let me dab some on these bad spots here . . . that's a boy."

Emmett cleared the table and then sat down again in the chair beside Jewell. He stole a glance into the boy's eyes; they were moving carefully now, all about the room, as if seeing it for the first time. Several minutes passed before Emmett was sure he could speak and be heard.

"Jewell . . . you better now?"

A tiny nod, the tip of his tongue passing over his lower lip.

"Good, that's good, Jewell. Listen close now. Is anything hurtin' you besides your hands? Inside, I mean, did he . . ."

"No. He only hit me once . . . in the face."

Emmett nodded, relieved, even though he had been almost certain that no such unseen wounds existed. But Emmett knew that there were unseen wounds—wounds of the mind which would have to be tended, and very soon.

"Good . . . good. What you need now more than anything else is some rest. I know you're wrung out." Emmett stood and helped Jewell to his feet then led him to the bed. "Lay down here and rest easy now."

Jewell stretched out on the bed and felt Emmett untie and remove his shoes. His body felt incredibly heavy now, but his mind was beginning to churn with images of his father's face; he could not discern between the real and the unreal. He knew something terrible had happened, something that had changed his life forever, and a great sadness came to him, like a wide stone on his chest, pressing him to the bed. For an hour, he drifted in and out of consciousness, the crazy images whirling, the pains in his fingers nagging reminders of the red world of rage that had claimed him for a time. A single tear slid from the corner of his right eye, but he did not wipe it away. He was not certain if he would ever again be able to weep, so the tear was a parting thing, a final reminder, and he allowed it to caress his cheek.

Jewell turned his head toward the center of the room. The light was soft now, the overhead fixture extinguished, and he could see that it came from the small lamp beside Emmett as he sat in the tattered chair near the window, the chair where he did his Bible reading. The little man read now. Jewell could see his lips move with the words, but he could not hear them. Jewell had no knowledge of where the desire to hear the words came from, but it did not matter. He wanted to hear them; he needed to hear them.

"Emmett."

The man's head jerked up as he closed the Bible, and Jewell could see that he intended to get up.

"No . . . no, stay there. I . . . I want to hear the words."

Emmett peered at him through the dim light, squinting to see Jewell's face, but he could not. His hands found their place under the Bible, and he pinched the marker in his fingers and flopped the book open to the book of Revelation. "I'm better at doin' numbers than I am readin' words," Emmett warned.

"I don't care . . . go ahead."

He had read the verse only minutes before, and he traced backward with his finger to the fourth verse of the twenty-first chapter. He read slowly, with great effort, attempting to pronounce each word correctly.

*And God shall wipe away all tears from their eyes; and there shall be no more death, neither sorrow, nor crying, neither shall there be any more pain: for the former things are passed away.*

Silence claimed the room for long minutes, but neither Jewell nor Emmett sensed unease. It was welcome, a semblance of peace coming with it, and both accepted it as a gift.

"When . . . when will it be like that, Emmett?"

"When the good Lord comes on back down here and cleans up all the messes folks made."

Silence again; the boy and the man could hear muffled night sounds—a truck engine gearing down on the long hill coming into town, a dog barking a block to the west, the low moan of the winter wind around the corner of the house—but they were not intrusions into the thoughts of either. They were but harmless pieces in the great puzzle of life; it was the hurtful pieces that clouded the mind of the boy, the same pieces that had long ago been accepted as unavoidable by Emmett Tragman.

"I don't want to wait, Emmett."

"Most days, I don't either, but He ain't gonna come till it's time. But He can take away all sorts of hurts now, Jewell." He paused and drew a long breath deep into his lungs, releasing it slowly between loose lips. "You go on back to sleep now . . . things'll already be a little better in the morning."

# Chapter 10

*T*HE KNOT in Annabelle's stomach felt as large as a grapefruit. It was six minutes before the morning bell, and Jewell's seat was empty. When she saw Emmett standing in the hall, the feeling turned to nausea. She walked quickly to meet him.

"What's wrong?"

"It was a crazy thing . . . a drunk snatched it from his pocket as a joke, made a scene . . . Jubal comes over . . . takes it from him . . ."

"Dear Lord, I should have known better. It was absolutely stupid of me to allow him to . . ."

"No, it wasn't stupid, Miss Annabelle. I had the same chance you did . . . right before it happened, and I let him keep it with him. He was so proud and all. I just couldn't . . . you couldn't . . . wasn't nobody's fault."

"What did he do to him? Is he all right?"

"It ain't so much what his daddy did to him as the other way around."

"I don't understand . . . how Jewell could have . . ."

"I don't exactly either, but somehow, after closin', he got the best of his daddy . . . messed him up fairly bad, but Jubal wouldn't let me get him the doctor. Just run us off."

Annabelle wrinkled her brow, attempting to understand the scene. "How did you know when there would be trouble?"

"I was bad worried," he looked down at his feet for a moment. "I never left after work . . . just stayed at the foot of the stairs and . . . listened."

"Where is Jewell now?"

"At my place. He was doin' pretty good. His hands are messed up some, but I tended 'em. His face ain't gonna be marked like last time."

"You're *sure* Jewell doesn't need the doctor?"

"No . . . it's more his mind that worries me. It's a heavy thing to mess up your own daddy, even if he did have it comin'." Emmett shuffled his feet, remembering the raised knife. "Could'a been a lot worse. Jewell was gettin' ready to take a knife to him when I got there . . . just did stop him."

"You don't think he really would have . . . used it, do you?"

He looked into Annabelle's eyes, held them for a moment, and decided to tell the whole truth.

"As I live and breathe, Miss Annabelle, he was gonna kill him."

Annabelle extended her right hand, as if groping for a handrail after stumbling. Emmett caught her by the arm, accepting her weight until she could steady herself.

"This is like a bad dream," she said.

"It is that."

"Somehow, I have to manage to get through classes today— without cheating any of the others—and I will. But I need to see Jewell this afternoon." It was both a statement and a question. Emmett nodded his agreement.

"Can you meet me back here at about three-thirty and take me to him?" she asked.

"I'll be here."

"You are sure he will be all right today? I suppose you will be with him?"

"Some of the time. I'll make sure he's doin' fine, but I have to be gone some too."

Annabelle's look was quizzical.

"Ain't employed no longer. Got to look for a job. Jewell might be stayin' with me for a good while, and you know how a young'un that age can eat."

Annabelle willed herself to the task at hand; there were twenty-six students whom she could teach this fine winter's day, twenty-six young minds to be filled with the necessary mental tools for life. They must not be cheated, not even for a day, and they were not. Annabelle taught the morning and afternoon hours away, wrapped around a quick lunch in her classroom. But once the classroom was empty, and faced now only by stacks of papers on her desk, the preoccupation set in with a vengeance. The long minute hand of the wall clock became a black slash in her vision until it was time to meet Emmett.

The steady footfalls of two people climbing the stairs came as no surprise to Jewell; he knew she would come. Emmett tapped three times on the door before turning the knob.

"Jewell, got company with me."

Jewell looked up from his seat on the edge of the bed. Annabelle's smile was wonderful to behold—without a trace of pity, but with the genuine caring that is the gift only a true friend may give to another. Jewell sifted the fingers of his right hand through his tousled hair and stood as Emmett and Annabelle approached.

"We missed you, number Twenty-seven," Annabelle said quietly as she extended her arms.

Jewell accepted her embrace with the lovable clumsiness of a boy too soon at the threshold of manhood, lost in a bittersweet twilight that made no allowance for the wrongs of life. A great sadness welled up within him that should have brought tears, but did not, and Annabelle was instantly aware of both the sadness and the void in his soul.

"Thanks for comin'."

Annabelle gently pushed him to arm's length and looked into his face before motioning to the table.

"Can we sit and talk for a bit?" she asked.

He nodded, and three chairs scooted quietly on the old wood floor. Annabelle folded her hands on the table and collected her thoughts for a moment.

"Jewell, I'm so sorry this happened . . . it was my fault mostly. I should have insisted that you leave the . . ."

"Wasn't nobody's fault," Jewell said. "Why should anybody have to worry about bringin' home a grade card? And a good one at that."

"That's true enough, but I knew who we were dealing with, and I'm sorry I took any chance at all."

"It doesn't matter now. It's over with."

"Jewell, we need to figure out where to go from here, come up with a plan for you," Annabelle said.

"Well, he's got a place here as long as he needs it," Emmett said.

"I can't stay here and just live off you, Emmett. You don't even have a job now."

"I didn't have one this morning, but I do now."

Jewell and Annabelle looked at Emmett. "Doin' what?" Jewell asked.

"Grave diggin' for a man named Rommie Rugg. Had a man move out of town just last week, and he's gonna give me a try. Won't be sorry, I guaranteed him. Besides that, I'll pick up odd jobs around. I'll make as much as before, maybe more."

"Just the same, it wouldn't be right," Jewell said. "A night or two is one thing, but . . ."

"No 'but' about it, Jewell. You can find some work after school and help out with the money. The landlady here is a fine woman, and I doubt she'll want more for the room if we come up with a little more for food."

Jewell lowered his head and stared at a spot on the table. There was really no choice; he had nowhere else to go, save for the county officials, and he would jump a freight train before letting them take him.

"Only if I can find some work to help pull my load."

"It's done then," Emmett said.

"Good," said Annabelle. "Just think, Jewell, you won't have to worry about studying out in the open here. I've got an extra small table that you two can bring over here. It will be perfect for a study area."

"We'll do it first thing," Emmett said.

Annabelle and Emmett made small talk for a few minutes about where to place the table to catch the best light, but Annabelle was busy forming an approach to the one thorny problem yet to be addressed.

"Jewell, there is one more thing we need to talk about . . . and I know it is difficult, but we can't ignore it."

"He won't ever bother me again." The words came with a coldness that belied the boy's age, and Annabelle was at once taken aback and saddened.

"Well, we can certainly hope that's true, but just the same I want both of you to know that if he should cause anymore trouble, I intend to get the proper people involved."

"I don't think it'll come to that, Miss Annabelle," Emmett said quietly as he remembered the sight of the bloodied man slumped against the wall.

"I hope not, but I'm through standing and watching from

afar. Someday, fairly soon I hope, I still intend to speak with him myself . . . when this situation calms down a bit."

Jewell and Emmett glanced at each other before Emmett spoke. "I wish you'd get that idea out of your mind. Jubal Cole ain't like anybody you ever tried to deal with."

"Do you both think that I've never dealt with anyone but children, for heaven's sake?" She had not intended to sound indignant, but knew that she did. She drew a measured breath before continuing. "I have known some very difficult people in my time, some of whom had trouble with alcohol, but I believe that *anyone* can be approached if the time is right."

"I'm not sure the time will ever be right with him, Miss Annabelle. It's hard to get across to someone who ain't been around him a lot like I have." Emmett waved his hand in frustration.

Jewell spoke, the hard edge still there. "Nobody knows him as good as I do, and the time will never be right." He looked at Annabelle with the eyes of a man, and it required a great effort for her to hold his gaze. "Promise me you'll never go near him."

The silence grew loud as the seconds that oozed by piled one on the other. Annabelle shook her head slowly and with a grim resolve. "That is a promise I may not be able to keep, Jewell . . . and I cannot make it."

The two men stood with the weak December sunlight of late afternoon on their backs, arms folded across their chests, as they studied the CLOSED sign hanging from the door to Jubal's Kingdom. The taller man raised his right hand to his chin and drew his forefinger thoughtfully across the black stubble, producing a rasping sound that was pleasing in a way that only grown men could understand.

"Second day in a row," he intoned, as much to himself as to his companion.

"Yeah . . . right strange for a man who likes a dollar bill good as Jubal Cole," the shorter man added.

"Never said nothin' about no repairs or such."

"Not a word."

They did not speak again for several minutes, paying no attention to the street sounds behind them. It was the tall man who broke the silence for the second time.

"Reckon we ought to go around back and check on him?"

"Don't know . . . seems like the boy or the idiot would be around to help him if anything was really wrong."

"Come on, let's go check."

They walked along the side of the building and turned down the alley, stopping in front of the door. Four loud raps of the tall man's knuckles echoed down the alley. There were no sounds from inside the Kingdom. Five more raps, louder this time. The tall man tested the doorknob; it was not locked. Cautiously, he pushed against the door and it opened a few inches with a low-pitched squeak.

"Anybody home?" the man called out.

He motioned for his friend to step close to him, and they could hear the heavy, shuffling sounds coming from the top of the stairs. They could see him now, a great hazy shadow looming in the dim light.

"This here's Henry, Jubal, and I got Alvin with me. We was . . . well, we thought we'd check on you to see if . . ."

"Leave me be."

The voice was weary, and if the two men had not known Jubal for many years, they would not have recognized it. They exchanged a wordless glance.

"We was just wonderin' when you'd open back up."

"You'll know when I turn the sign over. Now get out and leave me be."

When Jubal heard the door close, he considered for a moment

the effort required in descending the stairs to lock it, but he quickly rejected the idea. He did not yet have that kind of energy. He turned and made his way back to his chair, and when he reached it, he lowered the damp, bloody rag from the left side of his face and used both arms to lower his body. He reached for the neck of the whiskey bottle and cradled it to his side with his right hand, his left replacing the rag over the worst of his wounds. He took a long pull from the bottle and allowed the liquid fire to scorch down his throat and into his stomach.

It was a most wondrous and amazing thing, his medicine. He was very pleased that it lessened his agony but did not dull his hatred for the teacher-woman whom he would one day seek.

It was seventeen days before Jubal descended the stairs and turned over the OPEN sign on the door to his empty kingdom. The scabs covering the long slashes on his face were crumbling away, and the puffy reddish pink lines would soon mutate into the white scars that would mark the remainder of his days.

Within a few days, most of the former patrons of the Kingdom returned, and although, to a man, each of them harbored an abiding curiosity about the scars, none ever dared inquire. But it was not a difficult puzzle to piece together; the boy was conspicuously absent and with him, the idiot. And even though the marks appeared to be the work of a raging woman, the men knew that Jubal had long ago lost interest in women and had never kept or visited one. Emmett? Not the slightest chance under the sun.

It had to be the boy. Just how the fateful encounter came about was the mystery, and it was a mystery that would follow Jubal Cole to the grave.

# Chapter 11

A BONE-CHILLING wind swept over the high ground of the cemetery, rustling forlorn bouquets of sun-faded flowers scattered over weathered graves. The old man standing near the fire barrel with the spade in his hands had heard the winter wind sing its sad song hundreds of times, but the sound never failed to stir his soul. He was eighty-two years old, his face a parchment mask with wire-rimmed spectacles hiding blue eyes that still danced when he desired. He wore a cloth cap with ear flaps, the strap buckled securely under his chin. His coat was worn but serviceable, and the top button of his work shirt was closed high on his throat. Rommie Rugg watched as his two-man crew labored in the rectangular hole that would soon be a grave. He carefully worked the metal scrapper over the spade, peeling the sticky Missouri clay from the tool.

The new man was working his second grave, and Rommie was satisfied with his performance thus far; he was certainly much stronger than he looked, just as he had claimed. But Rommie had heard that claim many times before, and more often than not it had proven false. A grave was a very big hole to dig with hand tools. Big Hec, on the other hand, was a bear of a man, and he never appeared to be using more than a fraction of his strength. Hector Caldwell claimed that he could not remember ever being anything but big. Hector's own mother had crowed many times to anyone within earshot that her son was too weak for a horse and too strong for a man.

Rommie smiled to himself at the ten-year-old memory of the first grave they had dug together. It was a July grave, and the heat had wilted Rommie and the other worker to near exhaustion, but Big Hec seemed to gather strength in proportion with the sweat that poured from his body. Rommie shuffled over to the other man, who was taking his rest break, stretched full length in the shade of an oak. They talked for what Rommie knew could not have been more than a few minutes, but when they returned to the grave Rommie knew with a glance that Big Hec had already dug far too deep.

"Lord have mercy, Hec, you done dug too deep."

"Wanted to be done with it."

"Well you ain't done with it. Too deep's as bad as too shallow in the grave diggin' business, Hec. You're gonna have to put some dirt back, and that's a sorry thing to have to do."

Rommie rubbed a glove-covered hand over his chin and calculated that it had taken at least twenty graves before he could trust Big Hec with the last few inches. But the giant was steady now—quiet and steady, just the way Rommie liked a grave digger to be. It would not take as long for Emmett Tragman; of that, Rommie was certain.

He dropped the scrapper in his coat pocket and used the spade for a crutch as he stretched his back in the cold air. They were getting close to the floor of the hole now; it was nearly a grave. The old woman had lived for ninety-three years above the earth, and now her bones would lie beneath it for a time unknown. The grave measured one hundred inches long and forty-eight inches wide. It would soon measure fifty-six inches deep. Rommie walked ten steps against the wind and stood over the two men.

"Close, ain't it, Hec?"

Big Hec nodded silently from the hole as he reached out and pulled the measuring stick toward him, sliding it down the clay wall.

"Three more."

"Come on out and let Emmett floor it. He needs the practice."

Big Hec braced his back against one wall and walked his boots up the opposite side, popping out at one end and brushing himself off as he stood. Rommie paced slowly around the perimeter, his body hunched forward at the shoulders as he inspected the walls.

"Nice and straight, boys, nice and straight they look." He nodded approvingly. "Ain't ever laid a body down in a bad hole and don't ever aim to start." He nodded again, more to himself than his charges. "Everybody deserves a good hole."

"Reckon so," Big Hec said, "but I still ain't sure about them two back in thirty-eight."

They had buried two brothers who had been executed at the state penitentiary in Jefferson City for setting off a crude bomb in an escape attempt that claimed the life of a guard.

"Yes sir, them two included," Rommie declared, his passion now stirred. Big Hec was slightly irritated that he had set him off on his favorite subject, but it was going to happen sometime soon for Emmett's benefit anyway. Just as well be now, the big man reasoned.

"Can't hold up for what they done, no sir, can't do that, but they paid the toll for it and got on the long train, they did. Let the Almighty sort it out at the end of the ride, that's what I say. You remember their momma, Hec, I know you do, standin' over there yonder by that big oak, cryin' her eyes out for her babies gone wrong."

Rommie paused for breath and glanced first at Big Hec, staring penitently at a nearby tombstone, and then at Emmett, who had not looked up from his work.

"I'll tell you true, I couldn't a got a good night's rest for a year if we'd laid them boys in bad holes, their momma mournin' over 'em like that. No sirree, Hec, ain't nobody deserves a bad hole. Nobody."

Rommie stared a challenge down at Emmett. "What you say to that, Emmett? Man's got to have a proper attitude about this work, I figure, huh?"

"I reckon so . . . but . . ."

"But what?"

"Time they get to us, that long train you talked about has already got where it's goin'."

"I know that. For pity sake, I ain't no heathen. What I'm talkin' about is respect for the loved ones left behind, don't you see?"

"That's a good thing, Rommie, sure enough, but I don't see how the hole bein' a little crooked would make any diff . . ."

"Great day, I got a lot to teach you, Emmett, I'll swear."

Emmett disappeared back into the grave, the futility of arguing his point now apparent. The next half hour passed quietly, with Rommie instructing Emmett on the proper techniques involved in flooring the grave. Big Hec busied himself with gathering and cleaning tools. After jumping down into the grave with Emmett and satisfying himself with every detail, Rommie popped back out with apparent ease. Big Hec waited for the final pronouncement; the words never varied, and they were like a benediction of sorts.

"It started as a hole, and now it's a proper grave."

The three men stood silently for a moment, ignoring the sting of the wind, and then they slowly turned from the waiting grave and walked into the gathering gloom of late afternoon.

Although the man was but fifty-three years old, the age in his eyes gave him the appearance of a man ten years older. Harlon Allen stood alone at the corner of the weathered toolshed behind the house. The gray shed was more like a trusted friend than a building, its musty odors perfume to someone who made his living from things of steel and wood and black soil—things rooted deep in the earth. He reached up with a calloused hand and stroked the rough wood; the feel of it was comforting, though Harlon had never attempted to reason it out. The fact was that the feel of rough wood brought comfort; he did not have to know the reasons why.

The promise of more snow came to his nostrils with the sting of the late December wind. He shifted his boots and listened to the crunch of the three inches already blanketing the ground. He felt the corners of his mouth turn upward in a weak smile despite the heaviness in his heart. Annabelle loved snow at Christmastime, and it was Christmas Eve, with his beloved daughter to arrive any minute. But the hint of a smile faded quickly in the stinging wind, for Matthew, too, had loved snow at Christmastime.

The familiar rumble of the old Ford engine in the pickup drew him away from the shed and toward the white house. The engine coughed to a stop in the gravel driveway, and he could see his two daughters peering and waving through the windshield, the tops of their heads level, with Annabelle, as usual, perched atop her suitcase. Hazel Lee had arrived home with her five-year-old daughter, Anna, the day before and volunteered to make the trip to the train station.

Harlon walked to the passenger door and opened it, catching Annabelle in an embrace as she slid toward him.

"Oh, Daddy, I've missed you so." She kissed both of his cheeks.

"You too, my little Annabelle," he said, a loud whisper in the wind.

"Let's get inside," Hazel Lee chirped as she hustled past them. "Daddy, the heater in that old truck's not worth ten cents. For heaven's sake, will you work on it?"

He shook his head at the comment and reached for Annabelle's suitcase. The door to the house swung open, and Anna raced onto the porch as her grandmother smiled behind her.

"Auntie Teacher!" she squealed. "Auntie Teacher."

Annabelle knelt to catch her and swung her from side to side. "Miss Anna, I'll declare you've grown two inches. What a pretty girl you are."

Annabelle lifted her right arm toward her mother, who stepped forward from the doorway and joined the happy knot of arms. "How are you, baby? It's so good to see you." They cheek-kissed over Anna's head.

"Oh, you too, Mom. It's good to be home."

"Come on, let's get around the fire," Madalene said, shooing them all through the door. "Be supper time in an hour, and we got a pretty cedar tree to trim before bed time."

After supper, the tree was trimmed and wrapped gifts were placed, with Anna's excited giggles floating about the warm, close air of the sitting room. She flitted from lap to lap, eyes shining into the faces of the big people, but she was never far from Annabelle's touch. Annabelle—ever the gentle magnet for human emotions, especially those of a child.

"Auntie, which one's mine from you?" The dark little eyes mischievously searched Annabelle's face before shifting to the colorful mound of gifts under the tree.

"Let's see if I can remember, Anna. Oh, I hope I didn't forget and leave it at my place."

"Oh, Auntie, you wouldn't forget *mine!*" The child giggled at the unlikely prospect.

"I guess you're right," Annabelle said. She turned her shoulders and head to the left and placed a finger over pursed lips as if in deep thought. "It comes back to me now. Yours is the one with the big red reindeer on it."

"Can I shake it?"

"Again, you mean?" Hazel Lee interjected with a laugh. "I believe you have checked them all out, child."

"Just once more . . . pleeeease."

"I don't think it will hurt it," Annabelle said.

Anna looked to her mother for final approval and received the nod. In three skips, she was kneeling in front of the gift, stubby fingers probing, feeling, guessing with their touch.

"All right, little missy, time for bed, and no groans please. You're tired, but you haven't slowed down long enough to know it yet."

"Oh, Momma . . ."

The look silenced her, and she began the obligatory round of goodnight hugs and kisses. Brown teddy bear firmly tucked under one arm, Anna followed compliantly as Hazel Lee led the way to the bedroom. When she returned, the conversation turned to Annabelle's teaching experiences and her adjustment to the little town that had been home for nearly four months now. She painted word pictures of the school, her classroom, the little Baptist church she had joined, her rooms in Sadie Armstrong's rambling house, the landlady herself, and a dozen other people and places. She said little about Jewell and Emmett—a chance to help a special student with family problems, and the quiet little man who had become a friend and who was a part of it also. She did not even mention their names. Enough, but not too much. Annabelle did not understand the whole of it herself, but she was linked with the two lives in a powerful way, of this she was sure. But at this juncture, little could be shared comfortably, even with her family, and they understood and did not probe.

First Hazel Lee, then Madalene, said goodnight and retired to their bedrooms, more by design than from fatigue. Harlon Allen had been at the edge of the evening's conversation, but there was little heart in it. Both his wife and older daughter hoped that some time alone with Annabelle would prove to be a tonic that would produce a bright Christmas morning for the sorrowful man.

Annabelle popped up from the couch. "Come on, Daddy, let's see if it's still snowing. Get our coats and I'll get us a cup of hot chocolate."

She did not wait for a reply, did not look into the eyes that she knew dreaded the sight of falling snow on Christmas Eve. But it was necessary, even if hurtful; wounded souls could not be tended if they were not bared.

The night wind had shifted from the west and now came straight from the north, whispering along the sides of the house before cutting toward them as they stood on the covered front porch. Annabelle linked her arm through her father's and nestled against his side. The snow came without urgency, little more than tiny frozen pebbles that swirled and pecked aimlessly at the wooden porch floor. But they were snowflakes, and with them swirled memories of Christmas Eves long past, sights splashed with reds and greens, and sounds of laughter, and sugary aromas wafting from the kitchen, and Matthew came to them when the wind parted the clouds for a moment—moonlight on the snow—and they both knew.

Harlon reached forward and set his cup on the porch rail. Annabelle listened as the calloused hand passed over his eyes, rough flesh on weathered flesh, and she loved him fervently, almost fearfully, but remained silent. A windy minute passed, another peek of moonlight on frozen snow in the yard, grainy pecks at their shoes. Annabelle watched, sidelong, as his head bowed forward, stopping only when his chin rested on his chest.

"Annabelle . . . I don't think I can stay here any longer."

"Just a few more minutes, Daddy, please . . . I don't want to be alone now, and you don't need to be." Annabelle reached forward with her free hand and set her cup on the rail. She turned to face Harlon, waiting for him to lift his head enough to look into her eyes. "It's been over two years, Daddy . . ."

"I know how long it's been."

"Daddy, you think that you have to figure a way to let him go . . . somehow to finally watch him drift out of sight . . . to wave one last time. I know what you're trying to do. I did the same for a while, and it will never work out like that."

The voice was throaty now, hot and broken. "If I just could have had . . . his . . . ," he could not say the cold word, "him back from over there . . ."

"I know, Daddy, I know. It would have been better that way maybe, but it's not to be. That's the part that ate away at me too . . . that's the part I had to come to deal with."

He nodded slowly and swallowed. "That's good, daughter . . . that's good that it's worked out for you . . . ," the words trailed away into the wind.

"Matthew taught me how to work it out himself a long time ago."

The half turn of his head, a silent question.

"You remember the day Boots died, when I was seven?" He nodded. "Matthew dug the grave and said some words over her— for the sake of a little kid sister. And after I cried it out and after we got the new kitten, I never really thought much more about it . . . until we got word about him after Pearl Harbor." She paused and gathered her thoughts.

"I'm not sure how the words came back to me. They were just in my head one morning when I woke up. He said that Boots was a part of God, even if she was just a cat, and that I was a part of God, and that if I stayed close to God . . . well, I'd always be close to her too. I wouldn't have to let her go at all."

Harlon wept now, in the fashion of a man—silently, fighting against the burning in his chest and throat.

"It's like that with me and Matthew now, Daddy. I don't have to let him go. In some ways, I feel closer to him now than when he was with us. Oh, part of me wants him back here and always will; I accept that. Daddy, what have you and Momma always taught us God is? God is . . . ? Please say it. I want to hear you say it again. God is the . . ."

The words caught for a moment in his throat, but he forced them out. "The . . . perfect love."

"Yes . . . yes, the perfect love. Some Japanese admiral didn't change that, Pearl Harbor didn't change that. *Nobody, no event,* can take him from the perfect love, can they, Daddy?"

He shook his head but could not speak.

"No . . . thank God, no. And you are a part of the same love, Daddy, so Matthew is as close to you now as God Himself . . . closer than when he was on earth."

Annabelle laid her head on her father's chest, talked out now, suddenly cold and tiny, and she sought the warmth of his thick arms as they enwrapped her. The words had gushed out of her . . . perhaps too fast. Who was she to preach to her own father? That is what it felt like now, in the cold night wind, a child again, pressed to her father's chest, wondering. Then Harlon began to rock her to and fro, and she could feel the sobs deep within his chest, the gentle touch of his cheek atop her head. They rocked for long moments, and she knew it was all right and that her words had been taken in love.

"You're shiverin', child. Let's warm by the fire a while."

He awoke with the first gray light of dawn and quietly pulled his clothing together, draping it over his arm, and tiptoed from the bedroom. He stopped in the living room and put wood in the fire before moving to the Christmas tree and breaking off a small bough. He took his coat and boots from behind the kitchen door.

The tiny grave was fifteen years old, and the little wooden cross consumed by time, but he thought he remembered the place. He had watched from the kitchen window as Matthew turned up the earth to accept the small box he had fashioned from scraps of lumber. He had offered to help, but Matthew wanted to perform the task alone for his beloved Annabelle, the little sister who would always be strangely little. In her seventh year, she knew. Everybody knew.

Harlon toed the crunchy snow with his boot, scraping out a square yard, exposing tufts of dormant grass. He brought the bough to his nostrils for a moment, drawing the green fragrance deep within him, and then he knelt on one knee and placed it in the center of the square of colorless grass.

He could see them up high, the man and the boy, in the yellowish light of the second-story window. The bite of the night wind was lost on the flesh of his face and hands; the fuzzy warmth coursed through his veins and soothed his thoughts for a moment. Jubal Cole stood in the frigid darkness fifty yards from the rambling house that held his son, his eyes cast ever upward, the yellow square beckoning, taunting, a friend and an enemy.

He watched for long minutes as they moved about, placing ornaments on the squat, green cedar that stood atop a small table in the far corner of the room. He knew when they spoke to each other, like mimes on a stage, their heads turning or bobbing slightly, and he wondered what words were spoken by the shameless son and his idiot friend. He grunted aloud, a hateful sound in the stillness. What did it matter? He cursed them under his breath. And then he cursed the runt teacher-woman who was the cause of the whole sorry mess. He had stared into her darkened windows for a half hour until he was certain she was not there. But she would come back soon, back to her snot-nosed brood, all clustered in the schoolroom with their open books and fawning eyes. He had seen her there too. Always carefully hidden in shadows or darkness, Jubal had seen her in many places. He was always close enough to examine her and yet far enough away to be invisible.

She would come back soon. He could find her any time he desired.

# Chapter 12

*S*PRING CAME late and was nearly brushed away by the first week of June 1944. Annabelle stood near the window of her classroom, her face turned slightly toward the breeze that carried the warm green fragrances that mix when spring and summer touch in the air. It had been a good winter and spring, as good as could be hoped for, given the great swirl of life-and-death news that swept across the land—relentless, triumphant, tragic—word came home from the great stages of the Pacific and European Theaters. None of Annabelle's students had lost a loved one since last autumn, and for that she was thankful. But other students had suffered loss, one in the third grade and another in high school, and the town was small and grieved as one.

Annabelle turned her head and watched as Jewell thoughtfully chewed the end of his pencil. She had broken the class down into groups of four or five for an assignment on the Normandy invasion. It had been three days since word reverberated across America and the world. D-Day, hopefully the beginning of the end for Hitler and his Nazi war machine. Hopefully. *War is a strange and winding road,* she thought to herself. *And long, dear God, ever so long.*

The four other students in Jewell's group poked with fingers and pencils and chattered steadily at the map spread over two desk tops. They were no longer afraid of him, despite the fact that word of the bloody fight with his father had leaked throughout the town like spilled oil, black and ugly—seeping over concrete, finding the crevices, turning corners like a living organism. Annabelle and Emmett had shielded him from much of it and he faced the remainder head on, dealing with a piece of life that could not be avoided. She was proud of him, deeply stirred by the fact that he had a chance now, a very good chance, to lead a life that would make a difference.

A tiny dread had picked at her for the last two weeks, and she had chided herself for allowing the thought to creep into her brain, but it could not be completely pushed aside. He would leave her classroom forever in a few days and be swallowed up in the bigger high school building looming a hundred feet away. But the bond would not be broken; he could always come to her for help with any problem, *would* always come, she hoped fervently.

Annabelle glanced at the open doorway and the small face of Edith Blyth, which had seemingly materialized in it. With only the glance, Annabelle knew that the news about Edith's little sister was not good.

"Continue with your work, students. I will be back in a moment."

When she reached Edith, she took both of the child's hands in hers and squeezed gently. Edith had been absent for two days, remaining at home to help her mother with her two younger brothers while the woman tended the baby named Nellie. The fever had come like a ghost in the night, and the tiny body had been bathed with an unnatural sweat as consciousness ebbed and flowed.

"How is she, Edith?"

The girl shook her head weakly, in slow motion. "Doc Nelson . . . he says he don't know nothing else to try. He told Momma he doubted she'd make it through another night. I heard him say it . . . wasn't supposed to, but I did."

Annabelle drew the child to her. "Oh, Edith, I'm so sorry, honey. I'm so sorry."

Edith sniffed and pulled away, swiping at her nose with the back of her hand. Annabelle fished a tissue from her dress pocket as Edith nodded her thanks.

"Anyway, Miss Annabelle, I ain't . . . er, I'm not supposed to even be here. Doc's not sure about the fever and all, but I had to get away from the house for a while. I hope you don't care."

"Of course not, Edith. We've all been waiting to hear about little Nellie. You stay as long as you like."

"Just for a few minutes."

The soft knock on the door came just after dawn, and at first Twila Rugg ignored the sound. But it came again, a weariness in it that she could hear in the old wood door frame. Rommie stirred as she arose and pulled on a nightgown. Again, the soft knocking.

He grumbled, "Who in tarnation . . . ?"

His wife returned quickly and said, "A woman asking for the grave digger." She shrugged and turned her hands, palms up.

"Reckon that'd be me. You ask her in?" Rommie reached for his coveralls.

"Said she wanted to wait out in the yard."

"She grievin'?"

"Couldn't tell."

Rommie padded barefoot through the small living room and out the front door. He had seen her before, exactly where, he could not remember. Her clothing was simple and very worn, but clean. She was a tall woman, but she made no effort to hold herself erect. There was a great weariness to her, in both her posture and her eyes; Rommie had seen the thing many times, in many eyes. Sometimes it came before the grief, sometimes after, and Rommie surmised that it was before for this woman. For now, she had things to take care of.

"Yes ma'am, I'm Rommie Rugg."

"Mr. Rugg, I'm sorry to bother you so early . . ."

"No bother, time to get up anyways."

"I'm Grace Blyth . . . and I've lost a child." She held his eyes for a moment before glancing at the ground, checking her emotions.

"I'm so sorry, Mrs. Blyth. Terrible sorry."

She nodded. "Anyway, me and my husband, he's in the South Pacific somewheres, we ain't church folks, and I ain't sure what to do exactly right now. Doc Nelson said he'd help me, but he's wore out from the last three nights and all . . . and . . ."

"You don't need to look any further for help now." She looked up into the old man's face and thanked him with her eyes.

"Is your little one down at Tucker's Funeral Parlor now, Mrs. Blyth?"

"Yes, she is. They said they'd get hold of you this morning, but . . . I wanted to see you myself . . . about money and such."

"No need to worry with that now."

"There is for me, Mr. Rugg. I want . . . Clarence would want . . . this done right. When he comes home . . . it'll help if he knows it was done right . . . somehow, I know him. It'll help a little."

"I got two men that work on my crew, and I'll take something for them. Seven dollars and fifty cents each will do."

"But what about you? It's your crew, and you can't make a livin' like that . . ."

"Mrs. Blyth, you ain't lookin' at no spring chicken. I ain't in much need of a great deal more money so much as I am peace of mind. If I can't help a soldier's family out a little, it'd cost me a chunk of my peace of mind, don't you see?"

"Well, I reckon . . ."

"No reckonin' about it. Just you don't fret with this part of it, all right? Go home and get some rest now. I'll look after the necessary things."

The weariness came over her now with the realization that she had performed her duties and made the proper arrangements. It came like a shroud from the shadows, enwrapping her, claiming her, and Rommie watched it come. She turned to leave, stopped, and made a half turn back.

"I thank you, sir."

"It'll be my honor, Mrs. Blyth."

Rommie outlined the tiny grave in the predawn coolness as he awaited the arrival of Big Hec and Emmett. It would be another twenty minutes before sunlight touched the place and the men began the digging. The old man squinted into the faint light as two figures emerged from the edge of the tombstones, two hundred feet away. As they neared, he could hear the sound of their voices, but the words were indistinct.

". . . always the same." Big Hec's low rumble, strangely soft on the morning air. "Rommie likes to dig the little graves at sunrise."

"Why's that?" Emmett asked.

"Ain't no use in tryin' to tell you myself when I know good and well he'll speak on it directly. 'Specially since this is the first little one we've dug since you came on."

Rommie took three steps forward to meet them. "Mornin', fellers."

"Same to you, Rommie," Emmett said. Big Hec nodded.

"Kinda early, I know, and this here ain't much of a job, but I like to work on these little ones at sunrise."

Big Hec and Emmett nodded in unison.

"Don't reckon Big Hec told you why?" Rommie directed the words at Emmett but looked half-accusingly at the big man.

"I ain't told him nothin', Rommie."

"Just as well . . . like as not you woulda messed it up some."

Big Hec shook his head and ran his thick fingers over the top of his head, but said nothing.

"Anyways, it's just my way of doin' things, I reckon. Old as I am, no children of my own, and as many of these little ones I've dug . . ." he paused and let his view wander over the markers, "you'd think it wouldn't bother me no more, but it still bothers me some."

He looked the question at Emmett, and it hung quietly in the air for a moment. "Nothin' wrong with bein' bothered by the passin' of a child, Rommie—seems fairly natural to be bothered."

"For most folks, sure enough it's natural, but I ain't a normal man. I been diggin' holes in the ground since Methuselah was a pup. Young ones, old ones . . . a lot of both. Shouldn't bother me no more . . . but it does." He paused again, tapping his hands on top of the spade handle. "Well, anyhow . . . I do the little ones at sunrise cause I think that's when the long train stops for them. The promise of a new day here for us . . . somewheres else for the little one . . . there must be somethin' else somewhere for them. It don't make no sense any other way."

Emmett said, "I think you've got it figured 'bout right, Rommie."

Big Hec shifted his feet uncomfortably, making a half turn away from the conversation as he passed a hand over his head again.

"Hec here, he ain't much on things of the spirit," Rommie said quietly.

"Now, Rommie, don't start in on me . . ."

"Hec, I got no such notion."

"Well, don't then. Just leave me out of it. If you got it all figured out for yourself, that's fine, but it don't sort out that easy for me."

"Who said anything about 'easy'? I watched enough tears fall to fill a good-sized pond before I sorted it out. You just ain't seen enough tears fall, Hec."

"Seen my share, I reckon."

"Well, I ain't gonna argue with you. I was just tryin' to tell Emmett why I got him outta bed so early for this one."

"Well, he knows now, so let's get on with it."

"Can't . . . not yet," Rommie said.

Big Hec glanced eastward, looking for the first orange slice of sunlight, but it was not visible.

"Take a little walk and quiet your mind, Hec," Rommie said, "the train's almost here."

Save for Jewell Cole, the classroom was empty. He stood beside the globe, his right forefinger gently brushing the tiny green splotches that represented the islands of the South Pacific. The Philippines, the Palaus, the Tinians, the Marianas, the Carolines, the Marshalls, the Gilberts—one by one the raised dots slipped under his fingertip, and his thoughts drifted from Missouri with an airy freedom, carried over the thousands of miles to the places where young men fought in the great war.

Aircraft carriers pitched and rolled on the waves like elongated gray buildings, decks bristling with fighter planes like swarms of deadly steel insects. The hulks of battleships crashed through the waves, the monstrous sixteen-inch guns angrily spewing their shells toward the enemy positions on islands fifteen miles distant.

*Yes, the islands,* the boy thought as he touched them. They were the places that captured his thoughts—the places where soldiers bled. He had read and heard many things about these jungle-covered chunks of rock rising from the floor of the ocean. He had heard that soldiers prayed for night to fall and then prayed again for sunlight to rescue them from enemies who crawled in the darkness, crawled silently with knives. Five years. Five years by birth was perhaps all that separated him from the young men under his fingertip. He wondered what kind of soldier he would be on an island in the South Pacific, in the jungle night.

He lifted his finger from the globe and turned to face the big desk at the front of the room, Miss Annabelle's desk. She was out in the hallway, chatting merrily with a smattering of his classmates and their parents on this last day of the school year. He could easily pick out her voice, though it was no louder than any of the others. Her voice was a song, soft and melodious, at once blending with and yet carrying above all the others. Jewell stood quietly and listened and waited for all the other voices to drift away and leave her alone. Then she would come and talk with him in the room where his life had changed with the crack of a rock on black slate.

Her footfalls now, soft and steady on the wood floor, and he turned to face her.

She said, smiling only with her eyes, "Come sit with me, Jewell."

She motioned toward two of the desks in the front row. They sat in silence for a few moments, listening to the fading sounds in the hallway, allowing the caress of June air from the open window to push at their clothing. Jewell had planned to say many things, but now, with the moment at hand, with her sitting beside him, the words hung in his throat.

"Well, number Twenty-seven, it's been quite a year, hasn't it?"

He glanced at her and then down at the desk top before nodding.

"I'm not sure what I'll do without my war correspondent."

He flushed with the sound of the fancy word she used on him and the knowledge that she was certain he understood its meaning.

"I figure you'll find somebody to step in."

"I doubt it." She laughed easily, but it quickly faded. "It disturbs me that your gift for geography is linked with the war. I understand that war is fascinating to young men, but remember that other places and peoples are worth studying without wars. I hope you remember that."

"I will. I promise."

"Good, I believe you will, Jewell."

Silence again, but no discomfort with it.

"I want you to know that I'm so very proud of your accomplishments. Under . . . ordinary circumstances . . . they would be noteworthy, but . . . given the problems you've dealt with . . . well, they are extraordinary. And I know that your high school years will be filled with more learning."

"I hope." The words were unsteady, cloudy with doubt. "Everybody knows about me . . . and him . . . and all the school trouble I got in before."

"That's all past, Jewell. It will blow away like tumbleweeds in Kansas. Your 'new' reputation has spread to the faculty over there." Annabelle pointed to the high school building looming a hundred feet distant. "Mr. Bellman and I have seen to that."

"You have?"

"We have indeed."

"Whew, that's kinda scary in a way, but thanks. I mean, it was awful nice of you to do that."

"Believe me, it was a great pleasure. So you charge over there next fall and get started on the right foot, all right? It goes without saying that I will be here to help you any way that I can."

"I know."

She laughed. "If you don't check in with me every so often, I'll come looking for you."

He smiled at her, quickly and beautifully, a bright flash of light that pierced her soul. She looked away and drew in a deep breath, attempting to hide the emotion, dealing with it. But she could not hide it. Jewell felt his throat thicken, and he knew that if he did not quickly speak at least some of his piece, the opportunity would pass.

"Miss Annabelle, I can't get out all I want to say . . . but I *have* to say this . . ."

She raised a hand and shook her head as if to assure him that no debt was owed.

"No, please," he began again, "I need to, for me." He squirmed in his seat and rubbed the sweat from his palms on his trousers. "That day . . . when I chunked the rock . . . I can't believe I did that, knowin' now what kind of person you are and all . . . but I *did* do it, and I never really said I was sorry. I mean, I know that you know I'm sorry, but it's not right that I haven't come out and said it."

He paused and sucked in a hasty breath. "Anyhow, I'm sayin' it now, for all I'm worth . . . I'm sorry."

He looked away, toward the window and the yellow light of afternoon, blinking at the tears. Annabelle slipped her hand into the pocket of her dress and gently closed her fingers around the smooth stone. She had carried it with her each day since the morning she lifted it from the floor of the classroom. It was time to return it now; it belonged to her no longer.

"Here, Jewell, I want you to have this back."

He turned his head and looked down at the rock, but he could not speak, could not move his hands.

"There is no need to be sorry any longer. I accept your apology. When you threw this rock, it was like a cry for help. Something like that had to happen, sooner or later."

Annabelle reached out and quietly placed the rock on Jewell's desk.

"I am glad that you threw it."

# Chapter 13

*A*T TEN o'clock on a sticky August morning, while he was sitting, nearly sober, in his favorite chair, Jubal Cole made the final decision to kill the little teacher. The thought had flickered about in his brain for many weeks, in the beginning only as a delightful, though remote, possibility, and then as a righteous act, a high judgment that only he could carry out. The Kingdom beneath his feet was dying, and his own flesh and blood had turned on him like a raging animal; someone had to pay. She was the one. She had brought the trouble on herself, what with her high-minded meddling and books and ideas— things that had shoved his son off the path Jubal had laid out. A fine business, to be passed from father to son, now in shambles, all because of her. Save for a handful of die-hard customers, the men with their quarters and fifty-cent pieces and dollar bills had shuffled their way down to Able Townlain's little hole-in-the-wall at the other end of town. Just last week, Jubal heard that Able had rented the adjacent storefront and was busy knocking out a wall to expand his growing business.

That there was little money in the bank was no real concern; there had never been a great deal, even in the best of times. Enough to conduct routine business, enough to let the uppity bankers know that Jubal Cole was a successful businessman, but not enough to tempt them to steal from him with their sharp pencils and complicated ledgers. He was certain that they pilfered in quiet, shadowy ways known only to them, these pinched-face men in their starched white shirts and dark suits.

Jubal smiled crookedly. No, they were no worry; they had never even known of the twenty-seven quart-sized Mason jars hidden in his cellar, jars stuffed with only tens and twenties. But now only four remained. At the start of the decline, Jubal had saved the empty jars, at first, certain that they would be refilled, and then with a fading, pitiful hope that they might, somehow— but he knew. He knew many jars ago, and then he began to smash them into tiny pieces in a corner of the cellar, with the rotting, sprouted potatoes and the rat droppings and the spider webs. Sometimes, when the light from the naked bulb probed just so, and when Jubal's blood was warm and tingly with whiskey, the smallest fragments looked for all the world like diamonds, and his troubles were over as he knelt to scoop the treasure into his hands . . . and then they were pieces of glass again, part of the filth, worthless. As worthless as his life. Sometimes he cried and sometimes he screamed with rage, but it did not matter, down in the cellar. Down with the ugly creatures that scampered and crawled, and did not care.

But the thing with the little freak would be made right, and now, that he had decided to act, there was a bit of solace for him. He licked dry lips and the fingers of his right hand twitched in anticipation of the feel of the smooth glass only inches away, but his hand did not move. He was thinking with a marvelous clarity now; his soothing medicine could wait a few minutes more. Jubal leaned forward and snared the crumpled pack of Camels with his thumb and forefinger and shook one of the cigarettes from the end of the pack, pinching it free in his lips. It was when he struck the book match into a tiny, hissing flame that he knew she would die by fire. He stared, transfixed by the yellow flame, until it burned his fingers and the unlit cigarette dropped from his lips. He shook out the flame and placed the smoking stub in the ashtray, and then picked up the pack of cigarettes and crushed it into a loose ball in the palm of his hand. Another match hissed to life, and he held it to the pack and marveled at the power to consume, to destroy, to make right—power that was in his hands. The flame grew in his mind, and the ball of paper became a two-story house, the flame a thousand times hotter, and he stepped back into the shadows of his brain to see it all unfold.

The righteous fire, the cleansing fire, swept up the walls of the house on the night wind with incredible speed as the smoke thickened and billowed in the tree tops. Upward, ever upward, yellow and hungry, it climbed toward her room, and Jubal could see her now in the window, wide-eyed with panic, knowing her fate. He steps from the shadows and allows the firelight to illumine his face as the eyes of the judge and the eyes of the condemned lock, and then she vanishes into the smoke and the flame. But not before she knows that Jubal Cole has tried her and found her guilty and carried out her sentence.

Jubal's room now, the faint stench of burned paper in his nostrils, the images fading slowly, beautifully, into the wall. Street sounds floating upward—engines churning, the chirps and chatters of children's voices, the shouts of men, the yip yapping of a dog—things of life outside the Kingdom. Useless things to Jubal, things beneath him, things to be ignored. He reached for the bottle and the glass. The Kingdom would not be opened today. Let them all go down to Able Townlain's pitiful hole. It mattered no longer.

By eleven o'clock, the judge over the Kingdom doubted that it would ever open again.

Emmett methodically chewed a mouthful of beans and corn-bread as he stared over the top of the newspaper page hiding Jewell's face. The boy had not moved for several minutes, and Emmett was becoming impatient; sweeping events were taking place in and around Paris in late August of 1944. The hounds were baying at Hitler, and people had begun to sense the beginning of the end for the madman running loose in Europe.

"Well . . ."

"Oh . . . uh, sorry, Emmett. I'm just tryin' to get all this straight in my head. Whew! This is good news."

"Exactly *what* is good news, Jewell Cole?"

"Well, remember how I told you last week that Patton and his tanks were rollin' toward Paris, and how the Paris folks made a stand and fought the Germans?"

"I remember."

"Well, nobody's real sure why Hitler didn't just try and blow up Paris . . . the way things were lookin' and all, but it didn't get done—least not soon enough—and our boys stood shoulder to shoulder with the Paris fighters and kicked their hind ends clean out of Paris. I mean, clean out, Emmett!"

"That's mighty good news, all right."

"More than mighty good. I mean, Paris, *free*. That's an awful big deal. They had Paris for over four years. I don't reckon Hitler figured he'd ever get kicked out of Paris. Whew, man oh man."

"You reckon it'll be over soon?"

Jewell closed the paper and laid it on the table beside his plate. He tilted his head back and looked up at the ceiling for a moment before answering. "Reckon so. They're talkin' months now instead of years. Reckon we'll whip the Germans and the Japs both before long."

There was an unmistakable wistfulness in the words, nearly a sadness, and Emmett knew that the boy regretted having missed the war, being relegated to reading and listening to radio reports, while the real men reaped the glory of battles fought and won. And with this knowledge, a sadness came to Emmett, a slow-moving sorrow born of memories of World War I—haunted faces and pieces of cloth flapping where arms and legs should have been, and the tears of parents and children. It was proclaimed to be the war to end all wars, but oh, how wrong the proclaimers had been. He lifted a quick prayer to the God who surely hated all wars that the man-child sharing his table would never have to fight in a war. He had already fought terrible battles as a child, battles where no victor could ever be declared.

"It ain't all glory over there, Jewell."

The tousled hair bounced as Jewell's head swiveled with surprise at his friend's insight, and his mouth formed a half smile, sheepish and innocent. "What makes you think I'm . . ."

Emmett filled in the words. "Dreamin' of bein' a soldier?"

The smile widened a fraction, still retaining its innocence, and then it was gone. The boy nodded silently and began to pick at his plate of beans with a fork.

"I been around a war before this one. It was long and ugly too. I was barely too young for that one, but I was old enough to be a close watcher . . . a good watcher." He paused and swiped at his mouth with the back of his hand. "I watched the boys go, and I watched some of 'em come home, and I promise you none of 'em was the same. No sir, not all glory, Jewell."

"I don't claim it is, Emmett. I ain't blind to the bad things, but . . . I still say it'd be somethin' special to be a part of that . . . fightin' for your country and all . . . come whatever."

"Well, I just pray that this here one is the real last one. That's what I hope."

"It surely will be. Who'd ever be fool enough to mess with us after this?"

"Don't know, but that question got asked after the first one too, and somebody was . . . somebody was."

The rich, brown aroma of the beans returned to Jewell, and he picked up his fork and shoveled in a mouthful. The thing had passed, and he was fourteen again, more boy than man, and Emmett was glad.

Only the light above snooker table number one cast its yellowish glare about the Kingdom, and it did not reach into the shadows along the wall where Jubal sat, tilted on the wooden bench. Perhaps because it was Saturday night, the stillness haunted Jubal more than it had for many days. Without closing his eyes or even halfheartedly attempting to remember, the old sounds of raucous laughter and clacking snooker balls came to him—unwanted now, derisive sounds in the half-lit pool hall. Saturday nights were always the loudest, and the most profitable. Gone now. Gone forever.

He took a thoughtful pull on the bottle and swallowed slowly, tasting the liquid fire. The big wall clock chimed twelve times, and a twisted smile took his lips with the realization that it was already Sunday, sweet Sunday—the day she would burn. The day she would pay dearly for his misery. The same day she and her holy friends screeched up at God Almighty and pawed and smiled at one another. *Oh, yes . . . sweet Sunday.*

Jubal had it all laid out in his mind. He had worked it out from the lovely clump of trees just beyond the corner of the big two-story house. The trees from which he could see her in the window, the trees into which he would retreat and watch the progress of the blaze as it snaked up the wall. Sundays had proven to be the best watching and planning days. Her routine never varied. A slow stroll with the idiot down the street, which followed a gentle slope from the church house, their merry chatter an ugly sound in Jubal's ears. A runt and a dimwit, acting just like a real man and woman, almost as if they were courting. But they never touched, not even when they parted near the porch. Then he would trundle away in his stupid gait, lost in the dusk. The light would flood the window, and Jubal caught glimpses of her from time to time as she moved about the room, but mostly she sat in the rocker, reading one of her precious books. And then at ten o'clock, always ten o'clock, she would disappear from the window, and soon the light would go out.

The lights on the first floor, where the old woman owner lived, never remained on for more than a few minutes, and were sometimes extinguished before those of her tenant. Jubal fought a twinge of regret that the old woman would have to be placed in mortal danger. But she was on the first floor; she stood a good chance of surviving. Whatever, it was her great misfortune to be linked with someone condemned to death; fate would provide the final answer for her. It was out of his hands.

Jubal pushed himself up from the bench and tested his balance before making his way to the back and up the stairs to his chair. He slumped comfortably into his place of rest. He would continue to think, deep into the night, of his coming duties; sleep could wait. He would sleep with the daylight. It would be as if this lovely night blended with the next, and when it came, he would rise up and leave his place of rest.

And then Jubal Cole would defend his honor.


Emmett watched from a careful distance as Annabelle moved about the small gathering of Sunday night churchgoers. She floated about like a butterfly, her pale yellow dress trimmed in brilliant white, her movements graceful and unhurried. Everyone she spoke with soon smiled with her, even those for whom smiles did not come easily. A human magnet, a beautiful, tiny human magnet who was at once set apart from and yet inextricably linked to every person around her. It was her gift from God, Emmett reasoned, in exchange for a body seemingly ill suited for the world.

A few people, mostly older, drifted Emmett's way and spoke a word or two or nodded pleasantly, and he returned their words and gestures in kind. He would never be comfortable in the crowd, with people milling all around him, with the conversations jumping from one subject to another. This fact had long ago ceased to bother him; it was not his gift. His gift was to observe, to learn the hearts of others, to lend a hand when he was able. This gift required little in the way of lengthy talk, and most others, believing him dull, seldom probed into his quiet world of observation. And so he was left alone and unbothered in his assigned task, as he watched and studied hearts, and cared. *It all worked out rather well,* he thought—Annabelle on center stage in her world, with her wonderful ways and words, and he, quietly busy in his world.

The Sunday evening walks to Annabelle's rooming house had begun months ago, at her request. The first time they walked away from the gathering, Emmett had his antenna up for covert stares or muffled snickers aimed at their backs, but nothing registered. He really had not expected anything like this; they were, after all, people of like mind and spirit, but still—they were an unusual couple in the eyes of most observers. Emmett hoped fervently that nobody thought anything untoward about him, trusted that they did not, and yet . . . he knew of minds that were given to such thoughts. Like tall weeds around the edge of burned-out yards in a drought, they required very little water to thrive. If Annabelle had ever shared his concerns, he could not sense it, and he doubted that he could miss signals about something as important as that.

They walked slowly away from the church building, down the long hill, into the cottony evening.

"I'm excited, Emmett. Only one more week before classes begin."

"Reckon you are."

"I think I'm ready for a calmer year." She made a sound like laughter, but it was not. "Just an ordinary class of sixth-graders . . . hopefully no war tragedies, no home problems . . . something like that . . ."

"I ain't sure there ever was a ordinary bunch of young'uns."

Annabelle did laugh now, full and beautiful. "How true. You caught me there, Emmett. It was a poor choice of words. I don't suppose anybody, child or adult, is really ordinary, much less a classroom full."

They walked several steps in silence. Annabelle said, "It was Jewell who made me say that."

"I know."

"I'm so happy he's doing well now. I must be very careful not to cling too closely, make him too dependent on me for his studies. Ha! Listen to me, will you? He is likely to plunge into the seventh grade and never look back, but I hope he doesn't do that altogether. Oh, great day, I'm talking in circles."

"I know what you mean."

"Yes, I'm sure that you do, Emmett."

He felt her hand close over his for a wonderful moment and squeeze gently, and the feeling was like a tiny electrical current, but he could not bring himself to squeeze back. For a magical moment they were a couple, linked hand in hand, but it passed quickly, and they were good friends again, walking side by side.

They were nearing the house now. The first-floor lights burned through the windows, and they could see the dark clump of trees beyond. The breeze was from the west, and it sang in the leaves and branches and passed by their faces. Soon Annabelle entered the house, and Emmett walked away, only to stop and turn for a last look. He must have imagined it, the faint odor of gasoline on the breeze a few moments before. There were no other houses or people or vehicles over there, beyond the clump of trees. Just a small field and then more woods. He shook his head and resumed his walk home.

# Chapter 14

*J*UBAL STARED from his hiding place in the gathering gloom as Emmett disappeared down the street. He reached for his hip pocket and the half-pint bottle, taking a loose swig and then twisting the top back in place. The drink helped a bit; he had stood in the same place for well over an hour, watching and waiting, and there were still two hours to pass. But he could sit down against a tree now; she was where he wanted her. All he had to do was wait for the lights to go out and then give her another quarter of an hour to go to sleep. He could rest easy now.

Jubal ran his fingers over the two long-necked beer bottles propped against the tree trunk—beer bottles that now contained gasoline. They were perfect vessels for the secretive transportation—small enough to fit in his hip pockets and under his shirttail and yet large enough to provide a sufficient amount of fuel for the righteous fire to come.

Jubal whispered a curse at himself, thinking back an hour to his arrival at the hiding place. After carefully removing the caps and filling the bottles in his cellar, he had tapped the caps back on with a small hammer. But somewhere along the route, one of the caps had worked free and slipped out under his shirttail. It must have happened within the last few steps before arriving, Jubal figured; very little gasoline had sloshed onto his trousers, and the odor was faint. No real harm done, just a minor aggravation. The open bottle was pinned in the deepest bark groove that the old burr oak had to offer. No more of the precious liquid would be spilled before its time.

The minutes slid by with a dark peacefulness, soothing the jagged nerves of the half-drunken man, and he focused, dreamlike, on the yellow rectangle of light on the second floor. To his surprise, the lights on the ground floor were the first to blink out. The flickers of movement in the upper window had ceased for what seemed a very long time, and he knew his enemy must soon lie down to sleep.

Twenty yards from the oak, the close-set pair of shining eyes drew ever nearer as a big boar raccoon approached through the tall grass. He was an old raccoon, a creature of the night, and he had lived with and stolen from man for his entire life, so the odors of human flesh and alcohol and gasoline did not alarm him. His curiosity drove him now, and he slowed his pace but crept forward until he could see the man. It was strange to spy a man in the darkness; they were not creatures of the night. They sought the places where their little suns could probe and show them things that he could see very easily. Strange things, these men, very interesting, but they were an enemy. The worst enemy of all.

The raccoon stiffened and sank low to the ground. The little sun in the top of the house was gone, and the man's clothing scraped the tree as he twisted his body and craned his neck upward. This one was as noisy as any the raccoon had ever been near, and by the time the human had gained his feet, the raccoon knew that every night creature around him was aware of the man's presence. The man stood, leaning against the tree, and the minutes passed on the night breeze, but the raccoon's curiosity held him; there was no fear.

It was when the man stooped to earth and picked up the bottles that the animal began to feel fear. The sounds the man made were like growls, unnatural things in the quiet night, and the strong odor from the bottles stung in the raccoon's nostrils as he melted away into the grass.

Jewell looked up from the magazine and watched Emmett pace stiffly from the window to the door and then repeat the process two more times. The man clearly had not been himself since returning from church services, a most unusual occurrence, since Sunday evenings were normally his most restful times.

"Emmett, why are you doin' that?"

Suddenly mindful of his action, Emmett halted abruptly near the window and cast a blank stare at Jewell, as if he heard the sound of the words but not the question.

"Huh?"

"I said, why in the world are you walkin' back and forth like that. You look like a dog in a cage."

"Sorry, Jewell . . . sorry if I was botherin' you."

"Nothin' to be sorry about . . . it's your place. It's just that you're makin' it seem like it's not Sunday night around here."

Emmett pulled a chair from the table and sat down with a plop. "You ever had some little thing happen and not be able to chase it outta your mind?"

The boy thought for a moment. "Reckon so. What kinda little thing?"

"I was walkin' Miss Annabelle home, like I always do after church. When we got close to the house, I got a whiff of gasoline . . . and . . . I can't put my finger on it, but it bothers me. It came from a little patch of woods past the house."

He paused, brow deeply furrowed, hands locked in a knot on

the table. "There's nothin' out there—in the woods or on the other side. It's the last house on the street, not even one close . . . no shops or sheds. Her landlady don't have a car. Just no reason to be smellin' gasoline there."

"Still," Jewell said, "don't seem like a big deal to me."

"That's just it, don't you see? It ought *not* to be one to me neither, but it is."

Jewell huffed. "I don't much like the smell of the dang stuff myself."

His face hardened. He had done very well at dealing with thoughts of his father, but now and then some sight or word triggered a memory. He had learned that it was best not to wrestle with it—just allow it to come and brush against him, and then it would go away. Bad memories did not tolerate being ignored.

"Remember back last fall when he made me try to clean that stupid tool set one of his customers gave him for money owed? Had a big jug of gasoline down in the cellar and a bunch of old rags. I like to choked to death down there rubbin' on those things. Him and his buddies had a lot of fun with me 'bout how I smelled . . ."

Jewell rambled on, but Emmett did not hear him now. The ugly wad of fear in his stomach grew with the passing of each second. The words hammered in his head like the clangs of a great bell . . . JUBAL . . . CELLAR . . . JUG . . . GASOLINE. What if Jubal Cole was in the patch of woods with gasoline, and a match . . . and a terrible hate?

"Lord God!" The words from Emmett's mouth were a cry and a prayer, stopping Jewell in midsyllable. He grabbed for the edge of the table as it pitched wildly toward him and watched spellbound as Emmett flung his chair away and dashed toward the door. It banged once against the wall and bounced back, but Emmett was already through the opening, pounding down the stairs.

The pungent odor was deep inside Jubal's head as he sloshed the gasoline along the base of the wall under Annabelle's window. It had all become like a strange dream now, Jubal's vision hazy as he watched, detached, floating on the night wind. He fumbled with the second bottle, and before he could direct his splashes to the house, an ounce splattered downward to the cuff of his trousers, but he did not notice.

Quickly now, quickly and silently along the wall the big man trotted until the last drops had been shaken from the bottle. His hands trembled slightly as he ripped a book match from under the cover, and he knelt slightly before striking it on the third swipe. The orange flames exploded at his feet, and he sprang backward as they raced down the wall. Jubal stood and allowed himself a long glance at his handiwork before he turned and began to run toward the woods. He ran twelve steps before the smell of his burning flesh reached his nostrils. Panic-stricken, he increased his pace, and had he not stepped into a depression, he would have been consumed to the point of death. He felt something pop in his right knee, and then he was rolling through the long grass near the edge of the woods. From a place deep in his brain, the signal came to reach down and beat out the remaining flames. The pain in his knee was far greater than the burning sensations, and he flopped backward in the grass and cried out in fear more than pain. The crystal points of stars winked at him and he screamed curses at them. The sound of his rage mingled with the roar of the fire a hundred feet away.

"Burn! Burn!"

It was his own voice he heard, but he did not recognize it. Another voice came to him through the fire—an old woman's scream, high and plaintive, but devoid of fear. He rolled onto his side and peered through the eerie light, seeking the sound. She stood near the front door, arms outstretched toward the second floor, her hair and nightgown billowing in the hot wind. To Jubal, she was the angel of death, her cries reaching from the earth upward toward the dancing tips of the flames, cries of mourning for the soon dead.

But Jubal's were not the only eyes fixed on the pitiful woman and the fiery monster. Emmett Tragman was only thirty racing steps away and from the leer of the monster he knew that the next few moments of his life would forever be sealed in his memory as a forty-foot square of hell on earth—flashes of brilliant yellows and oranges and ghostly billows of grays and blacks. The haunting keen of the landlady rose with the roar of the flames as he dashed past her, and then the only sound in his ears was the roar. Within seconds his lungs began to ache from the superheated air and smoke, and his eyes strained to locate the staircase. His first three leaps consumed half of the stairs, and then he saw her, an unearthly sight materializing out of the smoke. Then she was flying toward him, arms outstretched, almost like a child springing playfully at him. With no time to brace himself, Emmett staggered backward a step and twisted his body against the wall for support. Annabelle's arms were locked around his neck and her fingernails dug into his shoulders, but she did not cry out. All that mattered now was finding the clean, cool air far from the little hell.

When he burst from the house, Emmett shouldered past the picket of onlookers, mesmerized by the flames and their pitiful human inability to do anything against them. A few trailed after him for the thirty yards he struggled before collapsing on his knees. Spasms of coughing racked both of their bodies as Emmett gently laid Annabelle on the grass in the dirty light of a street lamp.

A hoarse cry from behind him, "Somebody go get Doc!"

Emmett prayed silently as he began to examine her. Both of her hands were still locked around his neck, and judging from the strength required to gently pry them apart, they had sustained no great damage. Her face was black with soot and filth but there appeared to be no severe burns, and her eyes blinked clearly at him, the fear subsiding. Her arms, too, appeared to be only dirty, but the lower eighteen inches of her nightgown were burned away and dark splotches on her legs appeared suspect to his untrained eye. Pairs of feet shuffled into Emmett's peripheral vision—some bare, others covered with slippers or shoes or boots—crowding closer now, curious feet, inching forward, and he barely controlled the urge to swing his arm at them.

"Give her room!" he shouted, and the feet obeyed, creeping backward a few begrudged inches.

"It's gonna be all right, Miss Annabelle . . . all right, you're gonna be all right."

Annabelle nodded and attempted to speak before the coughing spasm overtook her, but she could not.

Emmett could hear the shouts from firemen and engines chugging behind him, but he knew that they would save nothing. The fire had grown far too hot, too quickly, and the wind was still strong in the tree limbs above him.

Two pairs of feet quickly sidestepped, but the space was immediately filled with another pair, black-booted and striding forward. Suddenly, Doc Nelson's knees thudded to the ground next to his, and Emmett felt the great hand envelop his and Annabelle's and pat soothingly.

"Let's have a quick look here, young lady. We've got an ambulance on the way . . . you're going to be fine."

The round spectacles glinted into Emmett's eyes, and Doc nodded reassuringly, but it was also a nod of dismissal; Emmett had done his part. Trained hands would tend her now and bind her wounds and cleanse the filth from her lungs—things he could not do for her, and he squeezed her hands once more before pulling his away.

Emmett moved away from the small circle of people and

sucked hungrily at the clean air despite the wracking coughs. It was several minutes before he began to feel relief deep within his chest, and as his head cleared along with his lungs, he knew that he must soon run again, run to the clump of trees beyond the burning house. Jubal Cole would still be watching.

Town marshal Eldred Haynes waved and shouted orders at the onlookers who had gathered near the fire truck and the men scrambling around it. The house appeared totally lost, but Haynes acknowledged the necessity of an honest attempt to control the fire. Perhaps something from a lower-level room or two could be salvaged—a photo album, a family keepsake, an old love letter, a worn item of clothing—something small but of great value to an individual. He had seen people weep over the loss of such things many times.

Despite the chaotic scene unfolding before him, the running man caught his attention, mainly because he was running away from the fire. People were still running toward the great blaze; fires of this size, and especially killer fires, were like magnets to the human race. But this man was racing away from the magnet with a purpose, and the lawman in Haynes was more than curious. He turned and shouted instructions to his only deputy and began walking briskly after the running man.

Emmett was five strides from the long body stretched flat in the grass before his eyes found it. He stumbled to a halt, dropping to his knees, and stared into the half-mad eyes of Jubal Cole. Emmett could not discern whether the sounds coming from Jubal were cries or laughs, but they were terrible sounds for a man to make. Emmett's left hand closed around Jubal's throat, his right knotting into a fist that rose high above his head and then descended with all the power he could muster. His knuckles smashed into Jubal's mouth and nose with a fleshy whump, but before Emmett could raise his fist again, the sound stopped him. It was clearly laughter now, and as Jubal's eyes sought and found his attacker's, the sickening, sweet stench of burned flesh came to Emmett's nostrils.

"Go on, little idiot, pound away. It don't matter no more."

"WHY . . . WHY?" Emmett screamed the words.

The laughter stopped and the words hissed through Jubal's clenched teeth. "You know why! You don't part blood from blood without payin' . . . and she paid!"

"She *didn't* pay, you sorry crud, she didn't pay!"

"What you talkin' . . ."

"I pulled her out. She ain't close to dyin', and she'll never die by your rotten hands!"

Emmett's hands sprang to Jubal's throat and closed like steel bands, and his knees pinned the bigger man's arms to the ground as the death struggle began. In mortal conflicts without weapons, the sounds are muted and there is little motion, and witnesses are often unaware of the deadly nature of the contest. Such was the case for a frozen moment in time as Eldred Haynes spied the battle. As he neared the combatants he realized that the smaller man on top was dangerously close to settling the issue. There was no time for shouts or commands, or even hands. Haynes lowered his body close to the ground for his last two strides and caught Emmett full force with his left shoulder. For an instant there were three men flat on their backs in the grass, but Haynes popped back to his feet and poked a finger of warning an inch from Emmett's face.

"You! Stay right there till I say you can move."

With a final sidelong glower at Emmett, he knelt beside Jubal, who had both hands wrapped protectively around his throat. His gasps for air punctuated the tension surrounding the unreal scene. The odor of burned flesh wafted up to Haynes with the wheezing breaths as he made a quick examination of the man he recognized as the owner of Jubal's Kingdom. It made no sense. Why would someone attack the victim of a horrible fire? No sense at all, but it was Jubal Cole—and what was he doing here?

"Take your hands down . . . your wind will come back sooner." He reached down and pried Jubal's fingers loose. "Easy now, there . . . easy . . . rest easy."

He turned to Emmett and said, "You want to start talkin' now, mister?"

"You saw what you saw," Emmett replied, his chest heaving from the exertion.

"That isn't much of an answer for trying to strangle a half-burned man."

"Why don't you ask him if he's got the guts to tell you what happened here?" Emmett pointed to Jubal.

"I'm not sure he's in shape to be telling much of anything."

Jubal rolled onto his side to face Emmett and spoke in a loud, strained whisper, as if Haynes was nonexistent.

"What'd she look like when you pulled her out?"

Emmett lunged at him, only to be jabbed by Haynes's open hand, hard against his chest.

"I told you to stay put!"

Jubal again, the tiny wheeze of a laugh in his throat. "I 'magine she was blackened some, huh?"

Haynes snapped at Jubal, "What you talkin' about, Cole?"

Jubal's gaze remained fixed on Emmett's face, and he did not reply. Haynes, exasperated with the strange encounter, jerked his head back at Emmett.

"Mister, what is your name?"

"Emmett Tragman."

"Well, that's a start, I reckon. Do you know how he got these burns on his legs?"

Emmett narrowed his eyes at Jubal as Haynes steeled himself for another assault, but all that came was a question. "Tell him, brave man, if you got the guts . . . tell him that you're a woman burner."

The wheezing laugh stopped, and although his voice was still strained, the hatred in it was strong. "She set blood against blood . . . ruined me . . . she needed killin'."

"Got the gasoline from your cellar, didn't you?" Emmett again, his voice weary now, the fatigue lapping over his body like warm bath water.

"That I did!" Jubal spat the words at Emmett.

Haynes stood abruptly and passed a hand over the top of his head. "This has been a bad night," he said, more to himself than to the other men at his feet. "Tragman, I want you to go tell my deputy over there to find three men to help me load him in my car. Got to get him to the hospital, then I'm gonna call the county sheriff. Me and you'll talk some more."

Emmett stood shakily and took a moment to gather himself before shuffling away. Haynes took a deep breath and released it loudly through loose lips as he lowered his head and looked into Jubal's eyes. He felt as though he should say something, make a pronouncement of sorts regarding the sorry mess of it all, but the right words would not come to him. It was only a moment before he realized that it would not have mattered anyway; Jubal Cole's eyes were vacant, and if they saw anything at all, it was far away.

The words slipped from Haynes, under his breath, lost in the strangely lit night.

"Awful sorry mess . . . awful sorry."

The boy stood numbly at the edge of night, where the firelight faded to darkness. None of the three men involved in the struggle had seen him, but he had seen them, and although he had not heard many of the words, he understood. He understood it all, and the urge to flee grew within him like a fast-rising fever, but his feet seemed to be rooted to the earth, his gaze riveted to the long tongues of flame. The blessed numbness began to wane, only to be replaced by the cruel reality of it all, and the reality freed him. Jewell Cole began to run, half blinded by tears, beyond the muttering crowd of fire watchers.

# Chapter 15

**W**HEN EMMETT swung open the door to his room, he sensed that something was wrong. Very wrong. During the walk home from the marshal's office, Jewell's whereabouts began to cause a cloud of worry to form. Without doubt, Jewell would have followed Emmett after witnessing the mysterious dash from the room. He would have seen the half circle of bystanders surrounding Miss Annabelle, and certainly would have spotted Emmett. But after that, when Emmett raced to the clump of trees—had Jewell followed there too? Emmett hoped not, prayed not. It would be much better to talk with the boy now and tell him no more than he absolutely needed to know at first. The whole of it was far too much to deal with at one time, without the perspective of at least a few hours' time.

Not wanting to, but knowing that he must, Emmett walked to the small closet and looked inside.

"Noooo . . ." The word escaped from deep within him, as if someone had punched him hard in the stomach. Jewell's clothes were gone. Emmett felt a tiny glimmer of hope as he saw Jewell's stack of books and magazines, but it passed quickly; if the boy had seen it all, these things would matter no longer. Emmett paced about the room, looking for a note, but there was none. A haunting stillness hung about the room, and a cold barrenness crept into his bones, as if he stood in a great snow-covered field in moonlight. Emmett sagged to the edge of the bed, head in hands, as his tired mind began to deal with the new crisis.

The questions jabbed at him. *Where would he go?* He had no relatives or friends that Emmett knew of. How long would it be before the shock wore off, allowing him to return? *Should I go back to Haynes's office and try to get him involved? Can't talk with Miss Annabelle about it . . . at least not until morning, if then.*

"Lord, Lord, Lord . . ." The words bounced off the walls.

Emmett decided it would do no good to alert Haynes. He and his only deputy had their hands more than full, and it was unlikely that he could be made to understand the situation.

It was all slipping away from him, steadily, like water from a cracked pitcher. The two people who meant more to him than he ever dreamed possible were wounded, one in flesh and the other in spirit. He felt the guilt begin to cast a shadow over him as he remembered the wild-eyed look in Jubal's contorted features, and even then, in the death struggle, Emmett knew that he would pay for linking hands with hatred, but he did not stop the squeezing. There is great power in hatred, and he had long known this, always before as the object, the hated rather than the hater. And now . . . he had become the hater, the one he had always pitied. And his act had compounded an already terrible situation; there was no excuse. It was the last thing in the world Miss Annabelle would have wanted him to do. He should have searched for Jewell, led him away from the fire and his father, helped him deal with it, shielded him from hatred, not shown him an example of it. *Oh, God . . . God, what have I done?*

Emmett lay on his side, his knees drawn up near his chin, his fists digging into his eye sockets. He wanted to weep, but the tears would not come; he wanted to pray, but the words would not come. He wanted the night to be over, but he knew it would be long.

Jewell stood in the windy darkness, thirty feet from the screened window of Annabelle's hospital room. The squat building could barely be called a hospital, but it had served the small town for many years under the firm hand of Doc Nelson. The big man with bushy eyebrows and the ever-present Camel cigarette pinched between his lips had set bones and stitched wounds and delivered babies and soothed the dying for more years than most people could remember. Jewell had watched him and two nurses tend to Miss Annabelle, and now the boy was satisfied that she was in no danger of dying. He had actually seen her lips move once, when a nurse cleaned her face, and the nurse smiled, and Jewell knew that she would recover in time. He knew that she would stand before another class of students and love them and teach them and push them gently beyond their limits.

A flutter of quiet commotion in the adjacent room distracted Jewell, and his pulse quickened; it was the room that *he* was in. Jewell slipped a few steps to his left for a better view. They were moving him onto a gurney, the marshal and his deputy helping Doc and a nurse. They moved out of his view for several minutes, and then Jewell could hear the chug of the ambulance engine as it rounded the street corner and disappeared into the night. They were taking him to a bigger hospital, probably Columbia; he had evidently done himself great harm in setting the fire. Jewell wished that he had done himself the final harm, but it might work out better this way after all. Maybe he would die in the hospital— many days after he had begged for whiskey.

Jewell walked with small, silent steps back toward Miss Annabelle's window, closer this time, close enough to see her face in sleep. The time had come to say good-bye. The urge to sneak inside and touch her hands and whisper over her was almost more than he could overcome, and he clenched his fists and closed his eyes until it passed.

Instead, he crept to the window screen and touched it with his fingertips, and then he melted into the shadows.

Rommie Rugg peered into the haze of dawn, his old eyes narrowing as the solitary lumbering hulk of Big Hec came into view. It came as no surprise that Emmett was not with him. The story of the great fire that took Sadie Armstrong's house and almost killed the young teacher had spread with a ferocity of its own. Many of the townsfolk went to bed chattering excitedly about the sensational details—a set fire, Jubal Cole badly burned and whisked away by the marshal, Annabelle Allen in the local hospital. Some had even begun to put the pieces together regarding motive; Jubal had spewed considerable venom to his dwindling patrons during the dying days of the Kingdom.

Now, for the Cole boy, and certainly Emmett too, great difficulty no doubt lay ahead as the town absorbed all of the juicy details. Then the whispers and muffled conversations would begin to pop up, and the pointed fingers would indiscreetly take their aim, and the probing eyes would shoot cold stares, and so it would go. Although Emmett talked little about any subject, Rommie had drawn him into conversations about the boy and the young teacher who was working with him, and the old man sensed the depth of feeling when Emmett spoke. Rommie Rugg had lived a very long time and had listened to millions of words spoken by more people than he could remember, but the words spoken from the heart lodged in his brain, and he accepted them in trust, like fragile, priceless gifts, soft and airy things that contrasted with the stone of the grave markers.

Big Hec shuffled to a halt near Rommie and shook his head. "Said he ain't of a mind to come just now. His chin's pretty low."

"Figures. I thought it might do him good to get out here and sweat a while with us. Uncloud his mind maybe."

Big Hec nodded agreement and then said, "Said he might come on later after he looked in on the teacher."

"The boy doin' all right?"

"Well, that there is another thing. I asked him that myself, and he stammered around for a little before he told me he was gone."

"Gone where?"

"He don't know—that's what's worryin' him."

"He won't go far."

Big Hec hesitated; it was always a testy thing to contradict Rommie, but he plunged ahead. "I ain't so sure about that."

"Naw, he ain't goin' far. Where's he got to go? Naw . . ."

"I ain't so sure."

"Dang it, Hec, I heard your opinion the first time, and I'm tellin' you that he ain't gonna go far."

Big Hec pursed his lips crookedly and shook his head.

"Tarnation, Hec, how do you claim to be an expert on what a young'un will or won't do in bad times?"

"I ain't claimin' no sucha thing."

"Sounds to me like you are."

"Ain't."

"Well then, where did all your considerable learnin' come from?"

"'Cause I was a young'un once . . . and it ain't been that long ago."

"Meanin' that I'm such an old cuss that I can't recollect what it's like to be a young'un."

"Didn't say that."

"You dadgum well did, Hec."

Big Hec filled his lungs with air and pushed it out like a contracting bellows. "Rommie, I swear, we gonna try to jaw each other to death or start this hole?"

"If you'd a burned as much energy diggin' as you had opinionatin' it'd already be half dug."

Big Hec reached down and picked up a shovel and began to walk toward the grave site. "You got it laid out yet?"

"No, I was hopin' Emmett would come on with you and eyeball it out." Rommie shook his head. "How in the world does he do that? Down to the dadblame inch, square corners and all . . . just eyeballin'?"

"Just natural to him, I reckon."

"Can't be just natural to *anybody* . . . just can't be."

Big Hec opened his mouth to speak, but quickly sealed his lips for a moment, reforming his reply.

"You're right, Rommie. It ain't natural."

Shortly after eight o'clock the next morning, Harlon, Madalene, and Hazel Lee arrived after a three-hour automobile trip from Randolph County. The telephone call had come deep in the night, with the deputy sheriff doing his best to answer Madalene's frantic questions. Madalene and Hazel Lee sat now, huddled shoulder to shoulder, in the tiny lobby of the hospital. Harlon paced slowly between two windows, pausing for a moment before each one, staring into the street but seeing nothing. The nurse had told them that Annabelle was sleeping comfortably; she would let them know at once when they could go to her.

"I can't stand much more of this sitting around, Momma." Hazel Lee's voice was tinged with the strain of the last several hours. She popped up and began to pace along the wall opposite her father.

"I was just thinking," Madalene said, "of all the things we talked about on the way down here, we left out the one thing we can start to fix right now."

Both Harlon and Hazel Lee turned in unison and looked a silent question at her. "Not two blocks down the street . . . on the way in . . . I saw a little cloth shop. It would be nice if we could show her the makings of a new dress or two."

"Yes! Daddy, we'll be back in a jiffy," Hazel Lee said. "You don't mind, do you?"

"Lord no, child, it's a fine idea." He began to dig in his trouser pocket.

Madalene stood and touched his hand. "No, Harlon. Keep it for other things. I brought a little money with me."

She stroked his hand again, and he nodded silently as the two women made a quick exit. He turned back to one of the windows, seeing now, watching as his wife and daughter scurried down the sidewalk, past a little man who stood like a statue, eyes locked on another part of the hospital. It was the way he stared at the building that caught Harlon's attention. He was not looking at a building, or any inanimate object; men did not look at things of stone and wood with such eyes. He was dressed neatly but poorly, his hands clasped in front of his body, his shoulders bowed slightly as if supporting some unseen burden. He ignored the vehicles passing behind him as well as the people who walked in front of him; he ignored everything except—someone. Harlon Allen was certain that the little man was focused on someone inside the hospital. In the twenty minutes that passed before the women returned, Harlon was also certain that the man had not moved an inch.

Annabelle awoke in a medicated haze, and it was another hour before the nurse walked into the waiting room.

"You folks come on with me now. She's still a little fuzzy from the medication, but when I told her you were here, she perked up quite a bit." The nurse cracked a toothy smile for an instant, but it faded quickly. "The doctor will be along directly to give you more details, but I can tell you that there is no permanent damage . . . he's sure of that. Her lungs are clearing up nicely; that's what worried us the most. There . . . will be some scarring on her lower legs—not a great deal, mind you. Mostly first-degree burns, but some areas of second degree." She paused and nodded her head gravely. "A very lucky young lady, folks. It could have been *so* much worse if she had not been rescued so quickly."

"Rescued?" The word came from Harlon's chest and caught in his throat. "By who?"

"Evidently a friend of hers. She spoke incoherently last night . . . for the most part. But his name is Emmett, we do know that."

Harlon exchanged glances with Madalene and Hazel Lee. "Thank God for him, whoever he is," Madalene said softly.

"Well, let's go." The nurse motioned for them to follow her, but she stopped in midstride and turned back to them. "She doesn't know that it was . . . arson. Doctor Nelson and the marshal both thought you should break it to her first. Not necessarily right away, but whenever you think best."

She led them down a hallway to a room with a window overlooking the street. "Not too long the first time, folks. Let her get her strength back slowly. You need to do most of the talking. Her lungs will flare up if she overdoes it."

Six eyes peered into the room, but only Harlon's eyes clouded over with tears. It was as if he looked at Annabelle as a helpless child again. All the years rolled away in an instant; she was tiny and still under the stark whiteness of the sheets. The thought staggered the man—yellow tongues of death had actually touched her. Then Matthew came to him, filled him, loved him from beyond his watery grave.

*One by water and one by fire.*

*Dear God, it could have been.* He leaned against the doorway for support as Madalene and Hazel Lee rushed to her bedside. In the moments that followed, Harlon regained his composure, and when Annabelle's hand reached out to him, he hurried to her side.

Loving minutes were lost in hugs and soft kisses and whispers of reassurance. They would stay for as long as she needed them.

They would help put her life back together. Things would be made whole again, by whatever sacrifice necessary. Family was family . . . blood of their blood . . . it would all work out.

When Annabelle spoke, her voice was throaty and weak, but they knew her wits were about her. It would take more than drugs to rob Annabelle Allen of her wit.

"If you all don't stop dripping things on me, I'll likely catch cold and have to stay longer." She smiled with them as they pulled back from the bed and poked at eyes and noses with their handkerchiefs.

"Oh, it's good to hear your voice, child," Madalene said.

"Sounds a bit shaky to me," Annabelle said.

"Not for long though. They've told us it will clear up soon," Hazel Lee said.

"I certainly hope so. Can you imagine me without a good chatterbox?"

The tension in Harlon's body left with a rush, leaving him nearly giddy. She was whole . . . dear God, she was whole and joking and ignoring the pain. She was being Annabelle.

She looked up at them, the amusement no longer in her features. "Sadie . . . my landlady . . . the nurse told me she wasn't hurt, but she lost her house, everything. Dear Lord, what will she do, where will she go?"

Harlon was already nodding his head with a hand half raised before Annabelle spoke the last question. "I checked on her for you, Annabelle. Her daughter from Jefferson City came up and took her back there. She's goin' to be just fine. She's got loved ones to tend her." He smiled, crooked and manly. "Just like you do, daughter."

Annabelle reached for his hand with both of hers and touched it to her cheek as she thanked him with her eyes. The weight of one worry had been lifted from her shoulders.

"Do you remember last Christmas . . . I mentioned a friend . . . Emmett . . . Emmett Tragman?"

Madalene answered. "Yes, honey, I remember you mentioned a friend, but I don't think you told us his name."

"Well, he's the one who carried me from the fire. He saved my life, pure and simple. I want you to meet him."

"Oh, you can count on that, child," Madalene said, "you can count on that for sure."

"What does he look like, honey?" The question from Harlon drew quizzical looks from Madalene and Hazel Lee, but Annabelle heard something in the tone of her father's voice.

"He's not a big man . . . maybe thirty-five or so . . . short hair, no glasses." Annabelle paused and shook her head, laughed fondly through the scratching in her throat. "And he always has a serious look on his face."

Harlon walked around the foot of the bed and stopped in front of the window, parting the curtains an inch with one finger. He looked out for only a moment. "I'll be right back," he said over his shoulder.

When Harlon drew within ten steps of Emmett, he slowed his pace, allowing the little man time to acknowledge his approach. Emmett turned his head only after he heard his name.

"Mr. Tragman? Excuse me, but . . . are you Emmett Tragman?"

Emmett nodded silently but did not turn his body to face the stranger. The man stepped closer, respectfully, until he stood directly in front of Emmett.

"Mr. Tragman, I'm Harlon Allen . . . Annabelle's father." Harlon extended his hand, and when Emmett took it, Harlon quickly wrapped his other hand over Emmett's. "I know what you did . . . at the fire . . . and 'thank you' sounds downright silly, but if you know how *much* I want to thank you . . ."

"I'm glad it worked out like it did," Emmett said.

Harlon released Emmett's hand, but he did not want to. He wanted to pull the man to his chest and bear hug him until he grew short of breath, but he sensed a distance, not unfriendly, but real nonetheless, and he respected it.

"I reckon you know it wasn't just *any* life you saved, Mr. Tragman, and I don't say that just because she's my daughter. Annabelle is special."

Emmett nodded solemnly before he spoke. "God saved her, not me."

"That may be true enough, but He needed you to help."

Emmett looked down at his feet as an awkward moment of silence passed.

"Well, she's awake and talkin' now, and her mother and sister are in there too, waitin' to meet you, and Annabelle wants to see you. It'd be my honor to take you to them."

Emmett dug his hands deep in his pockets and stole a glance at Harlon's face. "I wouldn't want to get in the way."

"Mr. Tragman . . ."

"Just call me Emmett, if you would."

"Emmett, I can tell you're not a man who likes to crow a lot, and I do respect and admire that, but if you don't come on with me and put up with bein' a hero for a little while, I'm gonna have three women mad at me, and that's not healthy."

"If you're sure it's all right."

"It's more than all right, Emmett. Come on."

Harlon walked through the door first, with Emmett a step behind. "Everybody, 'cept for Annabelle, that is, meet Emmett Tragman, the man who went into the fire."

Emmett felt as if he were in a trance as the two women rushed toward him in a blur of color, the liquid motion of a woman moving with a purpose doubled, wonderfully slow and dreamlike, and then delicacy all around him—soft cheeks painted with tears and hair like corn silk and the fragrance of perfume in his nostrils.

It was overwhelming to the man who could not remember ever being touched in love and honor by a woman. For a dizzy moment, Emmett trembled from head to toe, allowing the women to brace him so that he would not fall.

Hazel Lee pulled back first. "Good Lord, look at us will you, Momma. We about knocked the poor man down."

"Mr. Tragman, forgive us," Madalene quickly added, "We've never hugged a man who saved one of our family before." She laughed self-consciously. "Lost our manners altogether."

Emmett opened his mouth to speak, but he could make no sound. His face blushed to the point of burning, the intensity so great that he wanted to reach up and touch it with his fingertips, but he did not.

Annabelle rescued him with an outstretched hand. "Emmett."

He moved forward haltingly, still unsteady, until she could reach out and close her hand around his.

"Oh, Emmett . . ." It was all she could say. With her other hand she beckoned him to her, and he leaned forward until he felt her lips against his forehead, heard her voice soft in his ears. "Thank you . . . oh, thank you . . . I don't know what else to say . . . nothing would be enough."

Emmett willed his voice to come alive. "You're alive . . . that's all the thanks I'll ever want."

"We must talk more later, just the two of us." She paused, blinked away tears, lowered her voice. "Jewell . . . does he know that I've been hurt?"

"Yes . . . yes, he does, but he knows that you're gonna get well too." Emmett swallowed hard against the feeling that he had lied, but it was not a lie; this was not the time to tell the whole story.

"Good, I wouldn't want him to be worried." Emmett nodded, but could not hold her gaze, and she saw it—the shadow on the truth—but turned away from it. She released Emmett, and he stepped back from the bed and made a half-turn toward Annabelle's family.

"I'll be goin' on now."

"Oh, please, Mr. Tragman," Madalene said, "stay as long as you like. You couldn't be more welcome here."

"I thank you, but I'll be goin' on."

Hazel Lee opened her mouth to protest Emmett's leaving, but Harlon silenced her with a glance.

"Mr. Trag . . . Emmett, it's been an honor to meet you. I hope we meet again soon." He extended his hand, and Emmett shook it, looked quickly back at Annabelle, and walked from the room.

Annabelle listened to the muffled sobs coming from the corner of the room where her sister lay curled in the lounge chair. Only a few moments before, she thought the sounds were part of her dreams, but as her mind cleared and focused, she remembered that Hazel Lee had pledged to pass the long hospital night with her. They had talked of many things before Annabelle tired and drifted toward sleep, but she could remember nothing that foreshadowed the sobs of grief that now filled her ears. Annabelle lay silently and thought. Matthew, she reasoned—it was probably the loss of Matthew that tore at her now. A precious brother lost to war, and now her sister nearly taken also—yes, that was the cause of the tears. But it was not.

"Sister," Annabelle whispered, "come here."

Hazel Lee stirred in the chair, struggling to stifle the wet sounds that now angered her.

"Annabelle, I'm sorry . . . this is so silly. I didn't mean to wake you."

"It doesn't matter. I'm already tired of lying here like a mummy. Let's talk about it."

Hazel Lee scooted the chair next to the bed and curled back up in the cushions, resting her head on the sheet near Annabelle's arm. Annabelle reached out with her hand and began to stroke the long, soft curls of her sister's hair.

"Oh, Annabelle, this is turned around. I'm supposed to be a comfort to you . . . and . . ."

"You are, Sis, you are . . . you always have been . . . my beautiful big sister." Annabelle patted her head. "You can be my little sister tonight."

Hazel Lee buried her face in the sheet and squeezed her eyes shut at the sound of the words . . . *my little sister tonight . . . oh, dear God, dear God.* The words penetrated her brain—haunting, reminding, hurting. *She was my little sister* that *night, the cold December night so long ago, the night that will not go away. She was my little sister through the long years of merciless torment at the hands of children . . . my little sister, peeking into the mirror behind me at the long, graceful lines of my body . . . my little sister watching as handsome young men came calling, knowing that none would ever come for her . . . my little sister, ever smiling, never questioning, never resentful.* The secret could be kept no longer. In a few moments, it would be over with, and Hazel Lee did not know if she would feel cleansed or stained by the unburdening of it. Her throat tightened as she reached for Annabelle's hand.

"You don't know the reason I'm crying." It was almost a challenge, and Hazel Lee's tone sounded a distant alarm in Annabelle.

"Sis, I think I have some idea, and . . ."

"No! You don't."

Hazel Lee wrestled with the emotion spilling from her, the silent battle palpable in the semidarkness for long moments. It would come out now, whatever it was, and Annabelle realized that she did not know the source of her sister's torment.

"That night . . . when you were hurt . . ." She pried the words free, knowing that if she did not find a way to somehow detach herself, to narrate the incident rather than relive it, she would blubber like a fool. She pushed away from the bed and straightened her posture in the chair, drew a long breath, and looked away from Annabelle toward the light spilling in from the hallway. She sat stiff-backed in the big chair, her hands folded in her lap and her feet resting squarely on the floor. It was the seat of judgment now, but she would be the judged; she would judge herself. In measured tones, she began again.

"That night . . . all you've ever known was that you took a fall when you were only a few days old. You don't know *how* it happened."

In the moment of silence that descended, Annabelle realized beyond all doubt how the story would unfold, but it did not trouble her. Exactly how The Fall took place had never troubled her, nor even intrigued her for that matter. It was a part of her being, and she had worked through all of the hard parts long ago, deciding to live life forward, not backward. All that mattered for the next few minutes was helping her sister wipe away the last tiny drops of blood leaking from the old wound.

"It doesn't matter how it happened."

"Annabelle . . . let me . . . I have to do this."

"Only if you want to."

"I *have* to . . . let me get it out . . . for me, if not for you." She checked her emotions again, determined not to break down. "Momma had just given you a bath, after supper, and I was already in my nightgown, crowding close to see if she would let me do something. I was always hovering around you, and Momma was always so patient."

Annabelle turned her head and watched as Hazel Lee shook her head slowly at the memory. "When she laid you on the towels, I reached out to you, and Momma didn't notice that she'd laid you partly on my sleeve . . . and I couldn't take my eyes off you . . . and then . . . I pulled away from the table to reach for a towel."

The thing was very hard for her now, and Annabelle watched

her sister's chest rise and fall, the words coming in measured spurts.

"Momma told me a hundred times to be careful . . . you were so little and all . . . and I was, except for then . . . just that *one* time . . . that one silly, little girl time. I felt your weight come with my arm, and I turned back and reached for you . . . and I almost caught you. I had my hands on you, Annabelle . . . and I couldn't hold you. I COULDN'T hold you . . . and the sound when you . . . and you were so still . . ."

"Sis, don't do this to yourself. You were little more than a baby yourself."

"No, I wasn't a baby, Annabelle. I was old enough to help with a lot of things. I'd helped with you before; I knew better." She paused, and her head began to move up and down in a long, slow nod. "And I knew . . . I KNEW that something was terribly wrong . . . even after Doc came and you seemed better and all . . . and I tried to put it out of my mind for those years before everybody found out what I already knew. And all those years you put up with all the stupid kids and gawking grown-ups . . . but I couldn't . . . I still can't. And now you lie there, hurt again . . . nearly taken from us . . . and it comes back so strong."

"Turn it loose, Sis. If I've turned it loose, and I have, then you can too."

Hazel Lee was no longer the judge. She turned in the chair and laid her head back on Annabelle's bed. "But I want so many things for you, Annabelle. I don't want you to be cheated out of anything in life, and I was a part of what cheated you, child or not. That's why it hurts so bad."

"Oh, Sis, I don't feel cheated, trust me. I know that there are . . . certain things that will pass me by, but there are so many other things—beautiful things, important things—that haven't and won't pass me by. Have I ever acted like an unhappy person . . . ever?"

Hazel Lee shook her head against Annabelle's hand. "I'm not an actress, Sis, it's really me. Some things have been taken from me; others have been given. I've just been given a part in the lives of twenty-seven children. I mean something to them; I have helped them with more than arithmetic and English. I see the world at their level. I know their worst fears. It is a gift, Sis, wrapped in ugly paper—not what I expected, but now, strange as it may seem, more than I expected. This could not be if I were . . . like everybody else."

Annabelle's throat burned from the talking, but it did not matter; she was too close to stop now, too close to setting her sister free. "I won't lie to you; there are times when I wonder what it would be like to live in a normal body, but they always pass, and I'm never left empty, Sis. I *like* me. I fight the mirror in weak moments, but it is not a curse to me. It doesn't show me who I am; it just shows me the shell that will carry me through this life, and it's doing a pretty good job."

They joined hands, and Annabelle drew Hazel Lee's close to her chest. "This is who I am, Sis." Annabelle tapped the joined hands squarely over her heart.

"Turn it loose; it's not worth holding."

# Chapter 16

ON THE morning of Annabelle's fourth day in the hospital, the day of her release, Harlon, Madalene, and Hazel Lee filed into the room with a solemnity that could not be hidden. Annabelle was both surprised and puzzled. Not a half hour before, Doc Nelson assured her that her recovery could be completed out of the hospital; it could not be a health concern. Room and board had been offered by Lela Parker, who had assured both Annabelle and her family that the arrangement was open-ended. Her life was quickly being restored to order. Why the long faces?

They shuffled to the edge of the bed, and after glancing quickly at Harlon and Hazel Lee for support, Madalene spoke first. "Annabelle, there is another part of all this that you have to know about."

A chill crawled up Annabelle's spine; it was no small matter, that much was very clear. "Go ahead."

"Well, the fire . . . there's just no easy way to say it . . . it was a set fire."

Annabelle recoiled at the pronouncement, allowing her body to sink back into the propped-up pillows. A wave of nausea rose from the pit of her stomach, and she swallowed hard against it.

The question was a mere formality, the confirmation of a known fact, and she asked it only to buy more time to gain control of the nausea.

"Who was it?"

"A man named Jubal Cole. The marshal says he's already confessed . . . from the hospital in Columbia. He caught himself on fire while he set it. Marshal says his legs are in bad shape."

Harlon spoke, the enmity alive in his voice. "It's a shame the sorry crud didn't burn himself to death."

"Oh, Harlon . . . don't . . . it won't help now," Madalene said.

Harlon turned and took three quick steps toward the window; he would trust himself to say no more.

A silence claimed the room, oppressive and complete, a loud silence that grew with the passing of each moment. But Annabelle did not hear it. Her thoughts were dreadfully ordered, and for a moment she nearly despised the ability of her brain to function in such fashion. She pushed the foolish thought away; sorting out the truth, even hurtful truth, was a necessary thing. Emmett's evasiveness regarding Jewell made perfect sense now; the boy knew the details and was not coping well. For Annabelle, this was a far greater concern than the failed attempt on her life. She must rise up from the sickbed and help Emmett deal with the crisis. There was no time to be sick a second longer. The nausea was fading; Annabelle willed the last of it away. She pushed up from the pillows and straightened her posture.

"It is . . . a difficult thing to deal with, but I will deal with it," she said.

"Annabelle, you won't have to worry about this man for a very long time, if ever," Hazel Lee said.

Harlon made a half turn from the window and raised his hand in a fist, but Madalene cut him off with a look and the shaking of her head before he could speak.

"If he lives to get out, he'll be a very old man, Annabelle," Madalene said.

"I'm not worried about him," Annabelle said, "I'm worried about his son."

"We know. Emmett told us what you've done for him and all," Madalene said.

"I need to talk with Emmett," Annabelle looked into Madalene's eyes, "and soon."

"Well, he'll be along soon, I imagine. At least that's what he told us last night."

"I understand why, but there was no need to hide this from me so long. It was my legs that were hurt, not my brain." The agitation was masked, but not well.

"Maybe so, Annabelle," Madalene said, "but what could you have done anyway . . . from here?"

Annabelle shook her head. "It doesn't matter now . . . you're probably right, Momma. I didn't mean to be cross, I just want out of here."

"We'll leave you be for a bit, till Emmett gets here," Madalene said. "There's a bunch more stuff to get over to your room. You won't believe the things from your school friends and the church . . . mighty fine people, I'll tell you, child."

"Keep a list for me of who gives what, all right? They will all get written thank-yous."

"We're keeping it. We knew you'd want it," Madalene said, patting Annabelle's hand. "Well, you two, let's get busy."

Hazel Lee and Harlon leaned over the bed and kissed Annabelle before Madalene did, and then they walked quietly from the room, but Annabelle did not hear them leave.

A half hour later Emmett softly rapped his knuckles on the door frame.

"Come in." Annabelle motioned to the chair near her bed before extending her hand to touch Emmett's arm in greeting. "They've told me everything . . . about the fire, that is. But only you can tell me about Jewell."

Emmett looked down and picked out a spot near the toe of his right shoe for a focus. "If it'd been up to me, I'd talked about Jewell before now."

"I know." She raised her hand and opened her fingers like the petals of a flower. "They were only trying to protect me. So . . . how is he?"

Emmett drew a deep breath and toyed for a moment with the idea of approaching the issue from the side, but the thought was without foundation; Annabelle did not deal with problems sideways.

"It ain't how he is . . . it's *where* he is."

"Where he is? You mean you don't know where is?" It was not panic in her voice, but it was far beyond concern.

"No. He was gone when I got back to the room that night. Took his clothes with him."

"His books?"

"Left them."

The rustles and clinks from the corridor spilled into the room, but they did not disturb the silence.

Annabelle's voice, a quiet pronouncement. "He knows it all then."

Emmett nodded before speaking. "Yes, I reckon he does, reckon he knows more than you do." Annabelle turned to face Emmett directly, her eyes asking the question. "I got to get this outta me . . ."

"Get what out, Emmett?"

"I'm still mad at him . . . reckon I always will be. But I ought not to have done what I did that night."

"Emmett, please tell me what you're talking about."

"On our way home from church, when we got close to your place, I thought I smelled gasoline. Blowin' on the wind, from that clump of trees, but I put it out of my mind. Then, when I got home, me and Jewell started talkin', and he said somethin' about workin' with gasoline in his daddy's cellar, cleanin' somethin' or other . . . and the smell of it on the wind came back to me . . . and I knew. I knew it was him in the woods . . . waitin'."

Annabelle listened, spellbound, to the story of the few moments in time that caused her life to be extended.

"Then, after I got you out and saw you was tended to, I went after him. Figured he'd want to be watchin' it all from close by. He was close . . . by that patch of woods, on the ground, legs burned and all." Emmett paused and shook his head against the hurtful memory. "And . . . and I lost myself. I had a mind to kill him . . . tried to kill him. The marshal pulled me off him. I think I woulda done it." He shook his head again, afraid to look Annabelle in the eye.

"Oh, Emmett . . . it must have been a horrible time for you. Times like that . . . people can do things that are not really like themselves. It was one of those times. Don't be too hard on yourself."

"But don't you see? The boy must have seen us all tangled up . . . me actin' like a wild man and all. I know he saw it. Maybe if I'd acted like I had some sense . . . looked for Jewell instead of him . . . tried to help somebody 'stead of tryin' to kill somebody. Oh, I done wrong . . . bad wrong."

"Emmett, whether he saw that or not, Jewell would have been hurt so deeply anyway. It wouldn't have changed his leaving. It wasn't your fault. Put it behind you. It doesn't matter now, won't help now. Let's think about Jewell."

They allowed the silence to claim the room again. For Emmett, it was a time to deal with the bitterness he felt toward himself; for Annabelle, a time to contemplate the fact that a kind and gentle man had nearly killed for her. It was an awesome thought, frightening when considering the consequences had the act been carried out, yet gratifying beyond measure. The force that had driven Emmett Tragman over the edge was immensely strong. She looked at him now, his head resting dejectedly in his hands, elbows dug into his knees, the picture of quiet sorrow. The feelings that rose within her were kaleidoscopic, a whirl of emotions she doubted if she could sort out—pity, tenderness, thankfulness, camaraderie, and yes, she admitted, a love not altogether platonic. Annabelle decided that there was no need to sort it out, at least not for now, and she allowed the strange whirl to continue for a beautiful moment longer.

"Emmett?"

He lifted his head from his hands and turned to face her, but said nothing.

"It did *not* happen. You did Jubal Cole no harm. It was not meant to be. It would be a great waste of your time to punish yourself for something that did not happen." He nodded with little conviction, and Annabelle pushed ahead. "And I'm telling you the solemn truth when I say that Jewell's reaction would have been the same whether he saw the fight or not. The damage was done . . . Lord knows the damage was done over long years by Jubal Cole. A boy can bear only so much, Emmett . . . only so much."

With the utterance of the words, Annabelle felt a shiver pass through her body, as if she had listened to some objective observer pronounce the dreaded truth. *Only so much.* The straw had broken the camel's back; the boy's wound was wide and deep and bleeding, and she could not bind it for him now, could not even touch him.

"Will he come back, Miss Annabelle?"

*Yes, yes, certainly he will come back in a day or two . . .* The words rang hollow in her head and she knew that she could not say them.

"I think . . . I believe that he will come back, Emmett, but . . . it may be a time."

"A long time?"

"Yes, a long time."

"I shoulda tried to get the marshal or the deputy to ride the main roads outta town that first night . . . but . . . I was so tired and mixed up . . ."

"It would not have mattered, Emmett. It is not likely that anyone could have found him. Jewell is old beyond his years."

"That's a sad fact."

"I want you to do something for me."

"Whatever you want."

"Gather his books and magazines and anything he might have written or drawn, and bring them to me at Lela Parker's house this afternoon. I don't think he would mind, do you?"

"I reckon he'd want you to have 'em, sure enough. I'll get 'em over there for you."

"Thank you."

"One more thing. Look for a small stone. It's brown and flat, about so big." She parted her thumb and forefinger, sizing the stone for Emmett, who could not completely mask the quizzical look in his eyes. "I've yet to tell you the story behind the stone, but I will . . . soon. Strangely, it is the object that bound us together—for a time at least."

The sadness had crept up on her, noiseless and cunning, like a cat on wet grass, and when it sprang, Annabelle was unprepared. But with the sadness came irritation at having been caught off guard, and she concentrated on the irritation. Suddenly, everything about the hospital room irritated Annabelle—the white bed, with its white sheets and the soft pillows behind her, and the antiseptic smells, and the breakfast tray that had been under her chin—things for the helpless. But she was helpless no longer. A classroom full of sixth graders would need her soon. The hospital room was not a proper place from which to begin another chapter in her life.

"Emmett, kindly go tell the nurse that I'm about to get up and get dressed and walk out of this place . . . and I mean right now."

Emmett stiffened in the chair and then popped up and took three quick strides to the door, only to turn back to face Annabelle.

"What's wrong, Emmett?"

"Dressed . . . in what?"

Annabelle pursed her lips. "That is a very good question." She tapped her forefinger on the bed for a moment. "Find Momma or Hazel Lee . . . or Daddy . . . or *somebody*, for heaven's sake, and have them bring me a jacket or a coat or . . . or a horse blanket . . . or a rug. I don't care *what* it is." She turned to the window and stared out in exasperation for a moment before turning back to the empty doorway. She spoke the sentence aloud anyway. "Lord knows, it won't take much to cover me."

The old man and the boy bounced along in the cab of the dirty flatbed truck, twenty miles east of Tulsa, Oklahoma. The old man had little to say, and that suited the boy; the tired groan of the engine and the song of the tires on the highway were the only sounds he cared to hear. The pitch of the engine changed with the downshift of the gears, and soon the truck lumbered to a halt where a gravel road intersected the highway.

The old man turned his head toward the boy, the hint of a smile leaking through the tobacco-stained corners of his beard. "Goin' north here, son."

The boy reached to the floorboard and grabbed the cloth sack with his left hand, his right hand already wrapped around the door handle.

"Wait a minute." The man rolled on his left hip and dug his hand into his right trouser pocket. His hand emerged with a fifty-cent piece pinched in his fingers, and he extended his hand to the boy.

"No, mister, I don't want to take your . . ."

"Son, if'n you're gonna run the highway, the first rule is don't turn nothin' down. If I couldn't spare the fifty cents, I'd a left it in my pocket."

"I thank you, mister."

"If you ain't got another ride in the next two miles, you'll come to a little yellow store and gas pump. Woman named Lucille runs it." He did smile now, the brown stains creeping sideways. "Uglier'n a mud fence, but a heart a gold. You tell her Arlie said to feed you right on that fifty cents, hear?"

"Yes sir, I thank you kindly."

The boy opened the door and stepped down into the dust on the shoulder of the road, but before he could close the door, the old man spoke again.

"California, huh? You got a ways to go."

"I know."

"Ain't never seen the ocean myself . . . don't reckon I ever will now."

There was a wistfulness in the old man's eyes, and for reasons he did not completely understand, it touched the boy's heart. Part of him wanted to say something kind and soothing and wipe the longing out of his eyes, but the part that did not was stronger.

"When you get there, throw a rock in it for me."

"Yes, sir, I'll do it."

The engine strained away in low gear, and a thin cloud of red dust whirled about the boy as he began to trudge west along the edge of the highway.

# Chapter 17

*T*HE LAST of the night breeze puffed weakly
against the predawn heat as Emmett and Big Hec
drove their shovels into the clay soil. It was September 3, 1945,
and the day before had been an occasion of great joy across the
land. President Harry Truman had declared V-J Day; Japan had
officially surrendered on the decks of the U.S. battleship Missouri
as she lay at anchor in Tokyo Bay. But the day had also been a
day of sadness for the farm family that lived four miles north of
town, the family of a man who had finally lost a long battle with
cancer.

Rommie peered down through the spectacles resting low on
his nose. "You boys sure you can see where it's laid out? I'll swear,
I ain't much good no more in bad light."

"We wouldn't be a diggin', Rommie, if we couldn't see the
blame lines," Big Hec said evenly.

"Well, I hope not, Hec, I sure hope not. Gonna be too hot to
do anything over."

Rommie hooked his thumbs through the straps of his coveralls
and began to rock slowly, heel to toe. The scent of the fresh-turned
soil came to him with the other heavy, green fragrances of early

morning, and the old man sucked them deep into his lungs. For as long as he could remember, Rommie had savored above all others the last minutes before dawn. Whether or not it was a grave-digging day mattered little any longer. There was a time, hundreds of graves ago, when Rommie did not enjoy the morning offerings on digging days; the sadness he knew others were feeling was somehow his also, if only in small measure, and it picked at him and robbed him of small treasures. But no more. No man, and surely no grave digger, could afford to bear the sorrows of so many. It was God's job, not Rommie's, and he learned to leave it to God.

"Hec, you're movin' kinda slow this mornin'," Rommie nudged at his spectacles as he spoke.

"They was carryin' on in the streets last night till dang near midnight," Hec replied.

"Was quite a night, wasn't it?"

"Reckon it was if you don't have to get up in the dark and dig a grave," Hec answered.

"Oh, Hec, don't grumble about a little lost sleep," Rommie chided. "How many times people gonna get to celebrate a war endin'?"

Emmett's voice, soft and low: "Never again, I hope."

"I'll go along with that, Emmett," Rommie said.

Whenever Emmett interjected himself into a conversation, Rommie was always a bit surprised, and pleasantly so. Even before last year's fire and the disappearance of Jewell Cole, Emmett was too quiet to suit Rommie. In the ensuing months, the situation had grown worse, and it was only lately that Rommie had been able to stir Emmett into anything resembling good conversation.

"I'll tell you one thing," Rommie said, "that old Truman must have a garbage can full a guts to wipe out two whole cities. Be a hard thing to lay down at night after allowin' them bombs to fall." Rommie paused and pushed a jet of air through his lips. "Jap soldiers is one thing . . . but the young'uns and the women and all . . . whew . . . reckon it had to be done though."

"Them Japs is a stubborn bunch," Hec said, "Momma claims that they'd a never give up till the last soldier was dead, without the big bombs."

"Deep down, I know that's right, but I'm glad it wasn't me had to drop 'em," Rommie said.

"He was thinkin' of his own soldiers," Emmett said as he wiped the sweat from his brow with the back of his hand. "A life's a life."

"Emmett, for a man who's never been in a war, you seem mighty partial to soldiers. Don't get me wrong now, I love 'em each and every one too, but somethin' about you and soldiers runs deep."

Emmett speared the ground with the tip of his shovel and draped his forearms over the handle. "I remember 'em comin' home after the first war . . . arms and legs missin', sad eyes. I was just a boy, but I remember that better'n anything else from back then."

"Any of your family hurt or lost?"

"Ain't got no family I know about. Grew up in the county home . . . till I walked away one day."

Emmett mopped his brow again and returned to his digging. Rommie had not intended for the conversation to take a hurtful turn, if in fact it had, and he was slightly irritated with himself at the possibility.

"Well, anyway, I'm mighty glad the thing's over, and if it took the big bombs to do it, so be it," Rommie said, clearly slamming the door on further mention of war.

"How's your teacher friend gettin' along?" Rommie asked.

"She's doin' all right," Emmett answered without pausing from his toil.

"Word's gettin' around a little about her and her way with the young'uns over at the school."

Emmett shook his head without looking at Rommie. "Ain't no mystery to it. She can think like them or she can think real smart, whichever she needs to do."

Rommie pondered the statement, pushing his spectacles up his nose with a gnarled forefinger. "Yeah, I reckon that does about explain it . . . 'cept for the carin' part. She must have a lot of carin' in her too."

"Powerful lot," Emmett intoned solemnly.

"Reckon the Cole boy not comin' back hurt her deep . . . like it did you." Thin ice, Rommie knew, but he was weary of skirting the issue.

Emmett nodded silently, a bit surprised that Rommie would bring up a subject about which he had made an incorrect prediction.

"I still think he'll come back," Rommie added.

"Ain't gonna be no time soon, I was right about that," Hec piped in.

"Yeah . . . yeah, Hec, ain't no need to remind me about your right thinkin' on the matter. If I was to remind you about all the times I was right and you was wrong, we'd be here long enough to grow a decent beard."

Hec mumbled under his breath and shook his head as his shovel began to jab the soil with greater purpose.

Rommie made a quarter turn from the deepening hole and tilted his head upward as the rich scent of the soil wafted to his nostrils. "Good Lord A'mighty, the smell of that dirt's a fine thing, ain't it boys?"

"Dirt just smells like dirt, Rommie," Hec said.

"Hec, you got no appreciation of the finer things in life," Rommie scolded.

"Now you take a beefsteak cookin' or a fat hen bakin' in the stove—*that* smell is a fine thing," Hec said.

"Hec, just cause you can't eat it don't mean it can't smell fine. Besides, without the dirt, your beef ain't got no pasture to graze on or your old fat hen ain't got no grain to peck at . . . pshaw! Takes a man that's done some deep thinkin' to appreciate the way dirt smells."

Rommie retrieved a clean shovel and extended it to Hec, who in turn handed his to Rommie for scraping. "You take a man like mean old Jubal, all laid up in the pen down at Jeff City, why he'd give anything now to smell fresh-turned dirt out in the open."

"He'd come closer to wantin' the smell of my beefsteak, I 'magine," Hec said.

"He wouldn't care about no such things as that." Even now, after a year, the bitterness still washed up easily in Emmett's mouth. "He's too busy hatin'."

"Maybe . . . maybe not," Rommie said. "They've got him dried out now without killin' him . . . which I didn't figure they'd ever do to start with. So maybe he's back to bein' somethin' like a regular man."

"Ain't likely," Emmett said, hoping the finality in his tone would change the direction of the conversation.

Rommie took notice and decided to honor the unspoken request; at least the hurtful subjects had been broached. Progress had been made.

"Let me trade you for a clean shovel, Emmett," Rommie said. "You boys are regular diggin' machines this mornin', I'll tell you for sure. This here is gonna be a fittin' grave for poor old pilgrim Conley."

Lela Parker rocked gently in the creaking chair, her bare toes pushing rhythmically against the wood floor of the front porch. Six feet to her left, Annabelle sat in the porch swing, content to remain motionless, bare feet curled beside her in the seat. With the exception of the rocker made by her father, swings and rocking chairs had never been more than just ordinary seats for Annabelle, but over the years, she had become accustomed to the stillness, even enjoyed it. The living arrangements with Lela and Evan Parker had worked out very well indeed. The youngest of their two children had left the nest three years before, and though Evan was hardly the conversationalist that Lela was, both enjoyed the addition of Annabelle to the rambling house on Lanning Street. The respective space of each occupant was honored, but Annabelle had become as much family member as boarder.

"There goes the Haskins's beagle sounding off," Lela said, "Evan's a block and a half away."

Both women chuckled. Evan's after-supper strolls were as much a part of the neighborhood as the maples and hickories that lined the streets. Lela could track him along the streets with uncanny accuracy as, one by one, the neighborhood dogs yapped and yipped their greetings.

"Someday I suppose he'll get tired of that walk," Lela said with a shake of the head. "If he ever does, I'll have to send out statements of termination to about thirty houses. Did I ever tell you about the time in the winter of forty?" Lela paused, but not long enough for Annabelle to respond. "Probably did, but I'm going to tell you again. Anyway . . . terrible blizzard, snow blowing sideways, fifteen degrees, Evan's half dead with a chest cold, and I finally talk him out of his precious walk. An hour passes . . . one single hour, and four people call over here asking after him and three more *walk* over here to find out if he's all right."

Lela hunched forward in her rocker, imitating one of the neighbors who had braved the storm. She threw her head back and laughed at the memory, and although Annabelle had heard the tale twice before, she joined in with genuine enthusiasm.

"You surely won't ever have to worry about anything happening to him on his walk," Annabelle said.

"That man is a frightening creature of habit, absolutely frightening."

"We all have our habits, Lela."

"I suppose, but few like my Evan. Seems like men are the worst."

"I won't argue that, Lela."

"Take your friend Emmett, for example. Every Sunday morning he shows up to meet you at nine-fifteen on the dot, and I mean *on the dot*. And he doesn't even carry a timepiece. It's almost like he waits just out of sight until the precise minute ticks by, and then springs out from behind a tree."

Annabelle smiled. "I suppose it does look like that to anyone who doesn't know him well. He's very meticulous about some things, and time is certainly one of them. Anything to do with numbers, it seems. He has a gift."

"Me and Evan would surely like to get to know him better. Maybe someday he'll say yes to one of my supper invitations. Must think schoolteachers can't cook."

Annabelle chuckled. "He's not worried about your cooking. It's just that . . . well, he is uncomfortable around people." She paused and turned her body toward Lela for a moment, needing to see her eyes for a moment. "He is . . . different, we all know that, and he knows that I am aware if it, but he also knows that it doesn't concern me . . . others, he can never be really sure about. As time goes on, I'll urge him to open up and be more trusting. He is a special person . . . to me anyway, and not just because of the fire."

*And not just because of the fire* . . . The words echoed lightly in her head. The pronouncement from her own mouth surprised Annabelle slightly; she had never said such a thing to anyone before, not even to Hazel Lee or her mother. For an instant, she almost regretted saying it. Even for someone as caring and thoughtful as Lela Parker, the idea that she of the abnormal body could harbor feelings for a man . . . well, it would be more than some people could understand. But the regret quickly gave way to guilt; Lela was gold, unrefined in many ways, but human gold. She would understand.

"Emmett is special to a lot of us in this town, even if he won't let us tell him, but we all respect his ways, Annabelle. You can be sure of that. We are all . . . different, in our own ways."

They passed a minute in silence, comfortable with things both said and unsaid. The old rocker creaked pleasantly, mingling with the sound of children's laughter drifting up the street. Lela turned her head to the sound and squinted into the gathering gloom. There were four children, but only three were laughing and racing about. One stood twenty feet away, as motionless and silent as the coming night, his hands buried in trouser pockets. Lela caught Annabelle's eye and motioned with her head to the cluster of children.

"The boy standing away from the others . . . Sarah Donley is going to have a time with him this year in fifth grade."

"Who is it?" Annabelle asked, instantly attentive.

"Charles Spurley. Could be a good learner. Something happened toward the end of last year . . . nobody's quite sure what, but he clammed up and stopped progressing. He's not antisocial exactly; he just doesn't seem to mix in anymore. Like that." Lela pointed down the street. "Always on the edge somehow. Anyway, Sarah, she's too proud to ask advice before things get really bad . . . eighteen years of experience and all, don't you know." Lela arched her eyebrows and cocked her head to one side. "Oh, she might chat about it with Nathan, but we all know she needs to talk with you about it."

"I'm not so sure about that, Lela . . ."

"Don't be modest, Annabelle, we both know you became a quick legend with Jewell Cole. And this boy . . . well, there are certainly some similarities."

The old pain came to Annabelle obliquely now, still pain, it always would be, but without the hammer blows in her chest. They had talked of Jewell several times before, Lela assuring Annabelle of her feeling that he would return before long. But with the passing of each day, Annabelle resolved to turn more and more of him loose. It was the most difficult thing Annabelle Allen had ever dealt with, even more difficult than turning Matthew loose. Matthew was in the hands of God—missed, loved, remembered, but gone  in hands far more caring than hers; Jewell was lost on earth, in whose hands she could not know.

"I would be happy to help in any way I could, you know that, Lela, but it may not be as bad as you think. Maybe just a passing thing, something he can adjust to."

"Maybe, but I doubt it. I just hope Sarah doesn't let him harden for a whole year before you get him."

"I'm not a miracle worker, Lela. Jewell . . . it was just something very special between us. We are two of a kind in many ways."

"Okay, not a miracle worker, but the closest thing we have to one. What about the Hanley girl? Little Billy Rainer and his big chip on the shoulder? And . . ."

"Lela, every class has problem students. You deal with yours very well, as I'm sure Sarah Donley does. We just all have different ways."

"But we've had *years* to figure out our ways, Annabelle, and you haven't. Yet yours seem to work better. Don't you see it's a gift? This is what you are supposed to do in life."

"I hope so. I'm sure it's all I ever wanted to do."

"Just remember to share some of your secrets with the rest of us who aren't so sure from time to time." Lela smiled, at once impish and from the heart. "Let us all be heroines once in a while."

Annabelle gestured theatrically, her right hand extended in a sweeping motion. "I shall hoard not the slightest whit of my vast knowledge."

Lela laughed. "That's a girl, that's what I wanted to hear."

The mournful bay of Tinsley Adams's bluetick hound rolled down the street; Evan Parker was two doors from home. Lela threw up a hand in greeting as he marched the last few steps across the long yard. Annabelle turned her body to the opposite end of the street. The three children still frolicked in the dusk, a tiny circle of joined hands and stamping feet. She peered into the shadows along both sides of the street, searching for the fourth child, but Charles Spurley was gone.

# Chapter 18

*October 1947, Ocean Park, California*

*D*AIN GODSEY stood facing the salt wind blowing in from the Pacific, his hands clasped loosely behind his back, black-booted feet spread shoulder width. The cries of the sea gulls pierced the sky over the busy harbor, the birds like gnats swarming over the great, steel monsters sleeping at anchor. Godsey reached up and stroked his well-trimmed beard, once black as ink, but now flecked with gray. He was a man of square corners—jawline, shoulders, hands. Even when he smiled, which was not often, the line of his mouth resisted curvature. Dain Godsey had been dock foreman in the merchant marine for sixteen years; his strange, square hint of a smile had served him far better than the softer smile with which he had begun his career.

He turned from the wind to monitor the progress of the loading team. Eyes trained to notice every detail of both men and cargo swept up and down the line of sweating bodies. All of the workers in the line knew when Godsey was watching, even when he was not standing openly before them as he was now. Older workers quickly passed the cold facts to new recruits: Godsey was never far away. He was a presence, not a man. In truth, Godsey cared for the men, far beyond the strength of their backs. He had found ways to aid many through the years, albeit anonymously, all the while allowing the iron man myth to grow. It was a useful tool, necessary to the success of his task, and now the myth could not be separated from reality. Besides, he had never been a man who required praise or thanks for a kindness extended or a job done well. He could quickly weed out those who would not pull their own weight, who had no intention of bettering themselves in the hard world of the dock and the sea. It was an honor to supervise men who persevered, men who were the wheat of the world, not the chaff. To work with such men was reward enough for Godsey; it always had been, it always would be.

The one the men called Soldier Boy glanced back over his shoulder at Godsey, and although they made eye contact, neither acknowledged the other. Godsey smiled inwardly at the sight of the boy; now little more than a faint reflection of the frightened child who had asked him for work a year and a half ago. Even today, Godsey remained a bit puzzled at himself for giving the boy work. Certainly pity played a role in his decision; Godsey allowed himself a modicum of pity, though always dispensed with great care.

The boy had popped up behind him one morning like an apparition, half-starved, a tattered sack of clothing clutched in his hand, hollow eyes asking but not begging. No man could behold such a sight and not feel a measure of pity. But it was more than that. There was a flicker of passion in the boy's dark eyes, and Godsey peeked into the soul behind the dark eyes and admired what he saw. After stuffing a dollar bill in the boy's shirt pocket and directing him to a cafe, Godsey instructed him to return to the dock ready to work. The boy put in a man's day without so much as a sidelong glance. That night, Godsey set up an account at the cafe and paid a week's advance on a room two blocks from the dock. The boy gave his name as Billy Allen, but Godsey knew he lied; the name did not come off his tongue properly, and Godsey had heard many men lie about their names. But he let it pass; the boy did not smell like trouble, and Godsey could smell trouble on a man like a rotting onion.

Days turned to weeks and weeks to months, and now the dark eyes were sharp and bright and the knotted muscles of a man were tight under tanned skin. In eighteen months, Godsey judged that he had come to know Billy Allen rather well, despite the fact that they had never spoken more than a few necessary sentences at a time. Godsey was certain that the boy was driven, both away from something and toward something. Though he doubted he would ever know what Allen was driven away from, Godsey knew that he was driven to be a soldier. The few dock workers who had come to know him at all quickly hung the "Soldier Boy" moniker on him after learning that he had hitchhiked a ride to the Armed Forces Recruiting Station in Santa Monica after a month on the job. As with the name, Godsey knew he had lied about his age and figured him for sixteen at the most. Because he lacked identification papers, the recruiters had turned him away.

Godsey stroked his beard thoughtfully and lifted his head to sniff the smells of the harbor. The boy could have a long career in the merchant marine, there was little doubt of that. Godsey could shepherd him along the way, pass the word about the young man who never grew tired or complained. Godsey could get him aboard a ship so that he could ride the great ocean and travel to ports around the world. But the only favor Billy Allen ever asked of Godsey was that he help him obtain identification papers— papers showing a birth date that could be taken to the recruiting station in Santa Monica. After considerable thought, Godsey agreed to help. In truth, obtaining the papers was not a difficult thing for a man like Godsey. He knew many men who could find ways to procure whatever he needed; that part of it required little thought or worry. What bothered Dain Godsey was the fact that Billy Allen desired life as a soldier. In the end, Godsey decided that the great war that had ended only two years before would certainly be the last. Enough blood had been shed by the Billy Allens of the world, enough blood for all time.

So, in two more weeks, Billy Allen, or whoever he was, would become a soldier. The square man in the black boots cocked his head to one side and listened to the music of the gulls. Dain Godsey, the iron man of Ocean Park, would miss the mystery boy, much more than he would ever admit to anyone, perhaps even to himself. He would miss him long after he was too old for the dock and the sea. He would miss him when he was too old to hear the music of the gulls. He would never fully understand why.

Arthur Shellman's brown prison guard uniform hung on his body the same way his soft flesh hung on his bones: loose and rumpled. The mere thought of wearing his uniform properly caused Arthur to perspire. The six-inch wooly worm of an eyebrow that extended unbroken across his brow bunched in the middle. There was enough tension in his life—dealing with the inmates, keeping his superiors off his back, putting up with a wife who pecked at him like a hungry chicken—no, he deserved to live loosely in his uniform; life was constricting enough. He could tug and stuff and button when the big dogs came to sniff around him; besides, it was never for long. They never mingled with the inmates for very long; they had all paid their dues down on the concrete floor where hard eyes bored like jets of light and sharp unseen objects passed within arm's length. The big bosses were happy to leave Arthur and his fellow guards the task of living eight hours at a time with the most hardened criminals in the state of Missouri.

Arthur scanned the rows of bolted-down dining tables and the men who ate from the metal trays with rounded edges. Things were quiet today, wonderfully quiet; there had been no real trouble since last month when an ugly fight broke out in the food line and a near riot ensued. The heavy man slowly made his way toward another guard who stood military style, his back against the wall, feet spread at parade rest, hands locked over the small of his back—a tightly coiled spring of flesh and bone.

Lewis Kiel believed that hatred of the inmates was a necessary tool for life on the floor—a silent, healthy hatred, one that the inmates could not see, but burned brightly enough within him to always give him an edge. He had lived among them for nine years now, and he knew the hatred would always be a warm, yellow flame in his head, a tool to serve him at a moment's notice.

Arthur stopped two paces from Lewis and did not look at him when he spoke. "Nice and quiet, huh?"

"So far." Lewis Kiel did not turn his head.

Arthur slowly swiveled his head toward the row of tables nearest the wall, his gaze resting on the tall man who walked painfully to the edge of the bench and slid his tray onto the table. He stared straight ahead, into the back of the man at the next table. Unlike most of the other men, he picked at his food, chewing machinelike when he poked a small bite into his mouth, apparently unmindful of taste or texture.

Arthur shook his head as he spoke. "Who'd a thought old Cole woulda made it this long?" He huffed a sound that was almost a laugh.

"Not me." Kiel answered. "This is a hard place for a drunk to dry out. May kill him yet though. Hope so."

Word of Jubal's crime had spread quickly through the prison, and even among killers and thieves, he was reviled as a woman burner. The code of the prison allowed for killing and stealing; the men believed that such actions were often justifiable. But a man who would attempt to burn alive a woman who had not wronged him was beyond contempt.

Kiel chewed thoughtfully on his lip for a moment before

speaking again. "We shoulda let Crazy Elmer kill him that first week. He ever jumps him again, I'm gonna be real slow gettin' there."

Elmer Dempsey was a giant of a man whose only fond memory of a troubled youth centered around a woman who had been his teacher as a boy. Elmer learned of the unforgivable crime two days after Jubal's entry into the prison population, and could only manage to wait three days without seeking to administer a fitting punishment. Such a man as Jubal Cole should have been hanged, Elmer reasoned, and on the fifth day of Jubal's incarceration, Elmer attempted to perform the execution with his hands, which he calculated were at least the equal of any rope. It was a week before Jubal returned from the hospital ward, and a month before Elmer Dempsey returned from solitary confinement.

"I can't figure what keeps him alive, myself," Arthur said. "I've watched him for weeks. Don't eat enough to keep a bird alive, sometimes nothin' at all."

"Must be hate," Lewis answered. "Maybe he figures he'll get another crack at the woman."

"Ha, ha," Arthur rumbled, "ain't no way he'll outlive his sentence, no matter how clean he keeps his nose."

"I know, but hate's a strange thing . . . hate like that anyway. Now a little hate's a good thing sometimes, like the way I hate all these cruds; keeps me on my toes. I leave it here. But his kinda hate . . . well, that's somethin' else altogether. That kind can put you to sleep at night, wake you up in the morning, do in the place of food, make you strong, give you something to look forward to. Ain't nothin' that kinda hate can't do. I've watched it in here a long time."

Arthur glanced sidelong at Lewis Kiel, slightly amazed; it was the longest speech he had ever heard the tight-mouthed man deliver. Arthur wondered how Lewis managed to keep his hate on one level, a thing properly shelved and meted out, like some sort of potent medicine. In his heart of hearts, he doubted that Lewis, or any man, could accomplish such a feat, but they would never speak of it. Arthur disliked many people but truly hated none; he hoped it would always be so.

"Well, one thing it'll never do is sprout him wings and fly him over the big wall," Arthur said.

"Yep. They'll carry his sorry bones outta here one day." Lewis paused for a moment, his head unmoving. "You believe in hell?"

"I . . . uh . . . I don't rightly know, Lewis. Don't like to think on it much."

"I figure there ought to be . . . for the likes of him. Be a righteous thing, wouldn't it? The old devil showin' Jubal what a *real* burnin' was like."

Lewis laughed softly, under his breath, his expression unchanging. Arthur made a halfhearted attempt at joining in the laughter, but no sound came from him, and he walked away.

Jubal swallowed the tasteless morsel of food and dropped the spoon beside his tray; he would eat no more this day. With both hands, he drew the tin coffee cup to his mouth and sipped the strong, black liquid, his eyes clamped shut, his mind winding backward, mercifully backward. The coffee was cool now, the way he preferred it, allowing the bitterness to reach its peak. It was the strongest taste in the prison, the cool coffee, and the only taste that meant anything to Jubal. It was the only taste that linked him with the taste of whiskey, and a pitiful link at that. But it was usually enough, and Jubal could hold it on his tongue and remember the bite of the whiskey and swallow it and remember the fire in his throat.

He wondered if the dream would come to him tonight, as it had a hundred times before. It was always the same. A shadowy, faceless man came to him, dressed in a robe, a small knife in his right hand. His voice was mocking and deep. "A finger for a drink, my old friend?" Jubal eagerly stretched out his right hand, fingers spread, waiting for the pain that came white-hot, causing him to scream. Then the faceless man passed the pint bottle under Jubal's nose before placing it to his lips and allowing him a long swallow. It was real in the dream, the bite and the taste of the whiskey, and Jubal always extended his hand to offer another finger, but the shadowy figure would not linger, would not make another trade.

Jubal opened his eyes and guided his trembling hands to the table, the coffee tin empty now, the acrid taste foul in his mouth. Oh, how he wished the dream could come to life this very day. For if it could, Jubal knew that he would take ten drinks in a row. He screamed a silent curse at his plight and began the ritual of putting himself back together for one more hour, one more day. He forced himself to deepen his breathing and straighten his posture; he forced his hands flat on the table until the trembling subsided. Very slowly, he swung his legs sideways around the end of the bench, taking the pain as the great scars stretched and rebelled against the movement. Pushing with his arms, he gained his feet and stood for a moment beside the table before picking up his tray and cup. Then he turned and walked away, careful to avoid the other men.

The light that filtered into Jubal's tiny cell was unclean and flimsy, like soiled linen. The night sounds of the prison echoed up and down the long corridors—sounds of muffled conversation, the labored breathing of fitful slumber, cries and groans borne of nightmares, mirthless laughter—they all came to Jubal in the stale air, living sounds from dying men. He lay on the thin mattress, his right forearm draped across his head, knowing that he was dying with the rest of them. The whole sorry lot of them was dying in tiny increments of time, lives slipping away like grains of sand in an hourglass. And Jubal Cole did not care.

# Chapter 19

O*N THE* Sunday night before Christmas 1948, with sleet pecking insistently on the window-panes, Annabelle made the unalterable decision to visit Jubal Cole. She pushed the covers away from her chin and rolled onto her right side to face the window and the icy tapping. She would not sleep this night until the burden had been completely lifted.

It was an easy and natural thing, the forgetting of Jubal Cole, during the months following the fire. Annabelle feared then, more than anything else, that hatred would come creeping into her brain—inviting, urging, tempting, whispering. So she shoved him far away, this strange, raging man who fouled lives. There were higher matters that filled her days; forgetting him was not a diffi-cult thing to do. In fact, several friends had praised her for not openly speaking ill of this man who had attempted to take her life, but it soon became hollow praise for Annabelle. In truth, until recently she had never been sorely tempted to hate Jubal Cole. But the unvarnished truth was that she had never considered for-giving him for the final act that cast Jewell away, into places unknown where no one could care as much as she and Emmett cared, places where teenage boys could be chewed up and spat out.

Annabelle despised with all her heart the set of circumstances that had fallen disastrously into place, and the fact that Jubal Cole was so central to the whole of it presented a grave danger. For the past several weeks, the line that separated hatred of the circumstances from hatred of the man had grown fainter by the day. Now, after days of teetering on the tightrope, the futility of the effort had been revealed. It was a mystery, this power of the spirit, this part of her that refused to tolerate even the hint of hatred. But it was a beautiful mystery, and Annabelle never questioned the power.

She tossed the blankets aside and reached to the foot of the bed for her robe, and then padded barefoot to the window, peering into the wintry night. The sound of the sleet was no longer bothersome; perhaps it would turn to snow before morning and cover the ground. She shook her head and huffed a little laugh at herself. It was a simple matter of forgiveness; if she did not forgive Jubal Cole, her spirit would be tethered to earth and, in time, become listless, perhaps even lose its desire to soar, windy and free.

First thing in the morning, before class, Annabelle would check the train schedule to Jefferson City, and she would learn of the visiting procedures at the Missouri State Penitentiary. She could not tarry now.


On the Sunday following Christmas, Annabelle and Emmett walked steadily but unhurriedly away from the blocky church building. Emmett had known of Annabelle's plan to visit the penitentiary for four days, but he had yet to reconcile the peculiar fact that she would confront Jubal Cole within hours. They walked in silence for another half block, the slanting shards of winter sunlight warm on their faces.

"I must find peace with this man, Emmett."

"There ain't no peace in him."

"There must have been once . . . very long ago, before the liquor took him. He must have been at least a bit like Jewell. I'll grant you, it's a dying ember now, but an ember nonetheless."

Emmett thought it strange that she would speak of fire and Jubal Cole in the same breath, but he said nothing.

"He'll never come to see you if they tell him who you are."

"That may well be . . . in the beginning. But I'll try again and again and again. Sooner or later, he will face me."

"Then what? What will you say?"

She slowed her pace and looked up into the leafless branches of a wide maple, the black arms one with the indigo heavens. "I have no earthly idea. I'm not sure what will come out of my mouth. But whatever the words, he will know I come in peace."

"But what if . . ." Emmett bit off the words and shook his head; it was not his decision, not his business.

"Go ahead, Emmett, get it all out." There was no edge to her voice.

"What if he stands there and cusses filthy at you in front of all the other men and guards and all? I can't stand even thinkin' on it."

There, it was out now, his worst nightmare—the possibility that Miss Annabelle Allen would be further sullied by the most vile man he had ever known. She stopped and turned to him, her hand closing over his. *Oh, sweet Lord, how the man cared.* How very much he cared. She smiled into his eyes, dissolving some of the pain lining his face.

"I'll risk that, but I don't believe it to be a great risk. Besides, for a very long time I have paid no attention to foul tongues and hurtful words." She paused for a moment. "Maybe it would be a good thing for him to get it all out at one time."

Emmett shook his head; there was no point in discussing the matter further.

"Whatever happens, I won't back down." She squeezed his hand and released it.

Emmett nodded in resignation. "I know that for sure." He wanted to smile, but the elusive form would not take shape.

"Come and eat some dinner with us. Lela has probably fried enough chicken for half the town. Then maybe you could walk me to the train station."

"I'd like that."

They began to walk slowly again, arm in arm, down the long hill.

Annabelle shuffled patiently and uncomfortably forward in the line of Sunday afternoon visitors. Since walking through the gates of the prison, foreboding sights and sounds continued to rush at her—dark shades of gray coloring her vision; hard, metallic clinks and clanks knifing into her ears—all conspiring to increase her apprehension. Five minutes before, when the initial processing began, Annabelle sought solace by attempting small talk with the woman behind her, but it went poorly, and Annabelle withdrew into her own silence, like most of the others. The only conversations Annabelle overheard were between relatives or people who knew each other; clearly, the line was not a place to make new friends.

Annabelle cradled the two boxes of oatmeal cookies with her forearms and hands. The boxes had been duly searched and each of the cookies cut neatly in half before the lids were replaced. She focused on the back of the man in front of her; the line inched forward at the pace of the blue flannel shirt. Suddenly, the shirt vanished and Annabelle stood before the metal desk, the flat eyes of the guard probing hers.

"Inmate's name?"

"Oh . . . uh . . . I'm sorry. It's Cole . . . Jubal Cole."

The guard's eyes narrowed for an instant, a flicker against the flatness, and then it was gone. "He's never had a visitor before."

"Does . . . does that matter?"

"Not to me. Your name?"

"Annabelle Allen."

The guard's pen froze on the second "l" of Annabelle. He looked up at her now, his mouth slightly open, unable to hide his amazement. He swallowed deliberately, his Adam's apple gliding up and then back down.

"Aren't you the one . . . who . . . he . . ."

"The same."

"I'll be right back."

He popped up from his chair and walked briskly to a wall telephone. Annabelle could feel the stares boring into her back, and her arms began to weaken under the weight of the boxes. The guard clomped back and sank into the chair.

"You understand, now, we don't allow any shouting or trouble of any kind. It causes . . ."

"Sir," Annabelle stole a quick breath and composed herself as she placed the boxes on the front of the desk, "if I desired to scream curses at the man, I would not have gone to the trouble of baking these cookies."

The guard flushed, glancing down the line. She was obviously a young woman, but she spoke with the authority of an old one, and she was waiting for his response.

"No, ma'am . . . I just meant . . . uh . . . just trying to be sure, you understand?"

"I suppose I do, sir. You may rest assured that no loud noises will emanate from my mouth."

The little woman was finished talking, of that, the guard was certain. It was a very uneasy feeling; he was supposed to dismiss her, but to anyone within earshot, it was clear that she had dismissed him.

"I'll send the runner for him, ma'am, right away. Please, uh . . . take a seat with the others, all right?"

With a crisp nod, Annabelle gathered the boxes with a neat swipe and walked away from the desk.

The inmate runner sneered unbelievingly at Lewis Kiel.

"You're lyin'."

"I ever lie to you before, Dalby?"

Kiel's voice was a steady breeze over ice. The inmate relaxed the sneer, but to himself, he smiled widely and wickedly. Kiel, the great hardnose—the one who thought he was smart enough to hate them and hide it—like some kind of slick shrink full of goofy questions. He made them all laugh, but there was no humor in their laughter.

"No, Mr. Kiel, you're a straight shooter, for sure."

"Don't smart-mouth me, Dalby, just do your job and go tell him he's got a visitor."

When the footfalls ceased in front of his cell, Jubal Cole did not look to see who had come. He sat on the edge of his bunk, hands on knees, staring at a large spider climbing the opposite wall.

"Cole, you got a visitor."

Silence; a statue, not a man.

"Cole! I ain't gonna stand here and yell at you all day. I said you had a visitor. You want your lock thrown or not?"

Jubal heard him the first time, and his brain struggled to process the strange information. *A visitor? The public defender with some stupid question? Not on a Sunday. Who could it be?*

"Who is it?"

"How am I supposed to know who it is, Cole?"

Dalby would not run the risk of spooking him and ruining the fireworks that were sure to explode in the visiting area. Real entertainment was a rare and precious commodity in prison.

Jubal opened his mouth to send the man away, but the words did not leave his tongue. *Could it be? Oh, could it be the boy? The* hair at the base of Jubal's neck pricked his skin, and he felt the blood rise to his head.

"I got others to get, Cole, I ain't gonna . . ."

"I'm comin'."

The chastised guard peered intently over the barrier and through a Plexiglas window set high in the thick steel door. Lewis Kiel nodded to him, and then the long face of Jubal Cole filled the square. The guard hopped to his feet and walked directly to Annabelle.

"Please follow me, ma'am."

Annabelle fell in step behind him as they walked over the thirty feet of concrete floor. He stopped in front of one of the visitor's stations and slid a metal stool from under a short countertop, gesturing with his right hand.

"Here you go, ma'am. He'll be coming from your right."

Kiel tapped on the door, and the guard on the inside opened it for Jubal. Kiel's voice, clear and cold, followed him through the opening. "Sweet memories, Cole."

At that moment, Jubal knew who had come to see him. The urge to spin wildly and lunge for the closing door was nearly uncontrollable, but the heavy thud had already sealed his fate. His brain whirred in spurts, clear for an instant, then lost in swiftly moving clouds of confusion. A voice inside his head: *Stop! Turn quietly and ask them to take you back. Stop your feet! You're moving toward her! No!* Another voice, softer but even more urgent: *Go on! Look her in the eye and let her see inside you!*

It was all beyond him now, pulled onto this crazy little stage of a crazy life; there was no escape. His side of the communication screen was three steps away . . . then two . . . then one. A quiet power that he could not identify turned his body to the left. The wire mesh stretched over the bars was very fine, and he could see her face clearly.

He had never seen it so close—the big, beautiful green eyes, serene and pleading, a single tear sliding from the middle of each, the lips quivering yet smiling. Jubal Cole did not bother to call on the hatred to come forth; it died in the stillness. He could only stand and stare, and his shaking legs assured him that he would not stand for long.

Annabelle had not anticipated that it would be like this. Surely, there would be some animosity to deal with—some charred, ugly remnant from the great fire that would float on the heated air and pass close to her, or a flash of old pain in her legs. But it was not so. Only pity filled her, spreading through her body like warmth from a woodstove in the dead of winter. She peered past the gaunt features, through Jubal Cole's eyes and into what remained of his very soul. The light was dim, like the flame of a small candle seen through a thick curtain, but it was a light.

The air would not come to Jubal's lungs quickly enough, and he sucked greedily with a half-opened mouth. His left knee banged into the hard floor first, and he teetered for two seconds like a tree just severed from its stump before strong hands jutted under his armpits and raised him up.

"Get him back to his cell," the taller of the two guards said evenly to the other. "Easy now . . . Harding, get that door."

Annabelle heard the door open and close, but she could not yet stand. She forced herself to breathe deeply and evenly and willed the strength back into her body. She reached up and gathered the cookie boxes before pivoting on the stool and turning to the open room. Several pairs of eyes shot furtive glances before turning away, but Annabelle did not mind. She walked steadily to the guard desk and set the boxes down.

"I would appreciate it if you would see that one of these gets to Mr. Cole. The other is for you and your fellow guards."

The guard could only nod a thank you, but Annabelle was certain that he meant it.

"Good day, sir. We will meet again."

The walk home from the railroad station was invigorating; the tingle from the cold breeze a welcome feeling to Annabelle. Without so much as a single word passing between her and Jubal Cole, much of the burden had been lifted from her shoulders. Annabelle wondered if the inmate runner had informed Jubal of her identity; she doubted it. Perhaps one day she would ask him, provided a relationship could be developed. And if the man lived long enough.

Wedged comfortably between a cushion and the padded arm of the sofa, Lela Parker thumbed through the pages of the *Saturday Evening Post*. Only splashes of color registered in her vision; the words were of no interest. She looked up at the big wall clock. Straight up six o'clock; Annabelle should be returning any minute. Lela tossed the magazine onto the coffee table and sat in silence for five minutes before she heard footsteps on the porch. She flipped the cushion from her side and stood as Annabelle opened the front door and stepped into the living room.

The words came in a rush. "Annabelle, I won't even pretend not to pry. Come sit down and tell me what happened, or we can sit at the kitchen table while you eat. Your supper's still warm."

Annabelle laughed wearily; the strain of the afternoon was beginning to take its toll, but she welcomed the opportunity to talk about it. She needed to talk about it.

"Let's go sit, Lela. I'm not really hungry right now."

The two women walked to the sofa and plopped down on opposite ends. Annabelle unlaced her shoes and pinched them off with her toes. She curled into the soft corner and turned to face Lela.

"So?"

Annabelle sighed and rested her head on the back of the sofa for a moment before looking at Lela. "If I told you that we did not speak a word, but that it went well, would you believe me?"

Lela's brow furrowed and then she arched her eyebrows. "If it was anybody except you . . . no. But it *is* you, so for heaven's sake, start talking."

Annabelle narrated the details of the meeting, patiently allowing Lela to interject an excited question or comment. Looking back on it now, the scene came to Annabelle in surreal fashion, slowly filtered through a cloudy lens. Even so, she could see and understand the confrontation better than when she actually lived it. Two characters on the concrete stage—would-be murderer and intended victim—eyes locked together for moments frozen in time, speaking only through their spirits. When Annabelle finished, Lela felt as if she herself had been in the cold, gray room, an unseen witness sitting on a metal stool beside Annabelle.

"Dear Lord, Annabelle . . . it's like you made a movie with your mind and played it back in front of me."

"Good. In a way, it was like that for me too. It means even more now that I have relived it."

"Do you think he'll live for very long?"

"Not unless something changes very soon. He's little more than a big skeleton with flesh hung on it. But as I said, I know I saw something in his eyes . . . a spark . . . something. Maybe I linked him with Jewell for an instant . . . whatever . . . but I feel strongly that I watched his hatred die . . . at least for that moment."

"Hopefully it died for good," Lela said with a nod.

"I won't know for certain until we make it to the talking stage . . . assuming he will see me again, and assuming the guards don't interpret his collapse as an 'incident' of some sort and try to prevent me from visiting again."

"Surely they wouldn't do that, Annabelle. No, they won't do that. And he will see you again, trust me on that. I don't claim to be the leading authority on cantankerous men, but . . . I just have a feeling. As you said, your spirits touched, and no man, not even Jubal Cole, can ignore that."

Annabelle nodded a thank you to Lela's affirmation, but her thoughts were already drifting to Jewell. If she could only tell him about the meeting, the tiny flicker in his father's eyes. If she only could.

"If only Jewell could know."

The words were whispered in the quiet room, and Lela realized that they were not meant for her. Annabelle closed her eyes and rested her head on the back of the sofa. Very quietly, Lela padded away from the sofa and toward the kitchen.

Three Sundays passed before Annabelle worked her way to the front of the line of visitors inside the stone walls of the penitentiary. The guard manning the reception desk glanced up at Annabelle, mild surprise registering in his features along with awe, although he did his best to mask the latter. In three weeks, Annabelle Allen had become a minor legend in the prison—the strange-shaped wisp of a woman with the forceful manner who had stared down the man who had attempted to burn her alive. Tales of the fateful encounter had spread like wildfire, gathering details with each retelling, some true, others created in the minds of the tellers. Annabelle doubted that any of the guards or inmates were aware that she had come in the spirit of forgiveness and love. She smiled down at the guard. They would all know the whole truth in due time.

Annabelle set two boxes of cookies on the front of the metal desk. "Butter cookies this time. I hope you enjoy them."

"I . . . uh . . . thank you kindly, Miss Allen, mighty nice of you. Have a seat and I'll send for Cole directly."

Jubal sat on his bunk, his back against the hard wall of the cell. It had been a strange and difficult three weeks. In the first few days after Annabelle's visit, he had endured a hundred crude taunts. The fact that his intended victim was diminutive, even for a woman, and apparently disfigured in addition, served as a strong impetus for his fellow inmates. In truth, the taunts hurled at Jubal when he first entered the prison population bothered him very little. But now, after seeing her, after touching spirits with her, the words were like sharp jabs in his ears. He had not completely sorted out his feelings toward Annabelle Allen, but this much he did know: he would never again hate her.

For reasons he could not understand, the robed figure with the knife had come to his dreams only twice in the three weeks. And even during these dreams, the man with the pint bottle did not seem as powerful, and Jubal hoped he would not return again.

"Cole, the woman's back."

The inmate runner's voice startled Jubal; he had not heard footsteps. He looked up through the bars at the man and nodded his head.

"Throw the lock."

Arthur Shellman tugged at his belt as Jubal Cole approached the visiting room door. Arthur eyed the tall man as he limped painfully toward the door to the visiting area. He was still a sack of bones, Arthur judged, but something about his face was different, and it was not until Jubal was three steps away that the guard was certain. It was the man's eyes; Cole actually *saw* people now, he did not look through them. The tall man looked directly into Arthur's eyes for an instant, but the guard did not feel uneasy, and he nodded at the prisoner as he spoke to him.

"You all right, Cole?"

Jubal nodded affirmatively, but it was partly a lie. His heart pounded like a heavy hammer in his chest, and he wished his legs felt stronger, but it was more from anticipation than dread. The door groaned open, and Jubal stepped through the opening. She was at the same position as before, in the middle of the rows of partitions. He dared not look into her eyes until he pulled out the stool and sat down. Even then, he could not look up. The fragrance from her light perfume wafted delicately to his nostrils, the most wonderful aroma he could ever remember.

"Hello, Mr. Cole." Young and feminine, but an unmistakable strength in the soft voice.

Jubal slowly raised his head. Those eyes again, so near, smiling even more than her mouth. Jubal could only manage a nod before he looked back down; his throat felt as if it had swollen shut.

"I . . . know that it will be difficult at first, Mr. Cole, and I certainly understand. The only reason it is not for me is that I have lived this moment in my mind a hundred times in the last three weeks."

Jubal nodded again but did not look up. The pounding in his chest had subsided; the air came to his lungs more freely.

"I have only one request," Annabelle continued, "I do not want to speak of that night . . . ever again. It is a thing far removed from me, and I very much want it to be removed from your life."

Annabelle paused, but Jubal sat, silent and unmoving, a gray-clad carving in stone beyond the tight wire mesh. Several seconds passed before Annabelle noticed the tears, thin and crooked on his leathery cheeks. She drew a steadying breath, hoping and praying that he would get it out this first time; there were many other important things to discuss.

The words came in a harsh whisper, pushing his lips apart. "I can't . . . lay it all on the whiskey. I'm . . . sorry."

"I forgive you."

Annabelle reached across the shelf at the base of the wire mesh and placed the palm and fingers of her right hand on the barrier. Sensing her movement, Jubal looked up, hesitated for the longest five seconds of Annabelle's life, and placed his left hand against the wire, opposite her own.

"Life can only be lived forward, Mr. Cole. Let the thing stay in the past from this day forward."

"I'll try."

"That's all I ask."

They lowered their hands, and Annabelle locked her fingers and drew them to her chin, ordering her thoughts. The murmurs of the other inmates and visitors were constants in the big room, and though none were intelligible, Annabelle could identify a profusion of human emotion—anger and joy and fear and doubt and love—all swirled together in this place of the brokenhearted, this place that held Jubal Cole. She could clearly see that he was emotionally and physically drained; he needed rest now, more than conversation. There would be time for that later.

"Let's leave it there for today, all right? I want you to rest, and *eat,* and gain back your strength. I'll help you any way I can."

"There's one thing . . . I gotta ask today."

Annabelle knew what was coming; she had already decided how she would respond.

"My boy . . . how is my boy?"

"We haven't spoken in a while, but I'm sure he is doing well, Mr. Cole." The lie was white and absolutely necessary at this juncture; Jubal Cole personified a fragility that was frightening. She would feed him the whole truth piecemeal, as he was able to receive it.

Annabelle pushed her stool away from the shelf, careful not to scoot it over the floor. She stood very slowly and guided the stool under the shelf, allowing Jubal time to draw his long body to full height. She smiled a farewell at him and raised her hand in a tiny wave.

"Remember . . . only forward now."

# Chapter 20

*June 1950*

G ENERAL PATTON was right. We should've whipped those Russians at the end of the war when we had the army right there to do it." Evan Parker's long forefinger jutted toward the ceiling like a thick white stick.

Lela Parker shook her head at Annabelle and then Emmett as she tapped the tines of her fork lightly on her plate. "Evan Parker, you hush such talk. The whole world is just beginning to put the war to rest, and here you are rattling your saber like Alexander the Great about another one."

The reports coming out of Korea had been building to a crescendo for several months, and many Americans were beginning to believe that a confrontation between the United States-supported South and the Russian-supported North was inevitable.

"It's certainly not something I want, Lela, but it's going to happen, mark my word." Evan lowered his head and peeked over his glasses, furry eyebrows bouncing for emphasis.

"I've followed the stories too, Evan," Annabelle said, "but I'm not so certain it will come to war."

"The Commies have ten divisions, most of which are combat-trained troops, and they have all that Russian stuff those sneaky devils left for 'em—artillery pieces and mortars and tanks . . . and ammunition to boot." Evan shook his head and stabbed at a bite of ham.

"Well, Evan, I certainly wouldn't claim to be the military expert *you* are," Lela said, "but it seems to me they can settle any differences they have without involving our boys."

Emmett listened intently, though careful not to look either Lela or Evan directly in the eye. This was the fourth time he had accepted a supper invitation, and his comfort level remained very modest. Still, he felt far more at ease than he had on the first such occasion. The memory sent chills down his spine. He had asked Annabelle a dozen questions about matters of etiquette and the like, but when the time came, the knot in his stomach was a spiked cannonball. He had wiped his mouth so many times with the cloth napkin that his lips were chapped for two days afterward. Thankfully, he was now beyond that point, but he doubted that he would ever feel completely at ease.

"South Korea don't stand the chance of an ice chip on a July sidewalk," Evan retorted, a white blob of mashed potatoes poised on his fork. "And Mr. Harry S.—A-bomb—Truman is not about to let the Commies have a chunk of earth as big as South Korea, you can bank on that. I suspect our boys will be over there before the summer's done."

"Oh, Evan, you're going to ruin everybody's appetite, for heaven's sake," Lela said.

"Well I'm sorry, folks, but we might just as well face the facts." He paused, wiping his napkin across his mouth. "But, great day . . . this won't be anything like a *real* war. I figure we can kick their tails back up north without a lot of trouble . . . once they see the United States is serious."

Emmett's voice was quiet, nearly apologetic. "Any soldier gets hurt . . . it'll be a real war to him."

All eyes sought Emmett's for a moment; it always came as a bit of a surprise when he offered a comment without being asked a direct question.

Evan nodded thoughtfully before speaking. "Well, Emmett, you do have a point there, I'll admit. I meant it more as a 'numbers' sort of thing . . . not so many soldiers involved."

Emmett said, "I hope nary a one goes over there." The words were spoken like a benediction, a haunting quality about them. He was finished speaking, that much was clear.

"I'm sure that speaks for all of us, Emmett," Lela said. "Very well said."

Annabelle reached over and gently squeezed Emmett's forearm before dabbing at her mouth with the checkered napkin. "Lela, I've been bragging about your spice cake to Emmett for two weeks now, and I think the moment of truth has arrived."

"I hope you haven't crowed too loudly, girl," Lela smiled. "It's probably only the second or third best in the world."

Everyone joined in her laughter. The warm breeze pushed through the window screen, an unseen cleansing hand, tossing the light, green fragrances of late spring into the room, and Evan Parker dared not taint it further with any mention of wars or rumors of war.

Twilight now, filtering through the maple branches, thick and leafy; Annabelle and Emmett strolling around the block of tidy frame houses.

"Even for Emmett Tragman, you're awfully quiet tonight. Was it the war talk?"

He nodded. "Reckon so."

"Jewell too?"

Emmett nodded again, silently.

"I'm more at peace about him now that his father has become . . . a person to me, a friend actually," Annabelle said. She made a pleasant humming sound. "I consider it a small miracle . . . Jubal Cole and I talking like old friends. It did take a while though. We've spoken many times of Jewell . . . and you, and everything for that matter. You should go with me to Jefferson City someday soon. It would help you too."

"Maybe someday . . . I ain't the person you are."

"Yes, you are, Emmett, but I won't argue with you about it. It has to be your choice."

Three white houses, milky and square in the dusk, passed to their left before Annabelle spoke again. "Evan sounds like he knows what he's talking about."

"I figure he does."

Each knew what the other was thinking, the thoughts and feelings crisscrossing like electrical currents. Annabelle could not let it pass.

"Even if he joined the military, the likelihood that he would ever be involved in . . . that situation over there . . . well, I just refuse to worry about that."

Annabelle waited for Emmett to reply, but he did not. She understood his silence; it was his way of saying that he could not chase the worry away, and she decided to say no more about it.

Despite the fact that he did not want to hear the words, Emmett spoke them. Maybe if he said them aloud they would leave his mind, at least for a time.

"The boy surely did like soldiers."

Jubal rested on his bunk, flat on his back, his hands folded over his chest. The fingers of his right hand inched down toward his lower stomach and abdomen; even lying on his back, the swelling was noticeable. He sensed that it had something to do with the puffiness in his lower legs and feet, and he knew that these were not good signs. He had never felt truly strong of body since coming to the prison, not the slightest hint of his might in the old days. Surely some of it, even a tiny bit, should remain, Jubal thought, but it did not. It was to the point now that short walks to the dining hall or to his workstation at the laundry were becoming endurance tests. The guards allowed him to sit and sort clothing for the most part; they were able to make the distinction between an inmate's lack of desire or lack of strength. They knew Jubal Cole was a sick man, but neither he nor they knew how sick.

Jubal moved his hands back to his chest and waited; it was the third Sunday since she had last come to visit him. Miss Annabelle would come today as she had promised. He smiled crookedly with the knowledge that the inmates living near his cell were looking forward to her visit also. Sometimes cookies, other times cakes or rolls—the sugary treats were of little interest to Jubal, and he quickly passed them on to the others. Miss Annabelle would never know. The first time, Jubal flushed the cookies down the toilet rather than give them to the other men, but it did not seem right, Miss Annabelle having made them and all. It was an act so far removed from her spirit that Jubal felt immediately guilty and resolved never to do it again. And though he could never be sure how the others felt toward him, they seemed genuinely grateful, and it came to be a pleasing ritual. Some of them would always hate him, Jubal had no doubt of that, but many now spoke to him in ordinary tones of voice, now that his intended victim was his friend. It was a strange and unknowable thing to Jubal, this spirit of forgiveness that lived in the little woman, but it was a beautiful thing, as real as the steel in the cell bars.

She had revealed the whole truth about Jewell very slowly and cautiously, and in fact Jubal had put all of the pieces together before she had finally stated the hard facts. He was devastated at first, then sorrowful, and now resigned. Resigned to the belief that he would never again lay eyes on his son. It had taken many visits for Miss Annabelle to lead him through that terrible storm. She continued to urge him not to give up, but Jubal could see it in her eyes; she had some doubts of her own when she spoke of Jewell's return.

Jubal rubbed his closed eyes tiredly and then draped his forearm across his head. Maybe it was better this way, to love the boy he remembered with all his heart. The boy was a young man now, and locked deep within him were a thousand reasons to hate Jubal Cole. Yes, maybe it was better this way.

Fifty feet away, a cell door clanked open, and the sound of steady footsteps echoed up and down the corridor. Jubal swung his feet over the side of the bunk and sat up, dizzy from the effort. The runner would soon arrive at his cell.

A voice from the opposite side of the corridor came to Jubal, a quiet urgency in it. "Remember . . . it's my turn to get first crack at the box."

"I remember, Hays."

Jubal nodded and returned Annabelle's smile as he sat down, then reached up and placed his hand opposite hers on the wire partition. Neither of them had attempted to keep track of the number of times they had greeted each other in this fashion, and both would have been surprised to know that this was the thirty-second time.

"How are you feeling, Jubal?"

"About the same, I reckon . . . a little weak today, but all right for an old man."

"Seems like you would put some weight on just from the sweets I bring," Annabelle teased.

"Well, I spread 'em around in there pretty good. Not many of the others get stuff like that." He looked into her eyes and held them for a second. "That makes me feel better than eatin' 'em all myself. I hope you don't mind."

"No, Jubal, I don't mind. It's a kind thing to do, a thoughtful thing. I was sure you shared them, but I do wish you'd *eat* more of . . . something . . . for heaven's sake. You need to get your strength back. I know you're tired of hearing that, but you just *must*."

Annabelle had recited the first key word in the chain of hoped-for occurrences, and now all of the words tolled like great bells in Jubal's head: *EAT . . . GAIN STRENGTH . . . HANG ON . . . JEWELL WILL COME BACK*. Annabelle had said the same things a hundred different ways, but it always boiled down to these words. But the tolling faded with each visit, ebbed with the passing of each week, and Jubal was weary of the sound of dying hope. Better to silence the bells.

"It ain't gonna happen, Miss Annabelle. Let it go."

"Jubal, don't say . . ."

The look in his eyes amazed her, silenced her. It was not a look of sorrow; had Annabelle detected that, she would have continued to speak. It was peace Annabelle saw, as distinctly as she had ever seen anything written on a human soul.

"It's all right, Miss Annabelle. You tried so hard . . . so awful hard . . . but it's time to let it go." He raised his hand to the wire, seeking the warmth of her hand, defying the callous strips of steel. "Thanks to you, I can live with it. I can love him like I remember him, before the bad times."

Annabelle swallowed against the burning in her throat and made no effort to stop him. Maybe it was a false hope that she extended; clearly, she had no right to force it on him. It was a time to be silent and listen and love.

"I know it's hard to believe, but me and him had some good times . . . long years ago, even after his momma left. I had this little old pond I knew about, back in the woods in a hickory grove. The bluegill in it weren't much bigger'n his hand, and I'd tie up a little hook and worm it for him . . . and he'd holler and squeal when he pulled 'em outta there, jerkin' on that cane pole like he had a whale on the line . . ."

His voice faded into the memory, and for long moments, he lived the scene again—saw the boy dance with delight in the long grass, heard his high-pitched squeal reach to the tops of the hickories.

His hand slid slowly down the wire, but there was still peace in his eyes when he looked at Annabelle. "I hang on to things like that now . . . ain't no bars can keep 'em from me. I ain't gonna lie to you . . . it cuts me deep when I figure he don't remember those times . . . but maybe he does. You reckon he does?"

Annabelle nodded, decided to trust her voice. "Yes, Jubal. I'm sure he remembers those times."

"Good God'a mighty, I hope he does . . . I hope he does."

The low murmur of other voices came to them, and neither spoke for a full minute. Finally, Jubal broke into the murmur, his voice suddenly weary, barely a whisper, and Annabelle strained to hear it.

"Tell me again about that day when he drew the war map. I wanna hear it again."

Annabelle drew a breath and cleared her mind, allowing the scene to return to her. She had told Jubal of the wondrous day many times before, but, like him, she never grew weary of the telling. She began to speak, the scene unfolding in her mind as if it had happened yesterday; she recited every word spoken, painted a portrait of each look on Jewell's face.

Seconds collected and became minutes, and with the passing of each minute, another memory was given as a precious gift to

Jubal Cole. Annabelle spoke for an hour and a half, bringing to life a dozen other fond memories of Jewell.

When Lewis Kiel came and informed Jubal that his allotted visiting time was passed, he would have seen the peace in the old man's eyes had he looked at his face, but he did not bother.

# Chapter 21

*Early December 1950, ten miles south of the Chosin Reservoir, North Korea*

*I*'VE COME all the way from Iowa to kill them Commies."

The young private smiled at the words of his proclamation; it sounded even better aloud than when he had practiced it in his mind twelve hours before. Cecil Larkin was a serious soldier, and his comrades in arms needed to know.

Along with two of the other men, Jewell Cole quickly glanced at the solitary figure standing defiantly and stupidly in the face of the icy wind, his gloved hands twisting nervously around the barrel of his M-1 rifle. Ten heavy seconds were lost in the moan of the wind coursing through the high mountain pass before Jarman Creed addressed the young soldier. Creed did not look at him as he spoke.

"I got bad news for you, Iowa boy."

"How's that, Sarge?"

"Them Commies have come to kill you, and there's more of them than there is us." He paused, allowing the words to sink deeply. "What's more, if they don't get you, the cold might."

"I reckon I weathered some bad winters back home, Sarge." There was no passion in the boy's voice now, no defiance, only a halfhearted attempt at saving face.

Creed stiffly hoisted himself from a squatting position, using his rifle for leverage. He turned and looked into the boy's face through the wisps of smoke rising from the small fire and smiled thinly despite the ache in his soul. There was a time when he would have said the same thing, a time before the bloody sands of Utah Beach, and a time before the blackened bodies at the Battle of the Bulge—a time on the other side of war.

"There ain't no mountains in Iowa, son. It's a mite different up here. Don't wish for trouble that's gonna find you anyhow." He turned to Jewell and nodded as he walked away. "He's in your squad, Allen. Get him squared away before nightfall." Creed stopped and looked up into the snow-covered mountains, the breath from his nostrils curling down like leaking steam. "I smell trouble. They can't be far back there."

Jewell motioned with a wave of his hand, and the new soldier slung his rifle over his shoulder as he walked forward. "What's your name?"

"Cecil Larkin." He started to pull the glove from his right hand.

"No, don't do that. It's okay to shake with 'em on up here." Jewell extended his own gloved right hand and shook Larkin's hand.

"Hope I didn't make him mad," Larkin said, looking in the direction of Creed's departure.

"Don't worry about it. The only time he gets mad is when the Chinks surprise us."

"That happen often?"

"Some . . . not often. You bring anything to eat with you?"

"I got three chocolate bars and a couple cans of C's."

"Make 'em last. Grub's been scarce up here."

Larkin nodded in thanks and fumbled in his overcoat pocket. "Here, take a bar . . ."

Jewell smiled. "No, you keep 'em. I eat somethin' that tasted good, I might go crazy and shoot you for the other two."

"Sarge said your name was Allen?"

"Billy," Jewell nodded. It sounded natural now, his acquired name. He was Corporal Billy Allen, United States Army.

Larkin looked up into the mountains in the same direction that Sergeant Creed had. Jewell judged him to be perhaps a year older than himself. The stubble on his chin was thin and boyish and a shock of black hair peeked from beneath his woolen helmet liner. Though not as tall as Jewell, he was heavier, broader in the shoulders, and Jewell remembered the strength in his hand when they shook. He would need the strength now; he would need all he could muster, but Jewell would not worry him with that.

"Sarge thinks we're gonna get into somethin' tonight, huh?"

"Oh, he sounds off like that once in a while; he just wants us to stay on our toes."

Larkin looked down from the mountains to the rifle barrel at his hip, patting it with his hand. Jewell saw the question in his eyes long before he finally asked it.

"What's goin' on . . . with this outfit, Billy? Nobody back there would tell me much."

"The whole battalion's movin' south, that's the short of it. Chunks of the Eighth Army strung out for miles around here. Whole army's movin' south, or tryin' to . . . marines too. Chinks pop up from anywhere, seems like, bang us around. We kill bunches of 'em, but not enough, I reckon."

"I heard tell there was a million of 'em come down from China," Larkin intoned, almost reverently.

"There's a slew of 'em, that's for sure."

Larkin tried to laugh, but the sound was not one of laughter. "Funny, ain't it? We come over here to fight North Koreans and run into a zillion Chinese. Man . . ."

"Don't waste time worryin' over politics, Cecil." Jewell

laughed at the memory, thankful he could still laugh at anything. "Sarge said a while back . . . when we was startin' to head back south . . . he says, 'I'd rather hear a donkey bray at midnight in a tin barn than some politician spoutin' off.'"

Larkin did laugh now, but only for a moment. He glanced back at the mountains, listened to the solemn wail of the wind.

"Come on," Jewell said. "I'll help you hack out a little hole in this frozen crud over by mine. You got a good sleepin' bag?"

"I don't rightly know. The supply sergeant got kinda short with me when I started to look it over."

"Yeah, they're all like that . . . think they own every piece in the shed. I wish Creed woulda been down there with you when you were drawin' gear. All of us that came up with him drew good stuff. He don't waste much time on supply sergeants."

"He's been around, huh?"

Jewell's helmet bobbed up and down several times. "Normandy invasion, came in on Utah Beach . . . Battle of the Bulge . . . all over Europe in the war. They say he's got four Purple Hearts and a Silver Star, but ain't none of us asked him directly."

"Funny, he don't look that—mean. He looks like some farmer back home, or a guy runnin' a garage or somethin'."

"I know what you mean, but you're dead wrong. Four days ago, in a blowin' snowstorm, three Chinks snuck inside our perimeter and he spotted 'em before anybody else. Shot two in the head with his .45 and then it jammed up. The third one whizzed a round over his head just before Creed buried the trigger guard an inch deep in his forehead. Me and two other guys saw the whole thing; it was over so quick I never even got my rifle to my shoulder." Jewell shook his head at the recollection.

"Buried the trigger guard?"

"Right up to the bottom of the pistol frame. The medic said he broke his trigger finger, but wasn't much he could do for him up here."

"How can he shoot now?"

"Ain't had to since then, but he says he'll use his middle finger when the time comes."

Larkin had a half-smile frozen on his face. "I'll swear, but he just don't look like . . . that."

"Well, he is, Cecil." Jewell bent down and began to hack at the frozen ground with his entrenching tool. "And you'd better be glad he is."

The snow began to fall at three-thirty in the morning, ghostly specks of white flying horizontally in the wind. It was a half hour into Jewell's watch duty on the perimeter; the temperature stood at five degrees above zero. Jewell shoved his left shoulder into the wall of the foxhole and pressed his hip and leg against the rocky floor; only his helmet-covered head and the muzzle of his rifle protruded above the top edge. The foxhole was nearly two feet deep and three feet across, and Jewell was thankful for the effort of the five men who had spent most of the afternoon digging it. Two flares and four hand grenades rested against the soles of his boots, but they provided little solace. He could barely see the driving snow, and the howl of the wind was the only sound in his ears. If the Chinese soldiers came in the darkness and the wind, they would come slithering over the barren ground, low and silent in their heavy, quilted uniforms. And if they could avoid the trip wires fifty yards to his front, Jewell knew that they would surely kill him.

Another half hour crept by; the cold had penetrated every fiber of flesh and bone. That the velocity of the wind had decreased measurably made no difference. The snowflakes had grown to the size of fifty-cent coins, millions of pieces of crystal ice, falling dreamily now, covering the ground and the boy. The shivers passed through Jewell's body like jolts of electricity, one violent wave pushing another out of the way. He strained to focus on the ground to the front of his foxhole and was surprised to learn that a fifteen-yard strip was faintly illuminated by the new snow. At least now they would have to cover a few steps within his vision before they reached his position. Maybe he could toss a hand grenade or two and hunker down until the others joined in the fight. *Maybe . . . maybe not.* The little fights of which wars were made were never predictable; this much Jewell had learned very quickly.

"Texas!" The password came from close behind him, in the direction of his platoon, but Jewell was startled momentarily, twisting in his foxhole to look for the man. Jarman Creed duck-walked forward, a B.A.R. automatic rifle cradled in his arms. He stopped a yard behind Jewell and flopped noiselessly onto his stomach in the snow.

"Nothin' shakin', huh?"

"N . . . n . . . n . . . no."

"Allen, I'll swear if you ain't laid there and froze up on me. Don't you boys listen when I try to tell you somethin'?" He did not wait for an answer. "You gotta move around in those holes, boy. You gotta be movin' some body part *all* the time. You don't have to thrash around like a fish outta water; just flex a muscle here and there . . . move a few inches back and forth . . . make a little heat."

"T . . . th . . . there ain't no h . . . h . . . heat in me, Sarge."

Creed shook his head and maneuvered to the front of the foxhole, his eyes never leaving the faint white ground to his front. He positioned his body directly in front of Jewell and spoke over his shoulder.

"Lay your rifle down and put as much of your body as you can against my back." Jewell did as he was instructed. "Now reach around me like you were tryin' to hang on to a run-away horse."

Ten minutes passed before Creed could feel Jewell's tremors begin to subside, five more before they ceased. Though the return of his core of body warmth was marvelous beyond description, Jewell felt a measure of shame. He should have known better than to lie there like a rock and freeze up. Maybe a newcomer like Larkin, or a dumbhead like Wilcox—but not Billy Allen. He withdrew his arms from Creed's body.

"I'm okay now, Sarge . . . thanks."

Creed said nothing as he resumed his original position behind Jewell, his head extending over the right side of the foxhole, nearly even with Jewell's.

"If this stuff quits before long, it'll be a good thing. They don't like a lit-up landscape . . . may keep 'em out there for the night. But if it stays heavy and piles up, that wouldn't be a good thing."

"You mean it'd slow us down more'n it'd slow them down?"

"You get the picture, soldier."

"How you know they're out there, Sarge? We ain't seen 'em in three days."

"Gut feelin', and in pickles like this here, my gut's smarter than my brain. Besides, you don't figure they'll up and head back north for China now that they got us on the run, do you?"

The question did not require an answer.

"Where's home to you, Allen?"

"Missouri."

"Missouri? Well, I'll be . . . ain't that where old Harry Truman's from?"

"Yeah."

"An old stubborn Missouri mule, that's what he is." Creed made a low whooshing noise. "Calls this here fight a 'police action,' like some bunch of gumshoes in Cleveland roundin' up drunks . . . police action all right." He whooshed again, louder this time. "Hundreds of thousands of U.S. troops run up against enough Chinese and Koreans to populate half the earth, and it ain't a *war!*"

"Does seem pretty crazy," Jewell said.

A minute passed, and Jewell thought Creed had cleared his mind of the aggravation, but he had not.

"Politicians . . . I despise 'em all."

Jewell turned his head a few degrees to the right and rotated his eyes even further so that he could study Creed's face without staring. Larkin was right; Sergeant Jarman Creed, soldier extraordinaire, wore a face as common as any man he had ever seen. His thin lips, turned down at the corners and framed by a rounded jawline, always appeared to be pursed, stretched even thinner than they should be. Even when he spoke, the lips parted only enough to allow the words to slip out, and then they were tightly resealed, once again forming the slit that passed for a mouth.

"You all right now, Allen?"

"Yeah, Sarge . . . I'm okay."

"Another half hour or so, I'll send the new guy out to spell you."

"Okay."

"I'll get in his face before I send him out, but you stay for a while and get him squared away."

"Why don't you just tell him to bring my sleepin' bag with him, and I'll crawl over there behind that flat rock. I doubt I can go to sleep anyhow."

Creed smiled inwardly, but only for an instant. This boy would make a good soldier one day—if he lived. "Yeah, that ain't a bad idea, son. I'm gonna thaw out some others now." He paused, holding his weapon across his chest, then jabbing it into the air twice. "I won't be far away if they come."

# Chapter 22

*A* THOUSAND yards to the north, spread over a half mile of pine-covered ridge, a full battalion of Chinese soldiers rested in the snow. They had pushed hard since nightfall, and their commander knew well the capabilities of his troops. Dawn would arrive late in the thick cloud cover; ample time remained for a brief respite, now that his advance patrol had informed him precisely of the enemy's location.

The commander clenched his teeth together and smiled darkly in the direction of the mountain pass which pinched the tail of the American snake. The respect he once had for the great American war machine was quickly waning. They fought well enough, he thought, at least when engaged, but the commander could not understand why they were so quick to retreat, so willing to give up ground they once held. He had contemplated this strange behavior at great length and could only surmise that the leaders were too protective of their soldiers. The knowledge that he would lose many of his own soldiers was distasteful, to be sure, but it was a necessary thing; they were all but tools in service to China as she repelled the invaders. But the American leaders appeared to lack the necessary resolve to conquer. Whatever—everything was out of his hands except for the leadership of his battalion, and he trusted his own grim determination to lead it well as much as he had ever trusted anything.

He lifted his head and tilted his chin upward, drawing the refreshing air of winter into his lungs. It had been a marvelous night to advance on the enemy. Just before dawn, his soldiers would charge out of the frozen fog like raging demons in a nightmare, and when one fell, another would take his place.

And then, as Chinese blood mingled with American blood, the snow would turn red.

Jewell unzipped his sleeping bag and poked his face into the cold. Even from ten yards, he could see Cecil Larkin's head and shoulders shaking. Jewell quietly unzipped the bag all the way to the bottom and crawled, rifle in hand, to Cecil's foxhole. Cecil turned his head to watch Jewell cover the last two yards.

"L . . . L . . . Lordy, I'm tryin' to w . . . w . . . work at not freezin' up but . . ."

"I know, Cecil, it's near about impossible . . . first light ain't far off now, and I'll stay with you."

"R . . . Reckon they'll let us build a decent fire before we move out? I got a c . . . c . . . couple of coffee packets for us."

"Dunno. Depends on how Creed and the captain see the situation."

Larkin was thankful to have Jewell close by; he felt warmer somehow, though he knew that it was only his imagination.

"Billy?"

"Yeah."

"I don't mind tellin' you, I'm fairly scared."

"It's all right . . . everybody's scared."

"Even guys like Creed?"

"I figure even him . . . a little bit, anyways."

They both peered into the gray gloom. The wind had kicked up again, whistling down from the right, and they tilted their faces away from it.

"Wonder if it's this cold in Iowa." Cecil said. It was not really a question, it was a memory.

Jewell did not answer; he had no wish to deal with memories now. Maybe later, when they were on the move again, when the sun broke through the clouds and they could see clearly for a mile to the north. *Please . . . not now.* But Cecil Larkin was already back in Iowa, Jewell heard it in his voice, and now he himself was powerless against the flood—Miss Annabelle in front of the class, her eyes bright as she looks up from the book. Emmett across the little table from him, thoughtfully carving up an apple with his pocketknife. And then, like a ghost from the dead, his father's face, younger somehow, eyes unclouded, before the whiskey. And then it changed to the old face, the whiskey face—and love and hate whirled together, and he could not untangle them, did not try to untangle them. He simply turned his face to the cruel wind and allowed the memories to be blown away into the mountains.

"When I get back . . . I don't care if it's summer, I'm gonna get Daddy to build me a fire to beat all and I'm gonna lay up in front of it like an old hound . . . have Momma carry me hot chocolate till I'm ready to puke."

Cecil turned his head and peeked at Jewell, who nodded back at him. "Yeah, Cecil . . . that'd be good."

"What's the first thing you want to do when you get back home?"

"Oh, I don't know exactly . . ."

"Well, whatever . . . just have your family wait on you hand and foot for a while. I figure it'll take a good long while, and we ought to make the most of it."

"Yeah, you're right."

"I'll tell you something else I'm gonna . . ."

Jewell's hand punched into Cecil's side, and he swiveled his head to the right. When he looked into Jewell's eyes, the hair on the nape of his neck prickled against his collar, and it was then that he first heard the sounds rising from the fog. It was at once a roar and a scream, and three seconds passed before he was certain that it was even human. In his peripheral vision, he saw Jewell rolling wildly like a dark log in the snow, and he heard him shout words as he rolled, but he could not understand them. The insane screaming filled his head, and he tried to move his hands and arms, but it was as if steel bands bound them to his body. It was all a bad dream, it *had* to be. His father would come soon and shake him awake for the morning milking chores. He would sleep a little longer . . . chase the nightmare away . . . then it would be morning in Iowa.

"Shoot! Cecil! Shoot!"

Jewell squeezed off two quick rounds as the Chinese broke through the fog, and then he glanced at Cecil. He would not shoot . . . now or ever, it was plain to see. He was half a world away. For an instant, rage passed through Jewell, but it was only a flicker, and it quickly faded to pity.

Jewell sighted his M-1 on another soldier, thirty yards away, and pulled the trigger. The man crumpled to his knees and then fell forward into a shallow depression, a human snowball, tumbling in the slow motion of death. The cacophony of noise was wild and relentless—spaced rifle fire and full automatic fire and the sickening whump of hand grenades, all mingled with the screaming. It had become a white hell in a matter of moments. Jewell rolled back to his left and fired the last two rounds from his clip and fumbled for fresh ammunition. He locked it in his rifle and slammed the bolt forward. Two more shots and then another roll and he was at Cecil's side. His eyes were opened wide, the whites showing clearly, and his mouth was half open, as if he were attempting to speak. The blur of dull white came from his right, and Jewell spun to meet the onrushing Chinese soldier, the eerie muzzle flashes from both the soldier's rifle and his own filling his vision. Simultaneous with the flashes came the strange sound behind Jewell. It was the sound of a watermelon bursting open on hard ground. The Chinese careened to his side, spraying red snow into Jewell's face as he slid forward, and then he was still.

Moaning now from the foxhole, low and pitiful. Jewell reached behind him and groped for Cecil with his left hand, his right holding the rifle to his front. His fingers sought the wound, and he stole a glance to check the location. It was just below the shoulder, high on his arm, a gaping hole through the heavy overcoat with little clouds of steam rising up. Jewell pushed him down into the foxhole as far as he could and tried to pull the compression bandage from the wounded boy's chest pocket. Two more soldiers were moving in his direction, and he raised his rifle to shoot, but they swerved away and he laid the rifle on the ground. He grabbed Cecil's rifle and laid it next to his own. Cold fingers stiffly worked the bulk of the bandage into the gory hole and tied the cloth tails up and around Cecil's neck.

Jewell snatched up his rifle and looked back to the front. The flow of the battle had shifted; the main body of the enemy soldiers was attacking down the line. Despite the din, Jewell could pick out the firing of Creed's automatic rifle—spaced, short bursts, unhurried and deadly. Jewell jerked his head at the movement. Four Chinese soldiers, moving right to left, clumsy in the rocks and snow. He raised the rifle and fired, killing the last man in line as the others disappeared behind a boulder. Cecil whimpered behind him, flailing about in the shallow hole, and Jewell reached back and found his hand and squeezed it tightly.

"Try to lay still, Cecil."

Two minutes passed without Jewell firing another shot; he would have to make a decision soon. He could take a chance and leave Cecil for the time being; it was unlikely that the Chinese would return to this area. They were a force clearly superior in numbers and would continue to push south. But what if he could not make it back to Cecil? What if the surge of the battle carried him away from the foxhole? It was too great a risk. Cecil would have to be taken with him, wherever that turned out to be. He knelt beside the foxhole and peeled the glove from his left hand; maybe the touch of his flesh would stir Cecil. He placed his hand over the side of Cecil's face and patted it gently and then slid it behind his neck as he spoke.

"Cecil, hear me . . . listen to me, we're gonna get outta here now. Get you to a medic. You're gonna have to help . . . get up."

"I'm shot . . . I'm shot . . ."

"I know, but it ain't bad, Cecil . . . come on now."

Jewell reached for his glove, but before his fingers could close over it, a bullet whined into the rocks a foot over his head, sending fragments into the air. He threw himself flat over Cecil and located his rifle, spinning on his stomach to face the direction of the shot. At first he could see nothing moving in the rocky landscape; only the lumps of dead Chinese soldiers appeared out of place, dull white rocks against the larger dark boulders. He strained to catch a glimpse of movement behind the boulders, but it was from behind a fallen soldier that he detected motion. The sniper was using the body of a fallen comrade for a hiding place. Jewell slowly raised his body with his elbows and took a solid prone firing position. He held the front sight pin on the upper middle of the dead soldier's body and squeezed carefully. The body rocked with the force of the bullet and then, like a trick in a magic show, another body appeared beside the first.

Jewell popped to his knees, slinging his rifle over his shoulder. He spun back to Cecil and pulled him from the hole by the lapels of his coat, ignoring the moans of pain; it was time to leave. He reached into the foxhole and grabbed two of the hand grenades, stuffing them into a coat pocket.

"Stand up, Cecil . . . help me! We stay here, we're gonna get it. You understand me?"

He draped Cecil's good arm around his neck and shoulders and began to drag the stumbling man through the snow and rocks, toward the sound of battle. They covered a hundred yards before Jewell realized that his left hand was bare, but the thought of going back to retrieve the glove did not cross his mind.

Jewell half-carried Cecil another fifty yards before he eased him to the ground behind a low boulder. The cold air knifed into his lungs, and he struggled to control his breathing. Cecil babbled incoherently for the most part, though Jewell could make out a word from time to time. The sound of the battle was steady now, but less intense and from much lower ground. Jewell tucked Cecil close to the boulder and scanned the immediate area; he would be safe for a few minutes. Jewell loaded a fresh clip of ammunition and began to creep forward, using the scrubby pine trees and the boulders for cover. From a clump of three pines, he squinted through the dim light into the valley below. What appeared to be the remnants of his company were dug in behind a low ridge, pinned down by heavy machine gun and rifle fire. The bodies of both American and Chinese soldiers were strewn haphazardly over the seventy-five yards that separated the two forces. Jewell guessed that the Chinese outnumbered the Americans by a ratio of at least three to one. Within moments, the tactics of the Chinese became clear. Like a slow-moving serpent, scores of troops continually crept toward the far end of the ridge in an attempt to flank the Americans. But the ground at the end of the ridge flattened into a fifty-yard circle nearly devoid of rock or tree cover. And in this place, perhaps fifty Chinese lay dead and dying as withering fire swept the open area.

Jewell moved forward another twenty steps and reconnoitered the near end of the ridge. If they could manage to pick their way down a slope littered with jagged rocks and only a few pines to hang on to, he and Cecil could work their way to the rear of the friendly forces. He retraced his path to Cecil's hiding place and found him in the same position he had left him in.

"Come on, Cecil, we're goin' back to the platoon."

"Don't . . . don't wanna move . . ."

"We got to move. I don't get you to a medic pretty soon, you're gonna be in trouble."

"Noooo . . ."

Jewell slapped a hand on both sides of Cecil's face. "You wanna get back to Iowa, Cecil? Or you wanna die up here in these stinkin' mountains?"

"I don't wanna die . . . not die . . ."

"Then take the pain and help me get you back to our guys. Yell and holler if it helps, but just keep movin'."

When they reached the bottom of the slope, Jewell wondered if he had done the right thing after all. Cecil was deathly pale, and the only sounds he could make were tiny whimpers. But they had made it this far. Bullets whined overhead, and the smell of cordite was heavy on the air. Jewell's lungs were on fire again, and his legs trembled under the burden of Cecil's weight. Shouts and curses mixed with the gun fire as he picked his way through the rocks and trees. His knees finally buckled, and it took all the strength he could muster to prevent Cecil from falling to the ground. The world was reduced to the inside of his eyelids—bolts of light, then waves of blackness crowded into his head. Time stood still.

When Jewell opened his eyes, the face of a wild-eyed American soldier filled his vision. Jewell blinked his way back to reality as he linked the soldier's face with a name.

"Cramer?"

"Yeah, Allen . . . it's me."

"What's goin' on? Where's our platoon?"

Cramer ignored the first question. "Dead mostly."

"Where's Creed?"

"Up there in a pile of rocks with a machine gun . . . ain't nobody left up there but him. He told us all to get out while we could."

"But where's the rest of the company?"

"Dunno . . . scattered all over, I reckon."

"You gotta do me a favor, Cramer. Stay here with him till I go check on Creed."

Before Cramer could reply, Jewell raced away. Cramer knelt down at Larkin's side, peeked under the bandage on his arm, saw the white edge of bone in the morning light. He placed his ear to Larkin's chest; the heartbeat was faint. No. He would not wait on a man who would soon be dead. He stood, stamping his boots in the snow, his toes prickly with cold, and then he began to run south.

Jewell crawled the final thirty yards to Creed's position, the deadly staccato of the machine gun pounding into his ears. Creed was on his knees, hot spent shell casings piled in clusters as they melted holes in the snow. Three B.A.R. automatic rifles leaned against the boulder nearest him, with dozens of loaded clips stacked nearby. Creed fired another short burst, and then the gun fell silent. Jewell crawled within a yard before Creed acknowledged his presence.

"Well, Corporal Allen, I see you survived the morning rush." The voice was the same as always, the soft words slipping through tight lips; he could have been in the chow line back in the States.

"Yeah, Sarge, I did."

"Your farm boy buddy?"

"Caught one in the upper arm . . . got the bone . . . I dragged him down from the top a little while back."

"Where is he now?"

"Back there . . . I left him with Cramer."

"What you doin' here?"

Before Jewell could answer, Creed fired another burst, longer this time, sweeping the muzzle of the gun to the right.

"I . . . I just figured you might need a hand for a bit . . . before you came with us."

"I ain't comin' with you, boy. Get outta here while you can. Our flyboys are bound to get here soon, and that Chink commander knows that too. He ain't gonna let me chop his boys up in that clearin' much longer before he sends all he's got at once, right over the middle of the ridge. He waits till the planes get here . . . he'll have to pull back."

Creed let the words sink in for a moment, his eyes never leaving the body-littered clearing. "Get the picture?"

Jewell did not answer. A great sorrow pierced his heart as he weighed what he was about to say. He heard the words inside his head, a whisper from his soul, and then he spoke them aloud.

"I'm . . . I'm willin' to stay, Sarge."

The helmet-covered head turned, owl-like, and Creed looked beyond Jewell's eyes and into the boy's soul.

"I know you would, son, but I ain't gonna let you."

"I can't just run . . ."

Creed's voice was hard. "You can and you will! Go on and see if you can get that farm boy back to Iowa. Go on and see if you can live to grow old. I'm through talkin' about it."

He calmed himself, his voice soft again, fatherly. "If it comes to it—and I hope to God it don't—if you see they're gonna take you . . . shoot Larkin. They'll just make sport of him. You might make it."

Jewell attempted to swallow, but he could not; he spat in the snow.

"One more thing. You got any grenades left?"

"Yeah, I got two." Jewell fumbled in his pockets, producing both.

"Put one back in your pocket."

Jewell did as he was instructed. Creed reached out with his left hand, his right remaining on the gun handle, and wrapped his fingers around the body of the grenade, making sure his thumb covered the arming lever.

"Pull the pin." Startled at the strange request, Jewell stared for an instant before following instructions. With an ominous ping, the pin jerked free. Creed carefully positioned the grenade in the hollow of his throat, pulling his chin down tightly over the arming lever, and in so doing became a human booby trap.

"You ever meet old Harry Truman, you tell him we didn't die for him. We died for each other."

The machine gun chattered a long burst, Creed's body vibrating with the recoil. Then, in the silence before the next burst, Jarman Creed spoke the last words of his life.

"Go home, boy."


Cecil Larkin's body looked like a dark piece of driftwood afloat in a white sea. Jewell muttered a curse under his breath at the soldier who had abandoned his wounded friend. He dropped to his knees beside Cecil and jammed the forefinger of his left hand into the soft flesh alongside his Adam's apple. The pulse was faint but steady.

"Cecil! Let's go . . . please!"

It was no use; if Cecil Larkin was to survive, he would be carried to the rear. Jewell tossed his rifle aside; it was no longer a tool of survival, nothing more now than excess weight. They would make it to safety, be killed, or be captured, and in the latter case, Jewell knew that he could never turn the rifle on Cecil under any circumstance. Jewell pulled Cecil to a sitting position and wrapped his good arm around his own neck, then wedged his way under his midsection. In an effort fueled by adrenaline, Jewell staggered to his feet and balanced the great weight over his shoulders and neck as best he could. He encircled his arms around

Cecil's arm and one leg and began to stagger to the south, following the boot prints of the soldiers ahead of him. For the first fifty yards, Jewell imagined he could see and hear the Americans, just ahead, just beyond the next rise, but he quickly rejected the silly mind game. They were far ahead, maybe too far already. All he could do was will one black combat boot to move in front of the other. That was all.

When he judged he was three hundred yards from Creed's position, the low-pitched rattle of the machine gun changed suddenly to the higher-pitched chatter of the B.A.R. Creed had spent the last of the machine gun ammunition; his death drew ever nearer.

His eyes blinded with tears of sorrow and strain, Jewell veered to his left and waded into a knee-high snow drift. With a cry of anguish, he collapsed into the drift and rolled to his back. Swirling patterns of blue sky and gray clouds passed overhead like moving pieces of a giant puzzle as he drifted in and out of consciousness. Precious minutes slipped by, but he could not force his body to move. Then, like a sputtering engine coughing to life, he could feel his body again, identify his arms and legs, and he raised his hands to his face. His bare hand stung agonizingly, and he slapped it against his cheek.

*Cecil!* Jewell rolled over and dug his hands and arms under the dark overcoat and dragged him from the snowbank. *Must go on now . . . cover more ground.* His head cleared, and he realized that the blue patches in the sky meant the fighter planes would come soon. *Oh God in heaven, let them come soon.* The great weight on his back again, still and bloody, though he was unsure how it got there. Find the boot prints in the snow . . . move . . . will the black boots at the end of his legs to move . . . they were carrying Cecil Larkin to Iowa.

When Jewell staggered a final time and fell into the snow, the first of the fighter planes roared overhead, the thunder of bombs and the dull chatter of .50 caliber guns following the roar. Jewell heard the sounds of war, but they were faraway, and he could not identify them, but it did not matter. The soft blackness came to him, whispering like a friend, and then even the whisper faded to silence.

"Cramer, you sure there were two behind you?"

"Yeah, Avery . . . the new guy, down and shot . . . and Allen. Said he was goin' back to find Creed. I tried to tell him . . ."

"I'm goin' back for a look," Avery said. "You go with me?"

Cramer hesitated for a moment before the guilt scratched at his insides like a tiny claw. "Yeah, I'll go."

"I'm gonna find a couple more to go with us," Avery said. "Wait here a minute."

Cramer looked to the north; the air show had been spectacular to behold. He was hoarse from a half hour of jubilant screaming. No doubt, the fighter planes had bought him and his fellow survivors a great deal of time—precious hours to push south and rejoin the main force.

Avery and two other soldiers huffed up the trail. Of the four, only Avery and one of the other men still carried their rifles. "Let's go. I found the lieutenant and told him where we were goin'."

The search party had not traveled five minutes before Avery stopped and pointed a gloved hand to the side of the trail.

"There!"

Avery and Cramer plunged into the snowbank, tugging at arms and legs, until the two still forms lay side by side on the trail.

"The new guy's dead," Avery pronounced.

Cramer was on his knees at Jewell's side, his hands slapping firmly against Jewell's cheeks. "I can't find any holes in Allen."

Jewell moved his head to one side, mouth half open, as a low moan came from deep within him.

"I think he's all right," Avery said, backtracking over the last few yards of Jewell's journey. "He was carryin' the new guy. Looks like he just gave out."

One of the other men looked back up the trail and shook his head. "Lord a' mercy . . . he lugged him a long ways."

"For nuthin'," the man beside him said. "And look at that hand; might have cost him some fingers."

Avery stared, cold and hard, at the man who spoke. "You can't say it was for nuthin', Collins. You ain't Allen."

The man looked down and made a half turn away from Avery. Silently, Avery and Cramer loaded Jewell on their shoulders while the other two men gathered up Cecil Larkin's body. The crunch of boots in the hard snow was the only sound on the trail.

# Chapter 23

*Christmas Eve, U.S. Army field hospital, Osaka, Japan*

"T URN THAT thing off!"

"Just once more, Hadley. I like it!"

Jewell turned his head toward the shouting men. The gruff command and the steely reply pierced the air near the end of the row of beds, to Jewell's right. The complainer lay only a few feet from the record player, and the words from "O Holy Night" had scratched into his ears for the fifth consecutive time. The other soldier sat on the edge of his bed, his heavily bandaged left arm slung and taped to his side. The offending machine sat on one side of a small table. The other side was occupied by a scrub pine that had been jammed into a makeshift stand. The ornaments ranged from strips of surgical tape to links of paper clips. The floppy white star safety-pinned to the top branch had been fashioned from a sheet of paper.

The precise footfalls of the nurse tapped by the foot of Jewell's bed, and then the needle popped free of the record, silencing the tenor voice.

The soldier with the arm wound spun on his hip and flopped into his bed. "I hope you're satisfied, Hadley. Merry Christmas, you sorry sack . . ."

"Hey, Pendleton, that thing was about to make me scream."

From three beds away, another voice piped in. "It already did!"

"That's enough already." Donna Atkinson spoke very loudly, but it was not a shout. She had learned early in her career that shouts were of no use in restoring order; it was simply a matter of volume and tone. "You guys would do very well to save your energy for healing up. It's time to get sorted out and down for the night anyway."

Pendleton mouthed a final protest into his pillow, but the words were mumbled and devoid of passion. The nurse shot a warning glance in his direction, and he pretended that he did not see it. She turned from the foot of his bed, took two steps, and looked down at the metal pan that was positioned directly under Hadley's oozing, frostbitten feet, the toes protruding like stuffed black sausages.

Donna Atkinson had tended many such feet and hands, but she knew that she would never become accustomed to the ghastly sight. Somehow, the wounds caused by jagged pieces of shrapnel and heavy caliber bullets were acceptable, if indeed the casualties wrought by any destructive invention of man could truly be deemed acceptable. But wars were waged with things of steel, and everyone understood the horrible mismatch between steel and flesh. But these wounds—these dark, weeping appendages that were once healthy toes and fingers, savaged by an invisible force— no, these were not acceptable.

"Are they doin' better?" Hadley asked, his voice soft now with little-boy hope.

"I'm not really sure, Larry, I'm not a doctor. They'll make a decision soon."

It did not feel like a lie, though in the strictest sense it was. She had only overheard the surgeons discussing Hadley's case, deciding that the toes could not be salvaged. They would take them tomorrow most likely, or certainly the next day. But tonight, on his twenty-second Christmas Eve, Private Larry Hadley would sleep with hope, and with the hope would come needed rest for the days ahead. That was her decision, and it was made without qualm.

"Get some sleep now." She patted his arm, nodding encouragement.

She walked along the row of beds, checking wound dressings and vital signs, perusing charts, speaking soft words—performing the quiet chores of nighttime. Donna Atkinson needed the quiet times, prayed for such times, but with them came the subtle danger of attachment. The wounded were not merely cases in the quiet times; they were fellow pilgrims in life—sons of mothers and fathers, husbands of wives, fathers of children . . . and brothers . . . oh, God, were they not all her brothers?

She stopped at the bed of the silent soldier, picking up his chart, looking at the carefully penned entries but not seeing them. Billy Allen's war was nearly finished. The frost had devoured the last two fingers of his left hand, half of his middle and forefingers, and the tip of his thumb. His nose had been a worry for several days, but the doctors were now certain that it would suffer no permanent damage. Thank God for that; it was a handsome face, more manly than boyish despite his age. Only his eyes were old beyond their years.

She replaced the chart and stepped to his bedside, adjusting the overhead sling that held his left forearm perpendicular to the bed. "How's Corporal Allen tonight?"

Jewell nodded but said nothing.

"This hand's doing great. We're going to have you on your way home before very long."

*Home. Where was home?*

"Pain?"

"None that matters," Jewell replied.

He studied her face, pretending to watch her tend the dressing. Her blue eyes were bright and watchful, the loveliest feature of a lovely face. When she concentrated on a task, as she was now, the tip of her tongue peeked through her lips, and Jewell judged that this is exactly how she must have looked as a little girl, maybe twenty-five years ago. Her blond hair was pulled up tightly into a functional bun at the back of her head, and circular wisps like golden thread billowed down, gathering the light from the bare bulb fixture.

"There, that's better." She smiled down at him, despising the old sorrow in his eyes. "Listen . . . the hand . . . I know the look of it will take some getting used to, but your thumb is nearly intact and you've got the strongest part of two fingers left to work with it. The thumb, that's the main thing, Billy . . . and you're right-handed anyway. I know it might sound crazy now, but a year from now you'll be doing just about anything you want to. I know farmers back home in Indiana who have suffered terrible hand injuries, and they carry on like you can't imagine. Why . . ."

She paused, listening to herself for the first time in several seconds. "Great day, will you listen to Nurse Pep Talk. Billy, I didn't mean to rattle on like that. I'm sorry, but I just want you to know that your *real* life is just beginning. The hand . . . it could have been so much worse."

*So much worse*—Creed, on his knees behind the machine gun, unpinned grenade tucked under his chin, resigned to death. *So much worse*—Larkin, lying in the red snow, dying minute by minute. *So much worse*—the ghosts faded from his vision . . . Donna's face now, imploring, caring, and he loved her for it.

"It ain't the hand."

She knew then, instantly, saw the tears pool in his eyes.

"Buddies?"

Jewell nodded, felt a tear spill from one eye, warm and clean.

"I'm so sorry, Billy. I didn't mean to drag all that up. Me and my running mouth . . ."

He looked up, made her look at him. "Don't be sorry," he said, "I can't get 'em outta my head for more than an hour at a time anyway. You didn't do nothin' wrong . . . tryin' to help me. I thank you for it. You're a good person."

Donna touched the cloth sling, just below Jewell's hand, then gently wrapped her fingers around his forearm. Part of her, urgent and judicious, solemnly instructed her to remain silent, but another part, wild-spirited and freed by love, overcame the first. She squeezed her fingers around his arm with a firm pressure, soldier to soldier. Yes, she was a soldier as much as any of them. She could count a hundred times during the past five months when she would have gladly traded her scissors and bloody bandages for the freezing mountain winds at the Chosin Reservoir. A hundred times when she would have rather seen her own blood spilled than that of some nineteen-year-old, broken and doomed on the operating table. Oh yes, she was a soldier, free to say it.

"You owe 'em, Billy Allen. You know what you owe 'em?"

Jewell backhanded his eyes, shook his head.

"You owe 'em a good, happy life. You have to love for them now, reach out to the people they can't reach out to, say the words they can't say, do all the decent and kind things they can't do."

Jewell looked away to the foot of his bed, pondering the weight of the words, but feeling no burden from them. It was as if Miss Annabelle joined in making the entreaties, speaking in unison with Donna—one woman, short and strange in the eyes of the world, the other, tall and beautiful—one woman locked in his memory, the other beside him.

"Billy, I wouldn't say that to just anybody. Some would strap it on as a load, and it might hurt them in time, but not you. I've watched you and come to know you even though you haven't said much. I read men in hospital beds like some people read books, and I know you've got backbone. You're not a quitter."

She sighed and cleared her lungs with a long breath, shaking her head as she released Jewell's forearm. "Whew! How did all that pop out?"

She glanced back at him, a flicker of fear in her mind despite the solid conviction that she had read him right, but the fear died quickly.

"No, I ain't a quitter . . . and I don't mind owin' 'em."

"I read you right, soldier." She smiled, quick and sturdy, then walked quietly away to another bedside.

Enwrapped for long hours in the netherworld of the hospital night, Jewell Cole was now certain of the fact that Billy Allen was dying. The long room stuffed with beds cradling men with maimed bodies and broken spirits was a fitting place for death. Even those whose wounds would not kill them outright would suffer partial deaths in the days to come—sweethearts who could not accept disfigurement, parents who would grieve endlessly with a bitterness that would one day consume them, children who would be unable to see them as whole men, employers who would offer regret but not work—yes, they would all die piecemeal, bloodlessly yet hurtfully.

Jewell stared at the bulky white dressing encircling his hand and wiggled the stumps of his fingers, testing the level of pain. It was very manageable now, the dull throbs little more than a nuisance, certainly not worth the mind-blanketing fog induced by drugs. A clear head was essential now, more than ever. Before dawn Jewell would decide if Missouri was a home to return to or just a memory.

The restless murmur of his fellow wounded ebbed and flowed in the semidarkness, a constant reminder of his bond with them, the bond that would endure until death. Jewell could identify many of the wounded by the night sounds they uttered—names of loved ones beseeched in dreams, babblings of the lightly sedated, labored breathing of the heavily drugged, pitiful cries from nightmares of fire and smoke—the wails and sobs of soldiers. Billy Allen would die tonight, and he too would become a part of the bond, a part of the memory.

Jewell closed his eyes, his clear thoughts suddenly mingled with the night sounds of the soldiers, and he could see the rock in Miss Annabelle's hand as she held it in her own, offering it back to him as a weapon of hate forever transformed into a token of love. He longed for the touch of the rock, lost in the snows of North Korea, longed far more for the touch of the dainty hand. Miss Annabelle whispered to him, her voice soft and near, as if an angel stood at his bedside. She was whispering to Billy Allen, but Jewell could hear too, and he would never be sure that what happened next was only a dream.

Slowly, ever so quietly, Billy Allen tiptoed up and down the rows of beds. His wounded hand was unbandaged and the stumps of his fingers were rounded and smooth, yet very sensitive to touch. One by one, he passed by the beds and brushed his wounded hand over the feverish brows, loving them, telling them good-bye.

Then Miss Annabelle whispered again, and Billy Allen and Jewell could see the faces of Jarman Creed and Cecil Larkin, smiling and free of blood and sorrow. Billy Allen smiled with them as his face became one with theirs and was lost in the brilliance that carried them away.

When Jewell opened his eyes, Donna Atkinson's face was radiant in the slanting rays of the early morning sun coming from behind his bed. He blinked himself awake, rubbing the knuckles of his right hand into his eyes before she came into clear focus. The long night had taken its toll on her; the blue eyes were still beautiful, but heavy with fatigue. The silky wisps of blond hair had fallen lower, now a lovely tangle at the base of her neck. The blood stains on the front of her uniform had already darkened to a deep rust color.

"Hey soldier, you were making some serious sounds there a while ago. You doing okay?"

"Yeah . . . what kind of sounds?"

"Oh, just . . . words . . . talking in your sleep like the rest of the crew around here."

"What did I say?"

"I don't listen to what you guys say. I figure it's a private conversation with somebody . . . maybe just yourself. My only concern is if you're hurting."

"I'm not hurtin'."

"Good." She blinked, in the slow motion wrought by weariness, and pushed a smile up from her chin. "You're gonna do all right, mister. I can tell. Home in three or four weeks I imagine—away from preaching nurses and the like." The smile widened.

"I didn't take it like bein' . . . preached at."

"I sure hope not."

Jewell shook his head. "Don't worry."

"Where is home to you, Billy?"

*Billy.* The name hung in the air for a moment. *Billy*—a soldier dead and far away now, high in the mountains south of the Chosin. It was a strange feeling, bittersweet and deep within him; the woman with the caring soul would never know Jewell Cole.

"It's . . . Missouri . . . little town you never heard of."

"Try me."

"California . . . that's the name of the town."

"Ha! You were right. Never heard of that one."

"Not many have."

"Atkinson!" The female voice boomed down from the nurses'

station. "You wanna do report already or maybe just work another shift?"

"Hold your horses, Ellen." She shook her head at the impatient nurse and looked back at Jewell. "I'd better go before I fall in a heap. See ya."

"See ya," Jewell replied.

Donna took two steps, stopped, and turned back to Jewell, wagging her finger. "Don't you dare slip out of here without telling me good-bye, Mr. California."

"Not a chance." Jewell lifted his right hand in a gesture that was more pledge than wave.

# Chapter 24

*W*E HAVE just begun the shortest month of the year, students. Who can tell me the number of days in February?"

Annabelle tilted her head back slightly and slowly scanned the class. Some heads dipped, hoping to avoid the probing eyes, while others turned sideways in a false nonchalance. Annabelle zeroed in on one of the turned heads.

"Jeremy Patterson . . . how many days?"

"Thirty?"

"That is incorrect. Oh, come now, who remembers the little rhyme about days in the months?"

A hand shot up in the third row. "Yes, Susan."

"I think . . . thirty days has September . . . April, June, and . . ."

"Who can help her?" Annabelle asked, and a hand in the first row popped up. "Clarence?"

"November."

"Good . . . now finish, Susan."

"November. All the rest have thirty-one . . . except for Febru`ary, and it has . . . twenty-eight?"

"Correct, except for leap year. A very short month indeed," Annabelle said. "It always seems to fly by for me. So we will need to work very hard to accomplish the goals we set out today. We will review them again tomorrow morning. Now, we have only five minutes until the bell, so you may read anything you wish or get a little head start on homework."

Annabelle returned to her desk and sat down to reflect on the day. It had been a good day with the children. She had finally managed to lead two of her poorest students in arithmetic to a reasonable understanding of long division without allowing them to appear inferior to the rest of the class. It was the never-ending challenge for all teachers who dealt with large classes: how to push the gifted children while at the same time pulling the slow learners along at a meaningful pace. Annabelle perceived the challenge as a marvelous opportunity to exercise her intellect, like an athlete who stretched and built up muscle tissue in preparation for a great contest. Only for Annabelle, the exercise was never self-serving; she accepted the fact that no one would ever pin a medal on her or splash her name across a newspaper headline. But this was of no concern. Her rewards came from the beaming faces of children who could work long division problems or find faraway places on the globe or write well-structured sentences. Her reward was touching a young life and knowing that the life had been made better by the touching.

Annabelle looked out over her class of twenty-nine students. Counting this class, two hundred and fourteen children had passed through her classroom doors, and she could remember them all by face and name—all different, all beautiful in their own way, all touched by her love. She wondered how many years would pass before the names and faces began to fade. Perhaps the time would come, far down the long road, but she doubted that it ever would.

Jewell Cole stood across the street from the elementary school building, watching the children scatter from the front door like quail in the winter wind, coveys of little people flying to their places in the world. Seven years had passed since he flew away on the great wind that carried him halfway around the world, and in the seven years it seemed as if a lifetime had passed. The memories came on the wind, strong and clear, both loving and hurtful, but he did not attempt to shut them out, could not shut them out.

The sidewalk was empty now, even the stragglers long gone. Several teachers had also departed, but not the one Jewell sought; she would come soon. What would he say to her? He should have written to her, if nothing more than a note from time to time to let her and Emmett know he was all right. He had simply walked away—no, *run* away on that horrible night, even though he knew how much they cared for him. It had been an easy decision to make in Japan, after Donna Atkinson had given him direction. But now—now, with Miss Annabelle about to step out of the school building, he was not so certain. But he could not run this time; he was no longer a little quail on the wind. So he waited and watched, oblivious to the cold.

He saw her first through the glass pane that covered the top half of the door, the thud of his heartbeat suddenly audible in his ears. Only seconds now, and the years would be peeled away like the petals of an old rose succumbing to a late summer shower.

Annabelle braced herself as she pushed open the big door and stepped out into the frosty air. Tugging first on her hat with one hand and then poking at her neck scarf, she lengthened her strides until her shoes clicked over the sidewalk in a steady cadence. She saw him first as a faceless stranger in a long black overcoat, stand-ing motionless and ignoring the wind, looking as if he could stay put until spring if he chose to. When she was three steps away, Annabelle raised her head to toss a perfunctory nod and smile at the young man who now had a face—a face with eyes that were strangely familiar. She halted in midstride, nearly losing her balance. *Dear God in heaven . . . dear God in heaven.* It was a song of praise echoing inside her head, and she did not recognize the voice as her own.

"Jewell?"

"Miss Annabelle."

Slowly, Annabelle raised her hands, as if reaching for an apparition she feared would be swept away from her if she drew too near. Jewell stepped forward and took her right hand, small and delicate and lost in his own. He drew it to his chest and held it there.

"Miss Annabelle . . . I'm sorry that . . . I'm awful sorry for . . ."

"Don't . . . there's no need, Jewell."

She rested her head on his chest, and he could smell the fragrance of lilacs as the wind swirled the curls that spilled from below her hat.

"Just let me hold you for a minute. Dear God, I'm so thankful that you're back. Have you seen Emmett?"

"Not yet."

"He won't be home yet. Come back in the school building with me for a while. I need to sit down, and you need to warm up."

Arm in arm, they silently retraced Annabelle's steps to the front door and then down the hall to her classroom. Annabelle led the way through the door and without hesitating, turned left down the outside aisle and walked to the corner seat.

"Sit in your old seat, number Twenty-seven . . . for old times' sake." She smiled and shook her head, a part of her still unbelieving as she took the seat next to him.

Jewell squeezed half of his body into the narrow opening and rested his right hand on the desk top. The blackboard beckoned beyond her shoulder, filling like a movie screen with images from the day when they were bonded forever—the day when love was exchanged for hatred.

"Oh, Jewell, I don't know where to begin . . . and I have a hundred questions. But I won't unload them all on you. Just tell me how you have been . . . what you have done with your life."

"I've been a soldier mostly . . . in the army."

"Are you still in the service?"

*May as well get it over with.* "No . . . not after Korea."

The name hung in the air, and Annabelle felt a tiny dread pass over her, like a filmy cloud blowing in front of the sun. It was the way the words came from him, the sorrow disguised, but not well. Yet he appeared whole—tall, straight, and strong, and his hands. No, his hand; she had yet to see his left hand.

"Coulda been a lot worse," he said, withdrawing his maimed hand from his coat pocket and placing it alongside the whole hand.

The stumps were still red and angry looking, and Annabelle fought against the wave of sadness that rolled over her. She wanted to scream at the top of her lungs against the thing called war—the horrible, wanton beast that roamed the earth and killed and crippled young men while old men talked calmly across polished tables—but she wept softly instead and cradled the wounded hand with both of her own.

"Oh, Jewell . . ."

"I'm right-handed, Miss Annabelle. It'll be all right. I'm already startin' to learn how to make up for it."

"Was this the only result of . . . whatever hit you?"

"It wasn't something that hit me. Frostbite took 'em."

Annabelle closed her eyes and raised her head slightly. Jewell sensed that she was praying, her hands cupped tenderly over his wounds, but the moment passed quickly, like sunlight bursting through a narrow crack in winter clouds. She shook her head, as if to clear her mind of the burden, but Jewell could see a different burden in her eyes now.

"You're correct . . . you will deal well with this change in your life. In time, it will become little more than a minor inconvenience."

A minute passed in silence, the other burden heavy in the room, an unseen presence that could not be ignored. Very soon, she would reveal it to him; he could only wait.

"Do you ever think of him . . . your father?"

*So that was it . . . his father.* Love and hate clanged together inside his head like a sword striking a shield, the suddenness of it nearly making him dizzy. He leaned forward, resting his forearms on the desk as he steadied himself, struggling to calm his pounding heart.

"I know it is a difficult question, Jewell . . . maybe even unfair of me to ask, but I have my reasons. You will have to trust me."

"I didn't think about him for years. He was dead and buried in my mind."

"But you have . . . recently?"

"Yes, I have . . ."

Annabelle nodded and smiled, but an unmasked sadness was in it. "He is a very dear friend of mine now. I know that must sound very strange to you, but . . ."

"No, it doesn't sound strange . . . but only because it's you. Anybody else . . ." He shook his head. "I reckon he's still in the pen?"

"Yes, he's in the state penitentiary in Jefferson City. I visit him regularly."

"How is he?"

"He is not well, Jewell. The liquor did too much damage over the years. He is a very sick man . . . in the hospital wing now." Annabelle paused, weighing what she would say next, but only for a moment. It was not a difficult decision; there was no time.

"Your father is dying, Jewell . . . they think only days. It is no accident that you have come home now."

*Dying.* The father he had wished dead so many times was on his very deathbed at last. But now, the thought brought emptiness instead of rage, sorrow instead of savage joy. *Dying.* Oh how familiar he was with the thing called death, the dark angel that flew with bullets and freezing wind . . . and liquor. Flew with a grim resolve—unswerving, relentless, tireless.

Annabelle studied his face for several seconds, attempting to get inside his head, but she could not. Whatever he felt was locked deep within him. He was a man now, with a face that did not mirror his every thought in the manner of a school child.

"Would you be willing to go with me to see him, Jewell?"

The nod came slowly, thoughtfully. "I'll go."

"We must go soon . . . tomorrow. I will make arrangements for a substitute teacher so that we can catch the morning train. Do you need a place to stay?"

"No, I got a room across town they told me about at the train depot. I . . . I thought about finding Emmett. Is he still living at the same house?"

"Yes." Annabelle smiled at the mention of Emmett. "Same Emmett . . . solid as a rock. Maybe the most decent human being I have ever known."

"Has he . . . gone down there with you?"

"No, but they have made their peace . . . through me. I have never pushed him to go with me. I think it was easier for both of them this way."

"I want to see Emmett . . . tonight."

"Don't worry about that. If I don't get you over there as soon as he gets home from work . . . why he'd never forgive me."

"Where does he work?"

"The new jacket factory. Well, not exactly new any longer. It has been open for three years now. He still works with Rommie

Rugg's grave crew too. Old Rommie is nearly a legend in his own time in this county."

"I've missed Emmett. I've missed both of you a lot. I should have written, I . . ."

"No need for that, Jewell. We both understood what you were dealing with back then. We don't live in the past."

Annabelle reached out and patted Jewell's right hand. "Come, walk me home. I want to tell you more about your father before tomorrow. Emmett can tell you more too—that is, after he gets over seeing you."

They pushed away from the desk chairs and began to walk to the front of the room. The blackboard grew larger with each step, and when they cleared the final row of desks, Annabelle turned away from the door and walked to the dark rectangle. She motioned for Jewell to join her.

"Put your finger here," she instructed.

Jewell reached up with his forefinger and touched the tiny jagged hole beside Annabelle's finger.

"I have thanked God many times for that day, Jewell. That strange, marvelous day of the rock."

"I reckon I have, too, Miss Annabelle . . . in my own way. I wish I still had it. I lost it in the mountains in Korea."

"Well, I imagine this blackboard will be here for a few more years. It may outlive the both of us." She looked up at him and smiled. "You may come touch it any time you like."

"I may just do that once in a while."

"Let's go now. I have much to tell you."


Emmett turned the water faucet off and cocked his head toward the door and the sound of footfalls on the wooden stairs leading up to his room. The footfalls belonged to a man, though Emmett was certain that they were neither Rommie's nor Hec's; they were too light for Hec and too heavy for Rommie. Besides, he had just spoken with them only a half hour before when they discussed their next job. Higher and louder the clumps came, onto the top step and then the short landing. The man stood on the other side of the door, but he did not knock. Seconds ticked by, turning into a half minute, and Emmett turned his body to the door and took a step toward it.

"Who's there?" Emmett called loudly.

A knock on the door, light and almost apologetic. Emmett reached for the knob, turning it firmly but slowly, cracking the door open a few inches. The man stood tall and dark in the shadows of the dimly lit landing, but even so, Emmett could discern the youthfulness in his face. He opened the door wider, allowing the light from the room to spill over his shoulder, and the handsome features of the young man's face filled in as if painted with quick, masterful strokes.

Emmett's voice was a whisper. "My Lord in heaven . . ." He reached out tentatively with his right hand, nearly groping for a second, before Jewell locked his right hand around Emmett's forearm. Louder now, but still a whisper, "My Lord in heaven . . . Jewell."

"It's me, Emmett . . . I'm home."

They stood frozen in place for a moment, mannish and clumsy in the silence. When Emmett realized that his weight, in large measure, was being supported by Jewell, he haltingly began to retreat back into the room, pulling Jewell with him. He needed to sit down, and very soon. He searched for a kitchen table chair with his left hand and dragged it under his body, plopping down still firmly attached to Jewell, who gently freed his forearm from Emmett's hand before pulling a chair from the table.

Emmett could not will his eyesight to leave Jewell's face, even though he knew his open staring would soon become bothersome. He desired to search every fiber of the young man's being, to reach deep inside him and learn something of the lost years, and he accepted the fact that he would never be able to accomplish this with words. It was a matter of the heart, and in such matters, Emmett Tragman required few words to probe the depths of a person.

Jewell could not hold Emmett's gaze, and he picked out a spot on the table top to focus on before he spoke. "Emmett . . . I'm awful sorry I never tried to . . ."

Emmett raised both hands from the table, extending his fingers upward with the heels of his hands remaining on the wood. "Ain't no need for that . . . I understand. Always did."

"Still . . . I shoulda . . ."

Emmett's hands again, begging for silence, the fingers swaying back and forth like tiny tree branches tossed by the wind. He looked deeper inside of Jewell, saw the old sorrows, the scarred heart that had grown old before its time. Saw love and agony and loss and gain. Saw the face of a soldier, as clearly as he had ever seen anything in his life.

"You been soldierin', ain't you?"

Jewell nodded silently, his eyes again fixed on the table.

"Korea?"

Another nod.

"Front line?"

"Yeah. Up by the Chosin . . . in the mountains." Jewell drew his left hand from his lap and rested it on the table, like an abnormal growth—separate, yet affixed to his being.

Emmett clenched his teeth and recoiled inwardly from the sight of the maimed hand, but it was a quiet reaction, controlled and hidden, and he was certain that Jewell was unaware of his turmoil. Jewell waited for him to speak, to pass judgment on the crippled thing, but Emmett waited several seconds, ordering his thoughts.

"Thumb ain't hardly hurt, and there's some fingers left to

work against it," Emmett said evenly. "Coulda been a sight worse."

"Yeah, it coulda." Jewell was pleased with the assessment and sought to affirm it. "I'm already beginnin' to get used to it. When the tenderness goes away, I figure I'll be able to do most any-thing . . . after some more gettin' used to."

"No other hurts?"

"That's it."

Emmett knew there were other hurts wrought by war, of the soul rather than the flesh, but he would not probe in those places. Only the one who bore the sorrows would know when the time was right to speak of them. That time might come soon or it might never come. It was not for Emmett to decide.

He smiled. "I reckon you already found Miss Annabelle?"

"Yeah, at the school." Jewell raised his head and smiled back. "She looks just like she did before . . . don't seem a year older."

"Reckon she told you about your daddy?"

Jewell nodded.

Emmett nodded his head in wonder. "It's a plain miracle, that's all I can say about it." He nodded again. "Nobody but her coulda brought that on."

"I know."

"You goin' to see him?"

"In the mornin'."

"Good." Emmett reached out and patted Jewell's right hand. "I never been able to bring myself to go down there, but I don't hold nothin' against him no more. We know how we feel, him and me . . . one toward the other now. It's kinda strange, but me and him sorta talk through Miss Annabelle . . . somehow . . . you'd have to ask her. I can't make whole sense of it . . . just know it happens."

"I think I understand, Emmett."

Emmett pushed away from the table and walked to the window. The fading winter light was leaking into the alley with little purpose. A bushy yellow cat, huge and dirty, slunk along the base of the building across the alley.

"My mind's cluttered up in here, Jewell. Let's walk for a while."

"Sounds good to me."

Emmett turned from the window and swiped his denim jacket from the foot of the bed. "Don't reckon it feels too cold around here to you . . . after the mountains, huh?"

"No, Missouri don't seem too cold now, Emmett. Let's go."

# Chapter 25

*T*HE RHYTHM of the steel rails flowed soothingly through Jewell's body, the great rattle and
hum steady and powerful, carrying him east from California
through the rolling hills. Annabelle had said little since they pulled
away from the depot, and Jewell knew that the silence was in
deference to him. The first few miles of the ride brought him only
confusion, a hundred different thoughts and feelings welling up
within him, taunting and scolding and reminding. Dark and sorrowful pieces of the old life rushed before his eyes like charred
scraps of burning paper, darting and swirling on seared air. But
then another wind began to blow, cool and clean, sweeping the
air free of the debris, and with the cool wind came a certain peace.
Jewell knew why the wind in his mind changed; it was the nearness
of the tiny woman seated beside him. How she had brought about
this change was a mystery, a silent, beautiful mystery, and he accepted
it as a gift, though they would never speak of the train ride.

The train slowed and the whistle sounded long and mournful
cries. Jewell wondered if the sounds could be heard from inside
in the prison walls, wondered if his father could hear them, down
in the stone belly of the beast.

Arthur Shellman poked a finger under his sweaty uniform collar as he led Annabelle and Jewell through the final set of doors separating the hospital ward from the cell wings of the prison.

"About there, folks." He turned and glanced over his shoulder. "Well, here we are." He nodded respectfully at Annabelle, wanting to smile, but he could not force it on his mouth.

"Thank you, kindly, Arthur," Annabelle said.

"It was good to meet you, son," Arthur stuck out his hand and nodded solemnly.

"You too." Jewell shook his hand, and the guard walked quietly away. It took great effort for Jewell to force the two words from his mouth. His feet felt as if they had been set in concrete, and the flesh of his mouth and throat was hot sandpaper. The door to the room stood half open, ten feet away, at once beckoning and foreboding. Acutely aware of his plight, Annabelle moved closer to Jewell's side and slipped her arm behind his lower back, patting him with her hand.

"Do you want me to go in first for a few minutes?" she asked.

Jewell slowly licked his lips, and Annabelle saw his nostrils flare in an effort to draw air deep into his lungs. "I'm . . . I'm all right . . . I think. I want to go in there. I just can't make my feet move."

"That's perfectly understandable, Jewell. Take all the time you need. We're here now; there's no hurry."

Annabelle listened to the sounds drifting through the corridor; they were unlike those in the main section of the prison. The sounds here were softer and less urgent, mostly devoid of the metal edges that served as a constant reminder of the nature of the place. It saddened Annabelle that a reunion such as this would occur in this setting, but it was of little import in the final analysis. The fact that it would occur in any setting was all that really mattered. Her arm moved a fraction of an inch with Jewell's back, and then again, several inches this time, as they began to walk toward the door. Annabelle moved ahead and entered the dimly lit room with Jewell close behind.

Jubal's eyes were closed, but he was not asleep. He had heard Annabelle's familiar voice in the corridor, as well as the voices of men, but he could not understand what was said, nor could he identify the men. He listened as two pairs of shoes shuffled quietly to his bedside, but he did not open his eyes.

Jewell looked down into the gaunt face, stifling a gasp of disbelief. Could it have been only seven years? The man before him had aged thirty years, the flesh of his face but a paper-thin covering of skull. Lines of pain and torment were etched into the corners of his eyes like jagged incisions. Even in the poor light, his hair was a ghostly white, thin and pitiful across the top of his head. The sheet was pulled up to his chin, with only the long, bony hands protruding near the edge of the bed.

Annabelle leaned forward and spoke softly near his ear. "Wake up, Jubal. Our dream has come true."

*Our dream has come true* . . . the only dream they had ever spoken of—that the boy would come home. *Oh, God, could it be?* Jubal's fingers moved as he sought Annabelle's hand, and she slipped her hand into his. Still, he dared not open his eyes.

"Yes, it's true, Jubal . . . open your eyes," Annabelle whispered. "Jewell has come home to you."

Tears oozed from under Jubal's closed eyelids, and when he opened them and blinked, two blurred figures came to him—one very close and another much higher and behind the first. The fragrance of perfume drifted to his nostrils as Annabelle dabbed at his eyes with her handkerchief. He blinked more of the tears away as Annabelle moved away from his bed, and he felt her hand slip from his. Without warning, a great fear stabbed his heart; he turned his head toward the opposite side of the room. His creaky whisper scratched the air.

"I'm . . . afraid."

Jubal felt another hand brush his fingertips, and long, strong fingers, warm and gentle, enwrapped his hand. "Don't be afraid, . . ." the name stuck in his throat for a fraction of a second, "Pop . . . it's gonna be all right now."

Annabelle grabbed a chair and slid it behind Jewell, motioning for him to sit. Jewell sat down and leaned forward, resting his forearms on the edge of the bed. He was amazed at the strength of his father's grip; the hand trembled slightly, but otherwise there was no sign of weakness. Annabelle stepped silently to the bedside, to Jewell an almost holy presence, somehow frail of flesh yet mighty beyond measure. Her tiny hand reached out and brushed the wisps of white hair, resting there for a moment, then sliding down to Jubal's cheek. With great care, she turned his head toward her and Jewell and then kissed Jubal's forehead, knowing it was a last kiss. She placed her hand over Jewell and Jubal's for a second before kissing Jewell on the forehead, then slipped from the room.

Jubal strained his eyes to focus on Jewell's face, not knowing what he would be able to read in it, still fearful despite what his son had said just moments before. It was a man's face, handsome with strong lines and masculine features. Long gone were the roundish lines Jubal remembered—long gone—so long gone. Slowly, like wet snowflakes sliding down a window pane, Jubal's fears melted away as the soft, dark eyes looked down on him. Eyes of tenderness and sorrow, eyes that bore no malice. A peace beyond anything Jubal had imagined possible infused him now, flowing in his veins as surely as the blood of life. Nothing else would ever matter now—not sickness, not pain, not even death. Jewell had come back to him, and he would never turn his son loose.

"Oh, son . . . I'm so sorry for . . ."

Jewell shook his head intently, stopping the apology early, once and for all. "No, Pop . . . don't even start. There's no use for any of that now. Let it lay . . . doesn't matter now."

Jewell scooted his chair closer to the bed and laid his head down against Jubal's bony hip. Jubal loosened the sheet that covered him and reached across himself with his right hand and touched Jewell's hair, his fingers drifting down where the close-cropped hair at the nape of Jewell's neck was thick and bristly. He stroked with his thumb and forefinger, the way he had in Jewell's childhood, when the days were still full of hope, when the coming darkness was far away and unknown to either father or son. And with the touch of his fingers, Jubal spoke a thousand words with an eloquence that could have been equalled only by an angel of God.

Arthur Shellman glanced at the black-rimmed wall clock. Three forty-five; his shift would end in fifteen minutes. He decided to check on Miss Annabelle one more time. She was sitting in the same chair near the door to Jubal Cole's room. The same hard, straight-backed chair that had been her only resting place for the last eight hours. He had offered to find her a better chair or even an empty bed on which to rest for a time, but she had declined. She looked up as he approached, and though he looked for it, Arthur could detect no weariness.

"Everything all right, Miss Annabelle?"

She smiled as she spoke. "Yes, thank you, Arthur."

"Reckon I'll be goin' home in a few minutes, I just wanted to see if . . ."

Jewell's voice, a plaintive cry from the room: "Miss Annabelle!"

Annabelle jumped to her feet and darted into the room, closely followed by the guard. Jewell wept softly, his head resting in the crook of Jubal's left arm, his hand still locked in his father's. The heavy overcoat hung in disarray from his right forearm, spilling over the edge of the bed. When she spotted the coat, Annabelle knew that they had not unlocked their hands since she had left the room, and a pang of sweet sorrow passed through her like an electrical charge.

"He's gone . . . he's gone . . ." The words were sobs.

"Arthur, go get a doctor, and please . . ." she caught his eye, "no big commotion. There's no need for that now."

She draped her arm around Jewell. "Jewell, the only reason he lasted this long was his hope that you would come back. You've given him the greatest gift of his life. You must cling to that now. Cry it all out . . . don't hold anything back. It's worth crying over."

Two pairs of shoes clomped down the corridor, sounding like soldiers marching at quick step. The doctor was a short, rumpled man, his white lab coat flapping behind him as he entered the room. Without a word, he nodded curtly to Annabelle and moved to the head of the bed where he flicked on a small penlight and peered for a moment under Jubal's eyelids. He switched off the light and looked down at Jewell's right hand, locked whitely in his dead father's.

"You might need a little help there, son . . . with that hand."

Annabelle took a step back and allowed the doctor to take her place. He reached down and gently tested the tension in Jewell's fingers.

"I . . . I can't move it," Jewell sniffed.

"I know, son. Don't fight it, just let me do the work."

The doctor's meaty hands began to knead Jewell's fingers, all the while working the other set of cold fingers loose until Jewell's hand was free. He carefully placed the cold hand on the bed and stepped back.

"The feeling will come back in a few minutes. Don't try to rush it." He nodded again to Annabelle. "You folks take all the time you need . . . all you need."

Arthur and the doctor turned and walked quietly from the room, the guard pulling the door nearly closed as he left. Arthur was gone for only a few seconds before he reentered the room, a chair in his hand. He set it beside Jewell and motioned for Annabelle to take it.

"Thank you, Arthur, that was very kind," she said.

He nodded once and retreated from the room. Annabelle scooted the chair closer to Jewell and laid her hand on his forearm. She waited patiently as the minutes passed, content to pat Jewell's arm as he regained his composure.

"We talked, Miss Annabelle . . . a lot . . . before he got tired."

"I'm so very glad of that, Jewell . . . so happy for the both of you."

"It was like I never hated him . . . not just because he was old and sick neither. I wasn't feelin' sorry for him. Does that make sense?"

"Yes, it makes perfect sense."

Jewell swiped at his nose with his handkerchief and stuffed it back into his trouser pocket. He shook his head as his chin began to quiver. "Ain't nobody . . . nobody ought to have a life as hard as his was, even if he brought some of it on himself. It just doesn't seem fair."

"Fair is a word this life has no place for, Jewell. Don't waste your time worrying about what's fair or unfair. He *did* have the life he lived, but you made it so much better for him. Back then, when you were a little boy . . . my, we talked for hours about those days. And now, these last few hours. That's all that matters now."

"He said somethin' that didn't make much sense." It was more a question than a statement.

"What was that, Jewell?"

"He said to tell 'that preacher' that he was right about the Kingdom . . . and that he was sorry he hit him. I heard things about him and the preacher, but I was pretty little. It's all fuzzy now."

"It happened long before I came to town, but some of my friends in the church told me about it. The preacher said something to your father about the name of his place of business. He considered it to be disrespectful of . . . the other Kingdom, God's Kingdom. And, well, your father broke his nose." Annabelle chuckled a little laugh, and it was not out of place. "It's still crooked too. Always will be. But, according to my friends, Noel Edwards never spoke of it again."

"Well, I'm gonna look him up," Jewell said softly.

"You should; he would appreciate that."

Jewell looked at Annabelle, his red-rimmed eyes riveted on hers. "You reckon . . . he would say somethin' at the funeral?"

"I'm certain he would, Jewell. He would be proud to preach your father's funeral."

"Seems like a lot to ask . . . considerin' what happened."

"Not of Noel Edwards."

Jewell looked around the room as he arched his back against the steel bands of stiffness. Carefully, he shifted his weight to the front edge of the chair and pushed up from it, leaning against the side of the bed for balance.

"What do we need to do about . . . gettin' him home and all?"

"I've tended to all that . . . a couple of weeks ago. Don't concern yourself with it."

He nodded. "Thank you."

"It was my honor."

Jewell looked about the room again, seeing it for the first time, taking note of the details. He sighed. "Don't look like a prison in here."

Annabelle stood and looked down at Jubal's body for a moment. "It's not for him any longer, Jewell. No more prisons forever. Let's go home."

# Chapter 26

"*JUBAL COLE* was a tall one, all right," Rommie said as he paced stiffly around the grave site. The cold wind whistled behind his glasses causing his eyes to water, and as he walked he jabbed intermittently at the corners with a rumpled wad of red handkerchief. "Dadblame this wind, it ain't supposed to blow like this till March."

"Blows when it wants to," Hec intoned solemnly, raising his bare head slightly as if honoring the power of the wind.

Rommie pulled his glasses off with one hand and gouged at his eyes with the handkerchief, muttering under his breath until the words finally became intelligible.

". . . cryin' out loud, Hec, don't you figure I know the wind blows when it wants to? I been on this here earth near 'bout long as black dirt. I reckon I know more 'bout when the wind blows than you."

Executing a majestic half turn into the wind, Hec appeared to ignore the fusillade of words, but Emmett knew that he did not. He had simply chosen the safe route this time. Sometimes, Hec chose to prolong the unwinnable arguments for several minutes, poking in only a word or two along the way for sufficient fuel to feed Rommie's verbal fire. But today there was a very big grave to be dug; better to end it early.

"Like I was tryin' to say," Rommie said indignantly, "this here's gonna be a whopper." He peered over the top of his glasses at Emmett. "You got it all eyeballed out, Emmett?" Rommie had already given Emmett the measurements in inches.

"Yeah."

Emmett tapped a twenty-penny nail into the frozen earth, quickly followed by three others, forming a perfect rectangle.

"String it out, Hec," Rommie said, pushing up the bill of his cap and shaking his head. "Dadgumdest thing I ever saw."

"You musta said that fifty times, Rommie," Hec said as he wrapped the line of white twine around the first nail.

"Yeah, and I'll say it fifty more if the Lord lets me watch that many more 'fore I lay down in my own." Rommie huffed a blast of frosted air in Hec's general direction.

"Dad . . . gum . . . dest . . . thing . . . I . . . ev . . . er . . . saw." Rommie repeated each syllable like a rap on a drum.

With Hec at one end and Emmett at the other, the dig began with whumps of tools resounding from the cold earth. The two men worked steadily and silently with Rommie circling like a wary predator, the earflaps of his cap floating up and down in the wind as he offered a word of direction or encouragement from time to time. He stopped his stalking after forty-five minutes, satisfied with the beginning.

"Take a break, boys. Hec, you're breathin' like a wounded buffalo . . . you healthy?"

"Took a little somethin' in my chest a couple days ago."

"I'll spell you next round then."

"Aw, Rommie, it ain't nothin' . . ."

"Don't you think I can still dig hard ground? Why, it wasn't a week ago that I . . ." Rommie stopped speaking when he saw the look on Emmett's face as the little man stared beyond him.

Rommie turned instinctively to look down Emmett's line of vision. A tall young man dressed in a dark overcoat was approaching. He was hatless, with both hands thrust into the coat pockets, walking steadily but slowly. He appeared to pay little heed to the cold.

"Who'd that be, you reckon?" Rommie asked.

"That's Jewell . . . Jewell Cole," Emmett said as he tossed his spade aside and began to walk toward Jewell.

"Well, I'll declare," Rommie said.

He watched as Emmett and Jewell embraced quickly and spoke just out of earshot. They turned in unison and walked to within a few feet of the grave site.

"Fellers, this here is Jewell . . . come home from the war."

Rommie hopped around the corner of the grave and yanked the glove off of his right hand, thrusting his crooked fingers forward. "Mighty proud to meet you, young fellow, that I am."

"The same to you, Mr. Rugg," Jewell said as he clasped Rommie's hand.

"Just Rommie. I feel old enough as it is."

"All right, Rommie."

Hec stepped forward, his right hand emerging from the sleeve of his dirty coat like a small animal from hiding. "Name's Hec," he drawled.

"Pleased to meet you, Hec," Jewell said, allowing his hand to be swallowed by the great paw.

A bothersome silence descended for several seconds as Rommie and Hec shifted from one foot to the other. Neither had ever dealt with a close family member at a partially dug grave that would hold the body of their loved one. It was strange indeed, and to Rommie, nearly a breach of the death protocol somehow, and yet, as the seconds ticked by, he could think of no good reason why the boy should not be there if he desired to be.

"Well, I don't mean to be a bother," Jewell said, "I just felt the urge to come."

"Ain't no bother at all, son," Rommie said, now peeved with himself at having allowed Jewell to become uncomfortable. "You stay long as you like . . . long as you like. I got a thermos of hot coffee yonder under that tree. You just help yourself anytime."

"I thank you, Rommie, but I won't be long." Jewell looked at Emmett and smiled. "Truth is, I came for a keepsake . . . from the grave. I know it sounds silly . . ."

"It don't sound nothin' of the sort," Rommie interjected, although he could not imagine what Jewell could take from the grave that would be a suitable keepsake. He took a step backward and watched as Jewell walked to the low mound of dug earth and knelt on one knee. Emmett moved forward to join Jewell, kneeling beside him. Carefully, as if searching for some lost bit of treasure, both men began to poke through the clumps of dark clay. It soon became clear to Rommie that they were searching for a rock, the size and shape of which carrying great import.

"There," Jewell said, pointing to a small stone near Emmett's boot, "let me see that one."

Emmett plucked the stone from under a clod of soil and handed it to Jewell. It was smooth, a slightly elongated oval, and fit perfectly in the curvature of Jewell's right forefinger. He tossed it about in his hand for a moment, feeling the heft and balance, and for an instant, Rommie thought that he might draw back his arm and throw it, but he did not. The handsome face clouded, and he blinked back tears as he stood, the stone secured in his right hand. He nodded silently to Emmett, who responded in kind.

"Reckon I'll be goin' on now. Sorry for the bother," Jewell said, looking first at Rommie and then at Hec.

"No bother at all, son. Stay as long as you like," Rommie said quietly.

"Thanks, but I'll be goin' on now."

Jewell turned and began to retrace his steps along the edge of the cemetery. No one spoke until he was fifty yards away. Rommie shoved the bill of his cap until it pointed to the sky.

"Emmett, I ain't one to poke around in another's business, but me and you been together a good while now and . . ."

"I'll tell you about the rock, Rommie."

"I'd be beholdin' to you."

"When he was a boy in Miss Annabelle's first class . . . well, he and his daddy was pretty messed up along about then. One day, he chunked a rock to the front of the class while Miss Annabelle was readin'. Hit her on the shoulder and smacked up against the blackboard. She knew where it come from, and didn't even let on that nothin' happened. They just talked after class. She didn't bring him to no trouble over it. Don't know exactly what she said. When she told me about it she said that she knew they were alike in their sorrows . . . the ways of the world and all . . . and that she knew she would do all she could to help him. Anyhow, the rock . . . she gave it to him as a 'membrance, and he lost it in Korea." Emmett pointed to the grave. "That one took its place, I reckon."

"Makin' peace with his daddy, he was," Hec said softly.

The sound of Hec's voice came as a surprise to both Emmett and Rommie. The big man had seemingly faded into the background during Jewell's visit. That he would offer an unsolicited comment on a matter of the heart was indeed unexpected, and Rommie could only stare in amazement. Emmett looked at Hec until the eyes of the tall man met his own. Hec lowered his head quickly, a faraway pang of guilt bouncing obliquely against his heart. After all, who was he, a doubter of God's very existence, to make such a declaration in front of two believers?

"Hec, I'm proud to hear you say that," Emmett said. "You got it just right. Jewell made peace with his daddy in his last hours, down to the prison. And this here was the last of it. Their peace is done for this life."

*This life . . . and if this life, a next life?* Hec pondered the words whispering in his head. A beautiful thought—but only a thought. The sea of gray stones spread before him was reality. The half hole at his feet was reality. Jubal Cole's cold body was reality. And yet, the peace he felt radiating from Jewell was reality also, even if he could not touch it or see it. It was a heavy thing to wrestle with, and though he always managed to untangle himself from it before it tied his mind in knots, he wondered if he would always be able to.

Emmett read his thoughts with little difficulty; they had toiled side by side for endless hours over the course of many years. A man could learn another man's heart in far less time than that. Emmett Tragman had known Hec's heart for a very long time.

Rommie was strangely silent, contentedly gumming the inside of his cheek as he looked out over the gentle hills of the cemetery, waiting for the sound. The wind was out of the northwest, passing over the morning freight train as it rolled eastward; in seven minutes it would rumble through town. The wind rushed ahead of the train and carried with it the first mournful cry of the whistle.

"The long train's soon passin', boys. Goin' to watch her . . . be back directly."

Emmett waited until Rommie was twenty steps away before he addressed Hec. "You want to talk or you want to dig, Hec?"

Hec drew in a long breath and then pushed it away in a long cloud of steam. "Dig, I reckon."

They both picked up their tools and returned to the hole, back to back. They dug in silence for five minutes before Emmett stopped and spoke back over his shoulder.

"Don't try so hard, Hec. Your heart's smarter than your head."

Hec did not stop digging as he answered. "But it ain't as loud as my head, Emmett."

They buried Jubal Cole under a brilliant winter sun at half past ten the next morning. Rommie and Hec watched from a little knoll as the small gathering stood in a half circle around the grave. The vantage point Rommie had selected was far enough away to be respectful and near enough to hear what was said. Noel Edwards spoke eloquently and read two passages from his leatherbound black Bible. Then, with Annabelle's voice sweet and clear above the others, they sang "Rock of Ages."

"I'll declare, the little woman can sing too," Rommie said softly.

"Good as any I ever heard here," Hec said.

The pallbearers gathered the ropes and lowered the casket into the grave. Annabelle took Jewell's arm and stepped with him to the mounded earth. Together, they stooped and each gathered a handful of soil, which was softly tossed onto the top of the casket. Still arm in arm with Jewell, Annabelle extended her right arm to Emmett, and the three turned from the grave and led the short processional away.

Rommie placed both hands behind his back and groaned softly as he pushed at the stiffness. "Hec, these old bones 'bout had it. I think I'm ready to leave it to you and Emmett."

"I heard that before."

"No, I mean it this time. You two don't need me no more."

Hec sneaked a sidelong glance at Rommie; it was different this time. There was something in his voice—a weariness, a certain finality—something that Hec could not precisely identify, but that was all too real. The thought of digging without Rommie was disconcerting, and Hec was slightly irritated that the old man was seriously considering such a thing.

"For cryin' out loud, Rommie, you ain't no more gonna quit . . ."

"I am, I tell you, Hec. You want me to keep on till I drop

dead in the wrong hole some day? You and Emmett have to fish me out like some old rag doll? Tarnation!"

Like a great, sad bear, Hec slowly raked a hand from the top of his head to his chin. "Why all of a sudden? Just like that, you decide it's done with. Why, you don't have to do no diggin' nohow. Me and Emmett can handle all that."

"You think I'm gonna stand around and watch you two and take a cut of the pay?"

"You're the one that gets the jobs. People for miles around here know you're the grave digger."

"Well, they'll just have to figure out that I ain't no more, and that you two are."

Hec brooded in a fitful silence for long moments; he could think of nothing else to say. The matter appeared to be settled, and he would have to live with it.

"Looks like you'd be glad to get rid of my aggravatin' ways, Hec. I'll declare."

Hec looked at him with sad eyes. "Never really bothered me that much, Rommie. You was right 'bout things most of the time."

Rommie reached up and clamped a gnarled hand over Hec's shoulder. "Come on, you big bear. I'll help you finish this one 'fore I hang up my shovel."

They began to walk toward the grave, Hec lumbering slowly as he allowed for Rommie's uneven gait.

"You'll never be able to stay away from here, Rommie."

The old man cackled as the words sank in. "One way or another, Hec, you're right about that."


"Let's just keep walkin' for a while, all right?" Jewell asked Annabelle and Emmett. They had walked in silence for three blocks since leaving the cemetery. Annabelle had invited the men to sit with her in the Parkers' living room, which had been graciously offered by Lela. But with Jewell's request, the threesome turned right on High Street and walked toward the middle of town. When they were still two blocks away, both Annabelle and Emmett knew of Jewell's destination. They approached it from the opposite side of the street, stopping when they had drawn even with the building.

"Let's cross over," Jewell said.

Once across the street, Jewell approached the building cautiously, like a boy fearing who or what might be inside and yet doing his best to disguise his trepidation. But the anxiety was weak and seemed silly after only a few seconds. The weather-beaten sign creaked loosely, with one end resting precariously atop the door frame. Hoping that neither Annabelle nor Emmett had noticed his initial reaction, Jewell reached over the top of the front door and twisted the sign free of the last nail holding it in place. He studied the faded lettering for a moment before leaning it against the side of the building. The windows were boarded up with a sturdy patchwork of scrap lumber; to Jewell, they were useless wooden bandages on a building long dead.

"I reckon the whole thing's about ready to fall in," Jewell said, as much to himself as to his companions.

Annabelle darted a quick smile at Emmett which Jewell could not see. "Oh, you never know what you might find inside. It's a sturdy old building," she said.

Jewell turned to look first at Annabelle and then Emmett, who ignored his quizzical gaze. "Let's go around back," Emmett said, already beginning to walk down the side of the building. He fished a key from his pocket and unlocked the back door, pushing it open for Jewell and motioning with his hand. "Go on, take a look."

Jewell stepped inside, quickly followed by Annabelle and Emmett, who flipped a light switch. The single bulb suspended from the ceiling cast a yellowish glow over the big room.

"The lights . . . still hooked up?" Jewell did not try to hide his amazement. He peered about the room, his head turning slowly as if taking in one of the wonders of the world. "But . . . it looks like . . . it looks all right . . . I mean . . ."

Suddenly the realization struck him like a warm wave of water in his soul. He approached Annabelle and Emmett with his arms stretched wide and gathered them to him. His chin touched the top of Emmett's head, and he could feel Annabelle's hair in the hollow of his throat.

"Oh, I don't know what to say to you two. Oh, thank you. Part of me hated this place for so long, and then . . . after we made our peace, I was hopin' that it wasn't a total wreck. Oh, thank you both so much. But how . . . ?"

"Emmett found some money your daddy hid in the basement . . . not a fortune by any means, but a substantial amount, and I opened a bank account for it. We've used some of it on the lights and some coal for the furnace, but not much . . . just when it's really cold."

"We was afraid the bad cold would ruin the pool tables. They're worth a good bit," Emmett said. "We shut the water off so the pipes wouldn't bust."

"Upstairs?" Jewell asked.

"It's been cared for too," Annabelle said with a smile.

Jewell released Annabelle and Emmett and took a step backward. "How long . . . how long did you mean to keep this up? What if . . . I never woulda come back?"

"I must admit," said Annabelle, "that we had some doubts from time to time . . . but deep down, where the real truth is, we knew. We just didn't know when."

"You know there ain't . . . er, isn't no law says a pool hall has to sell liquor and beer," Emmett said. "Maybe cook up some more kinds of food over there, make it bigger . . . the pool tables been covered . . . just need a good cleanin'. Who can say what might happen?"

"You still have some money in the bank to get started with . . . that is, if you're interested, of course," Annabelle added. "We certainly don't mean to push anything on you."

"My mind's in kind of a whirl right now. I got to think some more . . . but just havin' a place . . . a chance . . . whew!" He ran his right hand through his hair, tilting his head toward the ceiling, and then took another long look about the room.

Annabelle sensed that his thoughts were passing into another realm; his vision seeking a place far beyond the wood and masonry of the building. The chiseled features clouded for a moment, and she wondered if too much had been thrust upon him so soon.

"I'm gonna head north for a few days . . . up into Iowa, to find some folks."

"Korea?" Emmett asked, already knowing the answer.

Jewell nodded. "Parents of a friend." He huffed out a short breath of air. "I only knew this guy for a few hours, really. A farm boy, about my age. I was with him when he got hit . . . and I almost got him out . . . almost. I want his folks to know that he was with somebody who cared at the end. I tried so hard." He shook his head in confusion. "Maybe it's for me I'm goin'. Will they even want to see me?" He expected Annabelle to answer, but it was Emmett who spoke.

"You're goin' for you . . . and them, and it's right both ways. They'll be better for it. Don't you worry."

"I think we can manage to mind this place for a few more days," Annabelle said, taking Jewell by the arm. "Let's walk some more, and then we'll go to Lela's. She's fixed some food for us, and she'll be mortified if we don't put a healthy dent in it."

"Sounds good," Emmett said.

Emmett locked the door behind them, and they walked back to the front of the building. Jewell stopped and looked down at the sign leaning against the wall. "You don't reckon the preacher'd want that, do you?"

"He might . . . he just might at that," Emmett said. He reached down, picked up the sign, and tucked it around the corner of the building, safely out of sight. "I'll see he gets it for you."

They were alone now, Annabelle and Emmett, bundled side by side in overcoats, sitting on the top step of the Parkers' front porch. The winter darkness was draped over the yard, clean and still and powerful. Thin clouds had moved in an hour before, shutting out the moonbeams, but Annabelle and Emmett did not mind. The quiet night was a friend, warm or cold, bright with moonlight or thick with darkness; it did not matter. A friend was a friend.

"You think he'll stay here and try to start somethin' up there?" Emmett asked.

"Yes, I think he will. I think Jewell will find someone and get married and father children whom I will teach one day."

"That'd be somethin', wouldn't it?"

It was in his voice, the unspoken question, though he did not intend for it to be there, and Annabelle heard it as clearly as the peal of a bell on a quiet night. For a moment it saddened her, a dreadful little tug on the bottom of her heart, but she chased the small sorrow away. She would answer his question, and they would move beyond it and live the rest of their lives.

"It was on a winter night like this when I saw my sister, Hazel Lee, dance so beautifully. She and Charles were not yet engaged, but everyone knew they soon would be. They were alone on our porch, sitting on the top step. Momma and Daddy were in bed, and Matthew was off somewhere with his friends. I tiptoed out the back door and around the side of the house . . . to spy on them . . . see if I could catch them in a kiss. I watched for a few minutes, trying not to let my teeth chatter out loud, and then Charles whispered in her ear and they stood up. They began to dance, in total silence. I will never forget the look of Hazel Lee's hair that night. The light from the front window touched it as Charles whirled her about the porch, and it fanned out . . . long and beautiful. And then, for the shortest moment . . . I hated her. For even then, I knew . . . that I was different, that no suitor would ever twirl me on our front porch, that Daddy would never give me away at the altar, that I would never hold my baby to my bosom."

She paused, bringing back the moment in every detail, for it was a moment that changed the course of her life.

"But the awful thought left me as quickly as it had come. I believe that God chased it away. Then I felt only the purest joy for them . . . and knew somehow that I would dance in winter in my own way. I knew that there must be some reason why I was like I was. I have taught more than two hundred children so far, and if God gives me health, I will someday teach a thousand."

She turned her face to Emmett and then rested her head on his shoulder. "I will remember every face, every name . . . every sorrow. It is a gift I have been given . . . in exchange for a dance in winter."

She found Emmett's hand and took it in her own, lacing her fingers tightly with his. "And you, my sweet Emmett . . . with your quiet ways and soft heart, you have also been given the gift of love. And I cherish you, in a way far greater than you will ever know."

Two thousand feet above them, the wind stirred and pushed at the clouds, parting them so that the moonlight could find earth, and for a silver moment, known only to the eye of God, the two figures huddled together were illuminated as one.

# *About the Author*

Steven Wise, a graduate of the University of Missouri, is a licensed real estate appraiser. He lives and writes his stories on a wooded farm ten miles north of Columbia, Missouri, with his wife, Cathy, and their two children, Travis and Stacee.

Wise enjoys long walks in the woods, for there in the silence, stories sometimes come.

*Long Train Passing* is his third novel, following *Midnight* and *Chambers*.